KING OF THE SCREWUPS

Houghton Mifflin Harcourt

Boston   New York

For Dustin, king of my heart

www.hmhbooks.com

The text of this book is set in 12-point Fournier Mt.

The Library of Congress has cataloged
the hardcover edition as follows:
Going, K. L. (Kelly L.)
King of the screwups / K. L. Going
p. cm.
Summary: After getting in trouble yet again, popular high school senior
Liam, who never seems to live up to his wealthy father's expectations, is sent
to live in a trailer park with his gay "glam-rocker" uncle.
[1. Fathers and sons—Fiction. 2. Uncles—Fiction. 3. Behavior—Fiction.
4. Self-esteem—Fiction.] I. Title. II. Title: King of the screw-ups.
PZ7.G559118Ki 2009
[Fic]—dc22

ISBN 978-0-15-206258-3
ISBN 978-0-547-33166-9

Manufactured in the United States of America
DOM 10 9 8 7 6 5
4500293734

1

TAP, TAP, TAP . . .

"Is this thing on? Ha! Just kidding, folks."

The newsman with the microphone grins and winks at me.

Mom, Dad, and I are perched on high stools across from him, my legs dangling in the air. The cameraman does this thing with his fingers where he counts down silently from five to . . . live.

"Goooood day, America! It's a beautiful sunny day in Times Square this morning. I'm Josh Harmon, and I'm here with the Gellers. Now, if you haven't heard of Allan and Sarah Geller, you've been living under a rock. Sarah was a top fashion model for many years, gracing runways from Paris to Milan with her tremendous beauty. She's been a Vogue *cover model, a spokesperson for Shinefree makeup, featured in ad campaigns too numerous to name, and in her latest incarnation she's the proprietor of the Style Boutique in Westchester, New York. Welcome, Sarah."*

Mom smiles and nods. Her eyes glow, and I think she is the most beautiful mother in the world.

"Allan Geller," says the interviewer, turning to my dad, "rose from humble beginnings to become the CEO of MoneyVision, which as you all know is one of the most successful businesses in the United States. I think it's safe to say that this man is a financial genius, and if you'd like to learn more about him, you can pick up this month's issue of Business Today, *since he's being honored as their man of the year. Congratulations, Allan."*

Dad beams, then nods humbly. I stare at him, thinking how cool he is.

"And this . . ." The interviewer turns to me. "This is their son, Liam, who is now . . . how old are you, Liam?"

"Nine."

The interviewer smiles like we're good buddies.

"You look exactly like your mom," he says. "I'll bet people tell you that all the time, right?"

I nod and remember to smile. The interviewer grins back, but then he turns slyly, like he's telling a joke.

"But are you good at math?"

Mom and Dad laugh, but I don't get what's so funny. I shake my head no, and the interviewer straightens in mock surprise.

"You mean you haven't inherited the math-genius gene from your father?"

I'm not sure exactly what this means, but when I look at Dad his smile is so fake I can see the corner of his mouth twitch slightly. I slide a little farther back on my stool, but the interviewer presses forward.

"Do you like school?" he asks. "Maybe there's a subject you're particularly good at?"

I've just gotten my report card, so the memory of it is fresh in my mind. I think about what the media specialist said this morning: "The reporter won't ask you any hard questions, Liam. Just be yourself and give them truthful answers that are short and to the point. And don't forget to smile."

So I smile and say, "My grades are all very bad, and Dad yells at me a lot."

Mom coughs loudly and has to take a drink of the water that sits by her chair. Dad shoots me a look that is so quick, I'm barely sure I've seen it. There's loud laughter from the adults, but I know I've said the wrong thing.

The reporter can't suppress his grin.

"I'll bet a lot of parents can relate to that," he says, like he's trying to be nice, but I can tell there's something different about him now. It's as if he was our friend before, happy to meet us, thanking us for doing this interview, but now he's a shark that smells blood.

"It must be tough being parents with such busy schedules," he says to Mom and Dad, only he doesn't give them time to answer. "Do you miss seeing your parents when they're busy?" he asks me.

This wasn't a question the media specialist prepped me for.

"No," I say. Then I think maybe that sounds bad, so I change my answer. "I mean, yes." Then I say, "I see Mom a lot, just not Dad because he's always working."

"Ooohhh," says the interviewer.

Dad reaches out and takes my hand, squeezing hard.

"It's true I don't get to spend as much time with Liam as I'd like," he says. "Running an international business — which, by the way, is one of the leading philanthropic businesses in the country — is a lot of hard work, but Liam and I have fun together. We like to go swimming and we play ball whenever we can."

This isn't true. I stare at Dad, wondering why he's lying on national television. Why would he say we play ball together when we don't?

"And even though Liam hasn't inherited my natural aptitude for math," Dad continues, "he's very . . . uh . . . very . . ."

Dad sputters. I've seen him do a million interviews and he has never sputtered even once. It's like he's lost his train of thought, and there's a silence that stretches on forever.

Then Dad clears his throat.

"Liam is very social," he says at last. "He's Mr. Popularity. His mother and I always say, 'Just wait until he reaches high school. He'll be giving us a run for our money by then!'"

If you didn't know Dad, you'd think he'd said something nice, but if you knew him, you'd recognize the tone he uses for people who are less than worthy. The name echoes in my ears. Mr. Popularity.

My face falls. I glance toward the door of the studio, even though I know I shouldn't, but the reporter turns to me . . . again. His eyes sparkle.

"Do you think you'll grow up to be like your dad or like your mom?" he asks.

I look at Mom, sitting straight and tall with her long legs, blond hair, and blue eyes. Then I look at Dad with his dark hair and short, compact body. His craggy face looks nothing like mine. Even though I've been told every day since birth that I look like my mother, now I think it like it's a brand-new thought. "I look just like my mother. Only *like my mother.*"

I think about my report card and the question about math, and my heart starts to pound. There's something behind this question, and I'm surprised to realize that I now know what it is. It's like I've gotten a decoder ring to the adult world and in the past few minutes I've figured out how to use it.

I bite my lip and clench my nine-year-old fists.

"My dad," I say, defiantly. "Because even though I don't look like him and I'm not smart like him, he's still my dad."

For a single second my father's chest swells. His eyes go from hard to soft. But then, before I have time to savor the moment, I screw up. And it's not just any screwup. It's the mother of all screwups.

"I know," I tell the interviewer on national TV, "because they got the patermally test and everything. I heard Mom say it to my nana. She said if we hadn't got the patermally test, she never would have believed it."

2

"YOU'RE A SCREWUP, LIAM. Do you think being Mr. Popularity will be enough to get you by in life?"

I'm lying on top of Dad's desk, drunk and half naked, wearing only rumpled boxers and one sock, while a sobbing girl who never really liked me in the first place searches for her pants and top.

"Please don't call my parents," Delia pleads. "I can explain, Mr. Geller. I'll do anything. Just don't call my parents. Please."

I wonder if begging will work for her, because it never does for me. I close my eyes, letting the waves of nausea wash over me. Delia finishes buttoning her shirt and gets on her knees to straighten the stack of papers we knocked over. She sets them on the desk, but I accidentally knock them over again when I try unsuccessfully to sit up.

The world spins, and I'm vaguely aware that Dad is now yelling.

"Do you think it's okay to fool around in my office," he's saying, "...on my desk...when your mother and I are right downstairs?" He's looking at me, but it's Delia who answers.

"We didn't know you were here," she says, crying harder.

I ought to be pleading too, but I can't stop thinking how stupid I was to believe Delia was actually in love with me. She's totally smart, president of the honor society and everything, so why would she ever like me? But there we were at this party, both plastered, and she's telling me how she had this crush on me all last year, when we were juniors.

"You're so beautiful, Liam," she shouts over the pounding music. "You're sweet and funny and I'm totally in love with you."

That's what she said.

So who can blame me for ending up back at Dad's office? I wanted to show her all his awards and stuff, but the whole time I kept hoping I wouldn't say anything monumentally stupid, so I started kissing her to minimize the talking, and that's when everything went wrong.

As soon as a girl starts taking off my clothes, I can tell how she really feels about me. The first thing Delia took off was my watch. It's a really nice watch—just the right degree of tarnished, and the worn leather band is soft. I picked it up used at this shop in SoHo, but it's still a brand-name watch so it was a rare find. Delia dropped it on the floor beside Dad's desk like it was garbage, and that bothered me, but I was in the process of taking off her sweater, so I let it go.

Only then she unbuttoned my shirt.

[7]

The shirt itself — a Kenneth Cole from a couple years ago — isn't special. The thing about *that* shirt is the perfect metal buttons. Thin and sharp. But they could have been plastic buttons with Gap stenciled on them for all Delia cared, because she didn't even *see* them. She wadded up the shirt, popping a button in the process, and tossed it across the room.

Now, you could argue that she was distracted, but so was I, and I still noticed her black velvet bra, probably from Victoria's Secret, which told me that underneath her brainy exterior, she was sexy. I liked that. But I could tell that Delia didn't like or dislike anything about me.

And that's when I knew.

This girl doesn't love me. She doesn't even *like me*. She just wants to be popular.

Who the hell cares when she's taking your clothes off, right? But I cared. And the thing is . . . I kept going anyway.

Right until the moment when Dad walked through the door.

So now as he yells, I lie still and let my head spin, thinking of all the things in life I wish I'd done differently.

"ARE YOU LISTENING TO ME?" Dad bellows at the top of his lungs. Delia cringes.

"You've really compromised your future this time," Dad hollers.

This is a phrase I hear a lot.

"Despite everything I've done for you — you have no moral qualities. You are nothing I ever wanted in a son, and I don't say that lightly."

Although he does say it all the time.

"When a child has been given a fine upbringing and an international education and he still turns out to be delinquent, then it's not the parents' fault, is it?"

Dad is in the zone, and in his zeal his thick black hair falls onto his forehead and the vein in his throat throbs. I watch it pounding.

Actually, it's my head that's pounding.

"I told you last time I wasn't going to put up with this behavior. I've had enough of you. I'm sick of you, Liam. Sick of you."

The words are blending together, slurring, but Dad's not the one who's still drunk — I am — so it must be my brain that's slurring. Sick . . . of . . . sick . . . of . . . What's he saying? Truth is, I do feel kind of sick. Really sick, actually.

"I want you out of my house."

"Mr. Geller!" Delia gasps, but Dad gives her the same look he always gives Mom, narrowing his eyes until she shrinks.

I feel sorry for Delia right then. Sorry that I dragged her into this, and sorry that she has to listen to Dad yelling. I try to sit up again, and I think that maybe this time I'll finally figure out the right thing to say and Dad will take everything back, because he can't possibly mean it, can he? So I take a deep breath, trying to force my eyes to focus.

"If I can just have a second to apologize . . ."

But unfortunately, the moment I sit up, the world spins. Everything around me turns upside down and my vision narrows to a single tiny speck, then fades to black.

3

I'M FIVE YEARS OLD, playing on the runway after one of Mom's shows in Paris. It's late. Really late. There are clothes everywhere and people are hanging around talking in sharp accents. The place smells like smoke and perfume, and my ears are still ringing from the pounding music.

No one has noticed me in a long time, but it's okay because I'm busy imitating all the models, remembering the spectacle I watched earlier from behind a curtain with some woman who kept whispering shhh, as if I didn't know how to be quiet for a show. But now I don't have to be quiet, so I stomp real loud, taking extra-long strides like Mom does. I pull my shoulders back and stick my chin up. I even suck in my cheeks.

Then people do notice me, and I pick out the words I recognize — the ones that are in English or French.

"Oh, look at him!"

"Good god, Sarah, he's drop-dead GQ. He looks just like you."

"Ohhh, couldn't you just eat him up?"

There's laughter and a group of models throw kisses up at me. Mom is watching me from her position draped over a chair below, and she's got these soft, half-closed eyes, but she's smiling. She looks really happy, maybe even proud, and I haven't done anything special. So I vamp it up, but in a five-year-old way. I run down the runway as fast as I can, and I think I will leap off the stage and fly into her arms and she will catch me, only it doesn't happen that way. Mom just watches me fall into a pile of chairs.

When I open my eyes Mom is standing over me, staring at her crumpled mess of a son. I'm still on Dad's desk and every part of my body aches. Sunlight streams in through the office window, so I squint. My face is hot and I feel sick. I sit up very carefully, then slowly slide off the desk into Dad's office chair. The movement makes my head throb.

Mom hands me a mug of coffee, then she sits down in the oversized chair next to Dad's bay window. For a moment it's silent, and I wish it could stay like this forever, but I know it can't.

"Oh, Liam," Mom whispers at last. "Why do you do these things? Why do you have to upset your father? Were you trying to make him kick you out? Is that it?"

It sounds like she's attacking me, but Mom's not like that. She just wants to understand.

"No," I say. "I didn't mean to get . . ." The words stick like cotton in my mouth. Up until Mom said it out loud, I'd been hoping that Dad kicking me out was part of a horrible drunken fog. "He hasn't changed his mind yet?"

Mom looks at me sadly, but she doesn't answer.

"How much did you drink at the party?" she asks instead.

"A few beers."

"I'm guessing that's an understatement," she snorts. "Drugs?"

"Ma. *No.*"

Mom nods because deep down she knows I wouldn't do that. In a strange, twisted sort of way, she trusts me.

"And the girl?"

"Delia? What about her?"

"Do you even like these girls?"

I think how I almost hated Delia as she was taking my clothes off, but that doesn't sound right, out of context, so I shrug, and Mom shakes her head.

"You're such a little shit," she says, and for a second she's truly pissed, but then her face softens. Mom's got the kind of features that you can't help staring at. When she smiles it starts in her eyes, then spreads across her entire face and makes the room light up. That's part of the reason she was a fabulous model. She didn't just make people look — she made them linger.

I wish she'd smile now, but of course she won't.

"Your father's serious this time, Li. He means for you to leave. I'm not going to lie and say I stood up for you," Mom adds.

"Your father wants you gone by the end of the week. He's called your grandparents and arranged everything."

For the first time I sit up straight.

"Mom, he can't! Gram and Gramps *hate* me. You know that. Besides, I'm his *kid*. And it's my senior year. Isn't there something —"

She holds up one hand.

"You're right about your grandparents," she says. "If it makes you feel any better, they hate me, too. You'll end up with them over my dead body."

"But you won't tell Dad he can't kick me out? Where am I supposed to go?"

She breathes out and I can tell she's exhausted, but Mom is *always* exhausted.

"I've been on the phone all morning," she says. "I found someplace else for you to stay. It took some convincing, but your uncle Pete will take you in for a while. Just don't tell your father it was my idea. And be careful how you break the news, because he won't be happy about it."

She stands up as if she hasn't just changed my entire life.

"Mom . . ." I start, but there's too much to say.

"Your uncle's number is on the coffee table. I told him you'd call to sort out the details once you were feeling better." She pauses. "He's enthused."

She laughs a small, airy laugh at her casual lie, and she looks so sad standing there that I want to shake her. I remember how she looked on the runway with her perfect posture and the tall, regal way she carried herself.

"Ma, *please!* Can't we talk about this some more before —"

"No," Mom says. "Your father wants breakfast. Don't come downstairs."

Then she walks out the door and disappears.

4

I'M SEVEN YEARS OLD, and it's my mother's retirement party.

I'm slumped in one of the huge leather living room chairs at our new house in New York. I miss Paris, and so does Mom. She sits in the chair next to mine, staring out the window. Dad is outside grilling, and Gram and Gramps are sitting on the couch directly across from us. There are people swirling around outside — neighbors and friends of Dad's he decided to invite — but the silence inside is deafening. Finally, Gram clears her throat.

"Really, Sarah, there's no doubt you've made the right decision, leaving modeling," she says, giving my mother one of those looks that's half pitying and half disdainful. "Honestly, I don't know how you lived such a . . . fast-paced . . . lifestyle for as long as you did. Especially when it's obvious your son needs you home with him. We've been so worried about Liam."

Mom looks away from the window.

"I think Liam is fine," she says.

"I wouldn't call poor discipline and bad manners fine," Gramps laughs. "Would you, young man?"

I shrug and look down at my feet.

"All Nina's saying, Sarah, is that a boy needs his mother to be home, setting an example, not gallivanting around the globe. Trust me, we've got complete confidence that your parenting skills will improve now that you'll be in a stable environment again."

This is Gramps's idea of a compliment. Mom stiffens.

"I didn't realize my parenting skills were in question."

Gram and Gramps exchange a look.

"Well, obviously Allan can't do everything on his own," Gram says. "Boys need plenty of attention, and before long there will be sports and girls, and colleges to look into . . ."

"Or the army . . ." Gramps adds, giving me a meaningful nod.

"Why, if I hadn't stayed home with Allan when he was Liam's age, we certainly wouldn't be celebrating his new job as CEO."

"Oh really?" Mom asks sweetly. "And what about Peter?"

A moment later, as if on cue, there's a knock at the door. Mom smiles politely at Gram and Gramps and says, "Let me get that," and when she opens the door, in steps a man in a slinky red dress. I stare at him very hard, not because of the clothes he's wearing — I've seen men at fashion shows in all kinds of crazy outfits. No, I stare at him because for a moment I have trouble recognizing who it is. Then I see it's my uncle Pete beneath those clothes. He's wearing a floor-length gown, high heels, and a black wig.

"Hello, dahlings!" he says, bursting through the door.

I clap. "Aunt Pete is here!" I holler.

As soon as I say it, Gram bursts into tears, and Mom doesn't even attempt to hide the huge grin that spreads across her face. Then Dad comes in from outside and it's as if all the sound gets sucked from the room, then it all comes back again, louder than before.

"I want you out! If you think you can act this way in front of my son . . ." Dad bellows.

"Sarah, did you invite him?" Gram whines.

". . . a disgrace," Gramps says. "You're not any son I ever wanted to have."

The voices are so relentless that I just sit there with my jaw hanging open. My dad's and grandfather's faces are beet red as they shout, but Aunt Pete is smiling. And for the first time since the party began, so is my mother.

Aunt Pete notices me watching and winks.

"Catch you on the flip side," he says, as my father and grandfather simultaneously usher him out of the house.

That's the last time I ever saw him.

Aunt Pete.

I stare at the phone number written in my mother's swirly writing, and my breathing gets shallow.

This can't be happening.

I feel like I can't get enough air, so I tell myself to cool it. Living with my cross-dressing uncle in his trailer park will be a hundred times better than living with my military grandfather and the world's strictest grandmother in Nevada.

Won't it?

Honestly, how the hell would I know? The only reason I even know where Aunt Pete lives is because Dad always says, "You don't want to end up like my messed-up brother, living in a broken-down trailer park in the middle of nowhere."

I drum my fingers on Dad's desk and try to remember Pete other than that day at Mom's retirement party. Only I can't. Did he visit us in Paris?

There's no way I can live with someone I don't even remember.

I get up and walk down the hall to my bedroom. Then I pull on some clothes and, despite Mom's warning, I go downstairs to the kitchen to find Dad, because really, this has got to be a huge misunderstanding. He misunderstood the severity of my mistake, and I misunderstood how mad he is.

Or something like that.

When I find him he's furiously working on files that he rescued from his office floor, which is not a good sign. The fact that Dad is working on a Sunday morning is standard fare, but the fact that he's working at the kitchen table has got to be pissing him off.

I hover in the doorway, taking deep, calming breaths. Mom is at the stove cooking tofu and scrambled Egg Beaters. She's got a platter of fake bacon on the new marble counter she had installed last week to replace the "old" chrome counter that she'd installed only six months ago.

"Dad," I say, and my voice cracks.

Dad doesn't look up. He writes something in a file and punches numbers into a calculator.

"I'm, uh, really sorry about last night. Honest. It was a bad decision, and I know you say I'm always making those, and you're absolutely right, I am, but . . . I didn't do it to make you mad."

I wait, but there's no reaction from my father. Mom concentrates on scrambling the tofu.

"Could we talk about this?"

No response.

"I know you're angry, and you have every right to be, but don't you think kicking me out a week before the start of my senior year is kind of harsh?"

The tofu sizzles so loudly the sound fills the room and the smell makes me nauseated. Mom stabs at it with her spatula.

"Mom?" I say, but she won't stop cooking. I notice the way she's stacked the breakfast plates on the edge of the counter so they're almost falling over. Two plates, not three. I want to reach out and topple them. Watch the expensive china explode into shards.

The tofu sizzles and starts to burn despite her continued jabbing.

Dad punches numbers so steadily the clicking sound is relentless.

"*Dad,*" I say again, and it comes out sharp. Then Mom turns and it's like the china dropping.

"*Go,*" she says, slamming down her spatula. "He doesn't want you here."

Her face crumples immediately after she says it, so I know she didn't mean it to come out that way, but it's too late.

I leave the kitchen and don't come back.

5

I DIAL AUNT PETE'S NUMBER, then close my eyes.

"Do not screw up," I whisper. *"Do not screw up."*

It must be a cell phone, because the ring tone sounds weird — like horrible screeching guitar music — and I almost hang up, but then someone picks up the phone.

"Y'ello?" The voice on the other end is one of those deep, scratchy voices cross-dressers always seem to have in the movies. I wonder if it's a prerequisite or something.

"Hello, Aunt Pete?" I say, and then I think, *Aw, crap.* I can't believe this. One point two seconds into the conversation and I have screwed up.

"Aaauuuncle Pete? It's me. Liam."

There's a long pause.

"Liam. Oh, right."

Now that didn't sound too "enthused."

"Yeah, so Mom said she called and I could come stay with you for a couple months."

There's a choking sound on the other end.

"Months?! Your mother said 'weeks.' A few weeks. As in *two or three*. Just long enough for my brother to get over whatever hissy fit he's having."

Typical. Mom always does things halfway. Maybe she was being optimistic that Dad will change his mind, but I doubt it. For a second I'm pissed, but then I remember she still saved me from my grandparents.

"Did I say months? I meant weeks." I consider trying to make months and weeks sound the same, but think better of it. Aunt Pete doesn't say anything for a long time.

"Does your father know about this?" he asks, and I know right away that this is a crossroads. I can show some character and tell the truth, or I can simply lie like Mom does.

"Yeah," I lie. "He knows."

"And he agreed to this? I find that hard to believe. Your father and I haven't spoken in a long time."

"Well," I say, buying time so I can make stuff up, "he wanted me to go live with your parents (the truth) but they said no (okay, little lie), and there's really no one else to ask since Mom's mother is in Paris and you may have heard about the whole thing that happened last time I visited her sister? The thing with the party (unfortunately, true)?"

Aunt Pete snorts.

"Your mom says we'd have to get you enrolled in school here, even if it's only temporary. You're a senior now, right?"

I nod vigorously then remember I'm on the phone. "Yeah. That's right. And honestly, I'd hardly ever be around because I'd be in school and sports and stuff, so you'd barely even see me."

This is another lie. I'm permanently banned from sports because of my poor academic standing, so I never have anywhere to go after school. But Aunt Pete doesn't have to know this just yet.

He sighs really loud. "Tell me something, Liam," he says. "This was your mom's idea, wasn't it?" The question comes out of the blue and I don't know how to answer.

"Um, did she say it was her idea?"

Pete hesitates, but then he says, "No. She said it was your idea, and I was your first choice of who to live with, but I'm asking for the truth."

He sounds serious and I wonder why this matters.

"It wasn't my idea," I say at last. "Honestly, I don't remember you very well. Sorry."

When Aunt Pete answers he doesn't sound mad. His voice is different — choked up. "Hell," he says.

I think, *Great, now I've made him cry,* but then he clears his throat.

"You can come live with me until your dad decides to let you back home. A couple weeks, right? You're going to get yourself straightened out?"

"Yes," I say in a relieved rush. "Dad and I just need a little time apart and I won't be a bother because I'm really self-sufficient and . . ." I say the word "and" before I realize that requires thinking up a second redeeming quality. "Uh . . . entertaining."

This time Pete laughs. It's a big, raucous laugh, so I guess that was the right thing to say.

"Good," he says. "You'll fit right in."

6

"DAD, WANT TO SEE WHAT I MADE IN SCHOOL TODAY? I got a B on it and the teacher said it was creative. See, Dad? Look, it's a picture in a shoe box, and there's this big dinosaur who's going to eat this little dinosaur . . ."

Dad stops reading Business Today and turns to me.

"It's called a diorama," he says with a loud sigh. "And a B," he adds, "is nothing to brag about. I always said that no son of mine would end up a B student, but I guess I was wrong. After all, as the whole world knows, we did get the paternity test."

Dad says that last bit under his breath, then he snaps his magazine back into place. I stand there with the shoe box in my hands, not sure what to do.

"Li, let's put your diorama up in the parlor," Mom says, coming from behind and gently pushing me away.

"He didn't even look at it," I say when we're in the other room. "The teacher said a B was good."

"It is good."

"Then how come . . . how come Dad doesn't like me?"

Mom leans down and wraps me in her arms.

"Of course he likes you. Your father loves you. He's just . . ." Mom sighs. *"Oh, Li,"* she says. *"It's complicated. You just have to be patient and stop trying so hard. Okay?"*

As I stand there packing my clothes, I know Mom's advice was wrong. I should have tried harder. I'm attempting to dredge up some shock over the fact that I'm really leaving, but no one can say they didn't see this coming. Not even me. Delia wasn't the first girl I've been caught fooling around with, plus I lost my license for DWI, failed numerous classes, attended more forbidden parties than I can count, and hosted more of them than I should admit. I wonder if things might have ended up different if I'd tried harder.

I glance out the window and see Mom's car out front, waiting for me to bring out my last suitcase. I'm trying to decide what one wears in a trailer park anyway, and when I turn around to take some clothes out of my dresser drawer, that's when I see Dad standing in the doorway.

"Liam," he says.

I don't look up, just keep folding the clothes really meticulously, the way I do when I work for Mom in her boutique.

"You know this is for the best. Don't you?"

Arms back, smooth out the wrinkles, align the creases.

"I'm sorry it's come to this."

There's a long silence while I fold and Dad watches. I wish

that had been the end of things, because that would have been a decent ending. Not great, but decent. But, as always, I screw up.

"I'm sorry, too," I say. "Maybe I'll do better at Pete's. I'm really going to try to be different this time and I think that I can . . ."

Dad's whole face changes.

At first I don't know what I've said wrong so I do my usual panicked search through my brain. Then it clicks.

Crap.

I hadn't told him yet.

"What did you say?"

Dad strides forward and I take a step back without meaning to.

"I . . . uh . . . I asked . . ."

"Liam," he says, "spit it out. *Now.*"

"I asked Pete if I could live with him and he said yes, so Mom's driving me to his place."

"She's driving you to the airport," he says. "I told her to buy your ticket to Nevada. I arranged everything with your grandparents."

I shake my head.

"She didn't buy the ticket."

Dad turns purple.

"How could you?" he breathes. "Did you try to come up with the one thing that would hurt me the most? You must have given it a lot of thought."

There's something mocking about his tone, and I can't tell if he's trying to imply that I'm awful and vindictive, or that I'm too dumb to think of this, or both. I want to say that it was Mom's idea. Believe me, I *sooo* want to say it, but I don't.

"Dad, I can't live with Gram and Gramps. They're all the way in Nevada and they don't even like me. Where else was I going to go?"

I'm stammering and Dad takes one more step forward. He speaks very slowly, enunciating every word. "If you think there is anything your uncle can give you that I haven't given you, you're dead wrong."

Our bodies are physically closer than they've been in years, and I can feel Dad's breath on my face. Even though he's never hit me before, I find myself waiting for his fist to whip around from behind, but at the last second Dad takes a step back. That step frees my tongue.

"I'm sorry," I say in a rush. "I'm really sorry. I knew you'd be upset, but I didn't think it would be this big of a deal. Honest. If I'd known you'd be this upset, I wouldn't have done it. I just wanted someplace to go, and . . ."

Dad shakes his head. He regards me coldly, and while I admit that I've given Dad eight hundred worthless apologies, this one I mean. I really didn't think he'd be *this* upset. I thought he'd be just about as mad as he usually is, so what difference would it make?

But I was wrong.

"Liam," Dad says right before he storms out of my room, slamming the door behind him, "you never cease to disappoint me, do you?"

7

SO NOW I'M SITTING IN MOM'S LITTLE RED CONVERTIBLE, with all my stuff crammed in the back, on my way to a new life I don't want. Mom is driving and she chatters the whole way, telling me about what good times she used to have with Aunt Pete and his glam-rock band when they were in college.

Whatever.

I think about Dad, wondering if it's too late to change his mind. Would it be possible to become an entirely different person in the next couple weeks? Someone my dad wouldn't mind living with?

I shift my weight to stop my surfboard from poking me in the back. It's crammed half in and half out of the car. I should have left it home, but Dad gave it to me on one of our vacations in Hawaii, and even though he's kicked me out, it's still the best gift I ever got.

I wonder if Dad liked me when we were in Hawaii. He always seemed relaxed there. Maybe if we'd lived in Hawaii instead of New York . . .

"Liam, are you paying attention?"

I look up because apparently Mom's been trying to tell me something.

"We're here," she says, nodding at the side of the road.

We're pulling into a trailer park, and the sign out front says, GOLDEN MEADOWS. I wonder why trailer parks and retirement villages always have names like that, especially when this one doesn't have a meadow in sight. There's hardly even grass.

Back home we have a sculpted, two-tiered lawn that Dad pays a zillion bucks to have landscaped, but here there's mostly mud and lawn ornaments. There's nothing as tacky as a lawn ornament.

Bad sign.

Mom winds the car around a series of roads, then pulls up in front of one of the trailers. I'd describe it, but it looks like every other trailer. Long. Rectangular. Sand color. Mom stops the car and gets out. There are four guys sitting at a picnic table, and they all jump up and rush over to her. I stare at the dashboard, but really I'm watching them from the corner of my eye. I wish I could figure out which one is Aunt Pete, but I can't. Guess he must have looked different ten years ago in drag.

Mom, however, goes directly to the guy with the potbelly and he picks her up and swings her around. They both laugh and she kisses him all over his stubbly cheeks.

"Sarah, you look stunning!" he says. Mom looks beyond happy to see him. I haven't seen her smile like this in years. For a moment I see her on the runway again, my radiant mom, and then Aunt Pete puts her down and she hugs the other guys like they're her long-lost brothers or something. They pretend they don't notice me sitting in the car, but I hear them whispering.

"Is that Liam? He's a doll, isn't he?"

"Sarah, he looks just like you. Honestly, you could be sister and brother."

"Doesn't look too happy to see you though, Petey."

I lean my head on the dashboard because suddenly I'm super tired. When I turn I see this short girl with artsy, vintage glasses and long dark hair watching me from the yard next door. She's walking inside her trailer with her dad, like they don't want to intrude on the spectacle we're creating. He's got his hand on her shoulder, and when he whispers something to her, they both laugh and their faces mold into the exact same expression. I bite my lip really hard and it starts to bleed, so I put my finger up to my mouth, then pull it away, studying the bright red blood. Mom doesn't notice though; she's too busy laughing with Aunt Pete.

"Get out of the car and say hello," she calls in a sharp but humorous way that lets everyone think my sitting here is some joke we planned in advance.

I get out and for a second Mom hesitates, as if she can sense how much I don't want to be here, but then she launches in.

"Liam," she says, "these are the guys."

The guys? Not such an impressive bunch.

One of them, the one who gets introduced as Eddie, is wearing a nice shirt, but it's pink. Unless you're a masculine guy, you really can't carry pink, so it's best not to try. Eddie is not a masculine guy. In fact, he's probably the most effeminate man I've ever laid eyes on, and I saw some really effeminate men when Mom was still modeling. But Eddie takes the cake. He is super skinny and he has short blond hair that curls tight against his head. He's wearing white snakeskin boots, and when he says hello to me, his wrist literally dangles. It's like he matches every stereotype of a gay guy and I wonder why he doesn't do something different. Wear another shirt maybe?

Then there's Dino. Dino is the polar opposite, and I could swear Aunt Pete hired him as some sick joke. Dino is HUGE. He has the world's biggest biceps and he's wearing a black Harley T-shirt that is way too small. Waaaaay too small. He's bald and he's got tattoos up and down both arms. Plus, he's got one of those belts with the huge belt buckle on it, and the belt buckle is actually in the shape of a skull. I can't believe anyone really wears this stuff. I mean, if he were doing it on purpose as a fashion statement about clichés, then okay, but something tells me he's not.

Then there's Orlando. Orlando is not so bad. He's got on jeans and a plain shirt. White button-down. Classic style. The jeans fit right, and they break around the shoe in a good spot. Not bad. The clothes don't say much — pretty middle of the road — but in my head I add a touch of color and some really awesome shoes. And a modern jacket to offset the long brown hair he wears in a ponytail down his back.

Aunt Pete clears his throat. While I've been studying his friends, he's been studying me.

"You've grown up," he says. "You look good."

"Thanks," I mutter. Pete's got on a plain black T-shirt and ripped-up old jeans that tell me nothing. He's got greasy salt-and-pepper hair and stubble, and he's sizing me up like I'm the next archvillain in a franchise movie. I glance at Mom and wonder why she likes him so much.

And she really *does* like Aunt Pete. Mom stays for over an hour and she's more animated than I've seen her in years. After we take my stuff out of the car, we all sit around this old picnic table and talk, but you would think Mom was giving an interview to *Vogue*. She talks with her hands and tosses her hair like she used to during photo shoots.

I sink back and listen to their conversation.

"Remember the time we slept out on the beach after that concert?" "Remember when Dino mooned the security guard?" "You guys still play gigs after all this time?"

They steer clear of certain topics though. Me. My future. Our home life.

It's all boring crap about the good old days until just when Mom's about to leave, and then she says, "I remember the night I met your father, Liam. I was in the front row at a Glitter concert — that's your uncle's band — and anyway, I was with this guy I was dating at the time. He was the quarterback of my high school football team and everybody just *loved* him, but really he was a total jerk. I'd had to drag him to the concert in the first place, and then when we were there he kept heckling the guys, until finally I told him to leave. I was so mad I didn't even care that I'd be stuck out in the middle of nowhere with no way to get back to the Hamptons.

"I was crying and that's when your dad came up and asked if I needed help. You know, Li, when your dad was young, you could just tell he was going to be somebody important. That very night I thought, if this guy will have me, I'll marry him in a heartbeat."

Mom's eyes are far away, then she blushes.

"And he *has* become somebody important," she says, "so I guess I was right."

"Sarah . . ." Pete starts, but she stands up.

"Allan will be waiting for me. I've already stayed too long, and of course, he's furious about . . . well, anyway . . ."

Her voice trails off.

"Liam, you're going to love these guys. I promise." She brushes her fingers against my cheek. "This is only temporary," she says softly. "Your father will change his mind soon. Honestly, Li, he doesn't mean the things he . . ."

Mom stops and looks at her feet. I'm the one person she's never been able to lie to. The guys shuffle awkwardly as the silence stretches on, then finally Mom hugs me good-bye — a quick, guilty squeeze of my shoulders — then she climbs back into the little red convertible and drives away.

8

IN THE MOMENTS after Mom's car disappears from sight, I think about that football player. The jerk. *Mr. Popularity.* Then I think about Delia crying as she tried to find her clothes, and my cheeks get hot. I finger the cell phone in my pocket, knowing I should call her to apologize, but right then Orlando, Dino, and Eddie are getting ready to leave.

"It's good to see you, Liam," Dino says, and I try to smile or nod, but instead I just clutch the cell phone tighter.

Aunt Pete says stuff like, "You've got to go to the station now?" and, "I thought that wasn't until Thursday," until finally Orlando leans over and whispers in his ear, just loud enough so I can hear. "Relax. You'll do fine. You two just need some time to get to know each other."

I can tell Pete and I are thinking the exact same thing.

No. Really. We don't.

But once they're gone, we're left standing outside. Just me

and my long-lost, crazy uncle. My complete set of matching luggage is on the ground in his driveway, my surfboard is propped against the front door, and Pete looks like I feel — as if he wishes someone would shoot him.

"So," he says at last, "do you want to move your stuff in?"

I don't really. He gave me the tour when we first got here, and it was dark, cramped, and smelled like moldy Doritos.

"Okay."

We both grab a suitcase and I grab my board, and Aunt Pete opens the trailer door, which is this rusted old wire contraption with a hole in the middle of the screen. We make a couple of trips back and forth from the driveway through the living room and the tiny kitchen, which is overrun with beer cans and electrical equipment, into the minuscule guest room.

I don't mind, because while we're making trips we don't have to talk, but eventually all the bags are stacked and there's nothing left to do. My luggage takes up most of the space in the bedroom. There's a mattress on the floor, a huge blue dresser, and a broken macramé lamp. The carpet looks like it hasn't been cleaned since 1990. Maybe not even then. I look around for a closet, but there isn't one.

"Where can I hang my clothes?" I ask, but Pete looks blank.

"There's a closet somewhere, right? I have some designer stuff from Mom's boutique and it really needs to be hung up."

Aunt Pete runs his hand over his chin. "Mmm. No. No closet."

My stomach twists.

"An iron then?"

He shakes his head.

He's got to be kidding me. How can someone live without an iron?

"Do you want to talk?" Pete asks. "In the living room?"

I don't. I just want to go to bed and never get up again, but I can't exactly say no when my uncle looks like he's in physical pain from trying so hard.

"Okay," I say again, and my smile feels strained.

We go into the living room and he clears a stack of records off the couch. It's a zebra-striped couch with half the stuffing falling out, and Aunt Pete flicks chip crumbs off the arm. There's a long silence while we study our shoes. Mine — square-toed Gucci loafers. His — god only knows.

"So, what do you like to do?" he asks.

I try hard to think of something, but sometimes, when you're miserable, you can't remember a single thing that makes you happy. I shrug.

"Anything special you like to eat?"

"I'm a vegetarian," I say, and I can tell Aunt Pete is horrified.

"What do *you* eat?" I ask, and he cringes.

"Meat," he says. "Mostly all meat."

Neither of us can think of anything to say after that, so I study the stuff he has up on the walls. It's weird junk. There's a stuffed, mounted blowfish, and a huge framed picture of this guy in gold leopard-print spandex.

Garish.

"So, what's the surfboard for?" Aunt Pete asks when the silence becomes unbearable. I wonder if he's making fun of me.

"Surfing."

Pete narrows his eyes. "You do know there isn't an ocean anywhere near Pineville, New York? There isn't one for miles and miles, and even then there aren't really waves one might surf?"

Of course I know this. I'm not *that* stupid. Still, I'm not about to explain about Dad buying it for me.

"Yeah," I say. "I know that."

Aunt Pete gets up and does one of those fake stretches.

"Well, then," he says. "I guess I'll make us some dinner. I must have some vegetables around here someplace." He goes into the kitchen. "Can't say I have a lot to choose from." He emerges from the freezer with two boxes of frozen spinach. "I suppose we can have spinach tonight."

I'm waiting to see what recipe he'll use the spinach in, but he empties each box into a plastic bowl, sticks them in the microwave, and when they're done he hands one bowl to me.

That's when I realize my life has truly changed. It's like this whole time I've been playing some elaborate game, but the minute he hands me the spinach, I understand. This isn't a game. No one's coming to get me. I'm going to live with this man.

I will now eat frozen spinach straight from the box and wear wrinkled Kenneth Cole shirts until the day I'm released from trailer-park prison.

Life is officially over.

9

I'M DREAMING OF MOM.

She's posing at a photo shoot, and Dad and I are standing off to one side, watching her. There's a male model standing behind her and he's one of the best known in the industry. He's tall. Blond. Tan. Muscular. The model is wearing a football uniform and he's touching Mom, running his hands up and down the length of her body, but this is no big deal because it's part of Mom's job. She's explained it to me before. I stare at them, watching the way their faces change as the lighting changes, but Dad isn't watching them. He's watching me. I'm ten, and while most kids have probably started their awkward stage, I look like a smaller version of how I look now. Dad looks at the male model. Then back at me.

"Do you want to know who your real father is?" he asks.

I look over, startled.

"I'll show him to you," Dad goads.

"You're my father," I tell him, but Dad shakes his head.

"Look," he says. "This is your father now."

I look up and the male model is gone. Aunt Pete is posing next to Mom, his beer belly hanging out over a leopard-print Speedo. He turns to me and grins.

I sit up in a cold sweat. My heart is racing, and for a moment I think I'm at the photo shoot in Paris, but my surfboard is lying next to my head and there are suitcases everywhere. Then I think I'm at home, only I hear voices. No one's ever home at my house. For a second I think it might be the remodelers again, but then I realize the voices are whispering about me.

"We can't just wake him up."

"Why not? It's noon. I'm just going to —"

"No!"

"What do you mean 'no'? He's not going to spontaneously combust if I wake him up at noon."

"Teenagers need their privacy."

There's a snort. "At this rate he'll have nothing but privacy. He's got to wake up sometime."

"Just knock on the damn door."

I sit up and stare in horror. Everything comes rushing back, and I realize I'm in Aunt Pete's trailer in a trailer park in upstate New York. I flop backward and pull a sheet over my head.

"There's got to be something he'll want to do."

"The park!"

"What kind of a stupid...You can't take a teenager to the park."

"A museum then. Darleen loves museums."

"Guys, come on. Darleen's a freakin' prodigy. When we were seventeen, did we ever go to museums? No. We've got to think of what we used to do when we were his age."

"Cross-dressing at glam-rock concerts?"

"Shut up. Orlando, you're the teacher. You think of something. I'm going to knock on the door like this and then you say something. On the count of three. One, two..."

I can't stand it. I open the door and Aunt Pete's fist is poised just inches from my face. Eddie and Dino try to lean casually against the refrigerator but only manage to knock off a lot of plastic beer-shaped magnets. Orlando is sitting at one of the bar stools in the kitchen.

"Morning, Liam," Pete says as if everything is normal. I try to smile, but it comes off as a pained frown.

"Hi."

Aunt Pete sticks his hands in his pockets.

"We, uh...were going to see if you were awake."

I nod. "I am."

"The museum," Eddie blurts. "We thought you might want to go to the science museum a couple towns over. It's small, but I used to go there with my cousin and she liked it. You'll meet her soon because she lives next door. We could invite her today if you both wanted to go and..."

Dino grins. "Smooth, Eddie," he says. "Real smooth."

Everyone's staring at Eddie, and he turns a bright shade of pink. It almost matches the silk shirt he's wearing. I can't help wondering if there are any other colors in his wardrobe, but I don't ask. I also wonder if Eddie's cousin is the girl I saw with her dad yesterday.

"I'm sure you don't want to go to a museum on your first day here," Aunt Pete says, turning to me. It's somewhere between a question and a statement, and once again I can't tell which answer he wants. The honest answer is definitely no.

"We could, uh, go to the museum," I say. "I like museums . . ."

Orlando laughs from the kitchen.

"Liam," he says, "how about breakfast? You could take your time getting up, and whenever you're ready we could make breakfast. Or lunch for those of us who've been up since morning."

Aunt Pete nods, looking like he might collapse. "Yeah," he says. "That's exactly right. We'll make whatever you want."

Dino grins and Eddie sighs loudly. I take a deep breath. Breakfast is definitely better than a science museum.

I have the impression that "take your time" didn't mean an hour. The guys are draped around the living room while I make a hundred trips back and forth to the tiny, filthy bathroom at the other end of the trailer. I consider rushing, but getting ready is a ritual, so I do each thing carefully. I shower, shave, moisturize, and choose cologne — the one that matches my mood — then put together the right clothes. Nothing high fashion or anything — those are best left for the runway — just the brands and designs that will fit in but are interesting enough to catch people's attention.

Getting ready is the only part of my day I can be sure I won't screw up.

Back home I never let my guy friends know I do all this stuff. If they happen to notice all the product I've got around my room, I tell them I get it free from stylists who visit Mom's boutique. Which is partly true. But I buy a fair amount of it, too. That drove Dad insane. I can hear him now, "You're worse than my gay brother!" but in fact, Aunt Pete owns no product at all other than a large bottle of aerosol hair spray from the 1980s and a razor that's so rusty you could get tetanus from it.

I'm thinking how wrong Dad was about Pete, wondering if maybe he could be that wrong about me, too, only the whole time I'm thinking this, I'm also trying to devise an iron out of an old electric teapot that I've got plugged into the wall, and I don't know if it's because I'm distracted or because screwing up is in my blood, but the next thing I know I smell smoke. I look over and the teapot is smoldering on the cardboard box I was using as an ironing board. Outside my room I hear Aunt Pete saying, "Do I smell smoke?"

I lunge for the teapot and pick it up before actual flames emerge, but by then Pete's cracked open my door and he sees what's almost happened.

"Sorry," I say in a rush. "It was an accident. It won't happen again. Honest."

The words come out sort of hysterical, and Pete makes a concerned face.

"It's all right," he says. "No harm done."

No harm done?

I nod, but I can't help staring at the smoldering box, wondering if it's a sign of things to come.

10

EDDIE MAKES AN EGG-WHITE OMELET for my breakfast and burgers for their lunch. Aunt Pete puts on seventies music, which I can't stand but pretend to tolerate. Dino sits on the couch and air drums to all the songs, and Aunt Pete sticks close to Orlando. They hold hands, so I'm gathering that Orlando is his boyfriend. I try *not* to imagine them kissing as I listen to Pete telling me about Pineville.

"It's pretty small," he says, "population of about nine hundred fifty-seven and a half — that's you since you're temporary. And I won't try and tell you there's a lot to do around here. Mostly there are a lot of cornfields and cows . . ."

"Do you have a mall?" I ask.

"Not in Pineville."

"Outlet stores?"

"Uh. No."

"There's the radio station," Eddie offers.

Aunt Pete grins. "Maybe I'll take you in to work with me sometime," he says, like I'm five. "It's a couple towns over, but we broadcast throughout the whole valley. Maybe after lunch . . ."

I try not to look bleak.

"What are your hobbies, Liam?" Orlando asks.

"Surfing," I mutter, for lack of a better answer.

Eddie clears his throat and dishes out my omelet, but doesn't actually say anything. The guys exchange glances, and there's a long, awkward silence.

"So, how are things at home?" Pete asks at last, and then he chokes, like he realizes too late what a monumentally stupid thing that was to say.

"Uh . . . good. Other than being kicked out. Dad got another award for being businessman of the year. Mom's boutique is busy. She's selling a lot of jewelry now in addition to the clothes. People come all the way from Manhattan to shop with her."

Aunt Pete nods. "Your mother was always good with people."

"What about you, Liam?" Dino asks in his deep baritone. "What are you good at?"

This has *got* to be a trick question. If I were good at stuff, I wouldn't have gotten kicked out of my house, right? I think about using Dad's "Liam is very social" line, but instead I shrug.

"Well, what are your plans for the future?" Orlando asks. I figure what he really means is do I intend to be a lazy screwup mooching off Aunt Pete all year. Since Orlando is Pete's boyfriend, maybe he also means how long until they can have some privacy again.

[45]

I give him my most sincere look. "It's good that you asked," I say, "because I want you — all of you — to know that I've done a lot of planning, and what I've planned is to be as responsible as possible so my father will let me come home very soon. I imagine this will be like a short vacation really. Hopefully painless."

This is a total and complete lie, but I think it's what everyone wants to hear.

"I meant, what are your plans after you graduate?"

Oh.

I stare at my water glass, then take several controlled sips.

"I don't know," I say at last.

"No ideas?" Aunt Pete says. "You're a senior, right? Don't you have to decide these things pretty soon?"

I shrug again. "Maybe I'll get into business like Dad."

"Business?" Aunt Pete chokes. "Why the hell would you want to choose . . ." he starts, but Orlando nudges him violently as he passes by to go to the fridge, ". . . that fine career choice?" Pete finishes.

I pause. How can anyone think Dad's career choice is anything less than, well, perfect?

"Dad makes a lot of money," I say, wondering if he's testing me.

Aunt Pete scoffs. "Yeah, but money isn't everything. You've got to do something that makes *you* happy. If business is really it, then go for it, but . . ."

"But what?"

"Nothing." Pete puts his napkin down hard, and I can tell he wants to say something else, but Orlando cuts him off.

"Business is a fine choice if it's what you decide you want to study," he tells me. "Maybe you'll figure that out while you're here." Orlando looks from me to Pete, then back again. "You guys are going to enjoy getting to know each other," he says. "Petey has wanted this for a long time. Ever since . . ." He stops and looks down at the remains of his lunch. "Well, anyway, I'm sure you're going to do great here, Liam."

I think, *Ever since what?* but then Dino lifts his glass and says, "Here's to Liam joining us for a short, painless vacation!"

Five glasses clink loudly, but no one actually takes a drink.

11

AS SOON AS IT'S HUMANLY POSSIBLE after the welcome toast, I clear my breakfast plate, wash the dish, and grab my cell phone. I know I should stick around and do the obligatory social thing, but I want to call Delia.

"Do you mind if I make a phone call?" I ask.

The guys glance at one another.

"Nah," Aunt Pete says, hesitating, "but are you sure you don't want to go out somewhere? Maybe for a tour or, uh . . ."

"Some other time?"

He shrugs. "Well, okay."

The minute I'm outside I go over to the picnic table, lie down on top of it, and close my eyes. The truth of my life is like the refrain from a bad song I can't get out of my brain.

I'm living in a trailer park. I'm living in a trailer park. I'm living in a trailer park.

Finally, I force myself to sit up and take out my cell phone. I flip it open and attempt to dial Delia's number. Only I never got it from her, so I call my friend Brice instead. His cell rings just once before he picks it up.

"Dude," he yells when he hears it's me. "When are you coming back? There's this awesome party coming up next weekend and —"

I can't stomach hearing about a party right now.

"I'm not coming back for . . . a while," I say. "My dad's pretty mad this time. Listen, do you know Delia's number?"

"Delia Washington? Why the hell would I have *her* number? Besides, she probably hates you, man. I heard she got in trouble big-time over that whole thing." Brice pauses. "Did you fuck her? How was it?"

I swallow hard.

"No," I tell him. "My dad walked in, remember?"

"Oh. Right. I don't know why you'd want to anyway, man. You could do way better."

Part of me wants to defend Delia, but I know Brice and it's not worth the bother so I just play along. It's the easiest way to get what I want from him.

"I was kind of plastered," I say, "and I don't know, it seemed like, what the hell . . . Listen, can you just look up her number in the phone book or something?"

Brice laughs.

"Did you at least get her pants off before your dad came in?"

I'm losing patience. "Yeah, man. Pants, shirt, the whole deal. Are you looking up that number?"

"Panties?!" Brice asks with this high, shocked inflection. I can tell he is not going to focus until he hears every detail.

"Almost. We were pretty much inches away from doing it and that's when everything . . ."

I can't say the words. I wonder if Brice might react to my getting kicked out, but he doesn't.

"Was she hot once you got her clothes off?"

"What?"

"You know, was she a babe underneath . . ."

I take a deep breath.

"I don't know," I say, interrupting. "Sure. She was hot. I don't really care anymore, I just . . . did you find the number?"

Brice snorts.

"There's about a hundred Washingtons in the phone book. You know where she lives or something?"

I want to pound the cell phone into my skull.

"No," I say. "You know what? Forget it. It isn't that important."

"Okay. Listen, call me if you want me to come sneak you out of there or something. I could drive down and pick you up, then drop you back in the morning before anyone even knows you're gone."

"Sounds great," I say, even though Pineville is probably too far from Westchester to make that plan doable. "I'll call you."

I hang up the phone and close my eyes for a second, and when I open them that's when I see her. The girl next door is sitting on her front steps, and from the look of things, she's been sitting there the entire time. Crap, she probably heard everything I said.

"Oh, uh . . . I didn't know you were sitting there," I say lamely. "That was . . . well . . . you see . . ."

That's when her front door opens and her father steps out.

"I've got to head in to work," he tells her, resting his hand on her head. "I'll be home around —"

He stops when he notices me.

"Why, hello!" he says in that phony cheerful way adults have of introducing themselves to kids. "You must be Liam. Eddie mentioned you'd be staying with Peter for a while until . . . well . . . Have you met my daughter, Darleen?"

I stand up and shake his hand.

"Are you a senior? Maybe the two of you will have some classes together."

I nod dumbly, and Darleen's father puts his arm around her shoulder and pulls her close. This kid is his pride and joy. You can tell.

"Darleen is poised to graduate at the top of your class, and she's first cello in the orchestra."

"*Dad,*" Darleen says, "I'm the only cello."

Her father laughs and I can't help but stare at the two of them. Their eyes and mouths look exactly alike. They've both got that dark hair and the small chin. They could probably win a look-alike contest.

"I wanted her to apply to Juilliard," Darleen's father is saying, "but she's thinking about art school in London instead. What are your plans, Liam?"

"I don't have any," I mumble.

Darleen and her father exchange glances.

"Well . . ." says Darleen's dad, clearing his throat. "I'd better get going, but I'm sure the two of you will have plenty to talk about."

"Nice to meet you," I say. Then I watch as he kisses Darleen on the top of her head.

"Have a good day, Dad," she says, and it's like she's reading from a *Let's Reenact What Liam Doesn't Have* script.

He gets into his car and drives away.

"Do you want to sit down and talk for a minute?" I ask, thinking maybe I can explain about my conversation with Brice, but Darleen turns.

"Phone's ringing," she says, although I swear it's not. I open my mouth, but she's already gone.

12

I'M SITTING NEXT TO MOM AT DAD'S AWARD BANQUET. There are a hundred round tables made up with perfect white tablecloths and delicate, shining crystal glasses. Dad is giving a speech, so we're at the table in the front. Mom is wearing an original Valentino gown, and I have on an Oscar de la Renta suit that is one of the sleekest items of clothing I've ever worn. Mom and I have gotten a thousand compliments, and for once Dad seems pleased. Everyone smiles and nods in our direction.

When Dad gets up to give his speech, I'm honestly excited. It's not every day your dad gets a major award and has a banquet thrown in his honor. He's wearing a tux, and he actually let me give him advice about what style and color to choose. Black on black. Straight cut. Classic style.

Dad goes up to the podium and looks out over the vast ballroom. His eyes well up.

"Tonight," he says, "I feel like the luckiest man alive. Not

only am I the recipient of this wonderful award, but I am sur-
rounded by those I love best —"

I hold my breath.

Let this be it.

Let this be the time he says it.

"— the business community. I truly could not imagine more
worthy colleagues than yourselves . . ."

I stop holding my breath and my lungs feel like they might col-
lapse. My eyes sting and I stare at everyone as they watch Dad.
They're beaming at his compliment, captivated by him. They adore
him and he adores them. You could hear a pin drop.

Or a cell phone going off in my pocket.

I scramble to stop the sound, but I can't find the damn thing.
All eyes turn to stare at me, and Dad glares down from the podium,
but the phone just keeps ringing and ringing.

Aunt Pete's phone is ringing. I hear him shuffle out to the kitchen,
so I open my bedroom door a crack, and there he is in a silky but-
terfly kimono and orange tube socks.

Aunt Pete works nights at the radio station — 9:00 P.M. until
6:00 A.M. — so he sleeps during the day. I wonder who would be
rude enough to call on a Wednesday morning at eight-fifty when
Aunt Pete should be sleeping.

His eyes are half shut, but he takes a beer out of the fridge,
then takes a box of chocolate-frosted cereal out of the cupboard,
pours it in a bowl, and finally he picks up the telephone with one

hand just as he's reaching for the microwave sausages with the other. "Y'ello," Aunt Pete says.

I don't know what the voice on the other end says, but Aunt Pete says, "HELL!"

He flings open my door with the phone tucked between his shoulder and one ear. Then he dumps his cereal back in the box, although most of it spills on the counter. He's making horrible faces and I can tell I'm supposed to be doing something, but I can't figure out what.

"School," he whispers madly.

School? I think. *Now?*

Aunt Pete flags me toward the bathroom.

"School starts today?"

"Yes," he mouths. "Right now. You're late."

Crap.

I go into the bathroom and try to shave in record time, but now the ritual is ruined. I hear Aunt Pete hang up the phone and he yells, "I'll be ready in ten minutes." Then I hear footsteps pounding down the hall.

Maybe *he'll* be ready in ten minutes . . .

I expect Pete to knock on the bathroom door at any moment, but it turns out I'm ready before he is. That's because he's tearing apart his room looking for something. He's on his knees, digging around under the bed, and there's a lot to dig through because Pete's room is a mess. I mean, it's a pigsty. No amount of floor space shows through. There are records and CDs everywhere, half torn apart turntables and keyboards and stuff. Plus, McDonald's bags from god knows when. I wonder what he's looking for, but I don't have to wait long to find out.

"There was a manila envelope," Aunt Pete says, breathless. "Your mother FedEx'ed it here. It has everything. Your transcripts, the letter transferring temporary guardianship . . . shit. Where would I have put it?"

I never thought about the fact that there'd be legal documents involved. I'm guessing Mom probably forged Dad's signature — she's great at that — so they're probably worth nothing when it comes right down to it, but I figure I'd better get in there and help look anyway. Even though I'm wearing my favorite pair of jeans and my best Skechers, I wade into Aunt Pete's bedroom.

For a while the two of us search through everything in this really frenzied way, but when it's clear the manila envelope isn't going to be found anytime soon, I stop looking so hard and start watching Pete. He's really upset, and I wonder why he cares so much. It's not like it's *his* first day of school in a new town.

I study him the way he studies me when he thinks I'm not looking. I wonder how old he is. He looks about fifty. Maybe fifty-five. He's got lines all over his face, and he generally looks scruffy, but not in a terrible way. I wonder how come he doesn't look more feminine. I figured a guy who likes to dress up as a woman might keep his beard shaved at least. In fact, short of the kimono bathrobe, I haven't seen him in one women's outfit. Except for the red dress that hangs on the back of his door, but that was a long time ago.

I grin when I see the dress, remembering Mom's retirement party. Pete sees me looking and stops digging through his dirty clothes bin.

"You remember that?"

I nod. "Did you and Mom plan that entrance?"

I've always wanted to know.

Aunt Pete hesitates, but then he laughs. "Yeah," he admits. "We planned that days in advance. Laid out every detail ahead of time . . . how she'd be in the living room with my parents, and as soon as they started ripping on her — because there was no question they would — the maid would sneak out the back and tip me off."

"So you were waiting in the car the whole time?"

He nods. "Yup, only it almost didn't work out so well because I caught the train of the dress in the car door when I was rushing to get inside and . . ." Suddenly his voice trails off, then he stops completely. "You know," he says, "it was a stupid joke. If we'd known how your father would react, we never would have done it. I mean, we knew he'd be mad, but we didn't think . . ."

I remember Dad's face when I told him I was going to stay with Aunt Pete instead of his parents.

". . . he'd go ballistic?"

"Yeah." Pete nods. "Nuclear explosion. I never realized he was so much like our father until that day at the party, but by then it was too late. After that he never let me come back. Your mom and I screwed up, big-time."

I want Aunt Pete to say more, but for some reason he doesn't, so while the silence drags on I stare at the red dress.

"So, do you still wear it?" I ask at last. "The dress, I mean . . ."

Pete looks up, as if I've startled him.

"No," he says. "I've never worn it again."

He eyes the dress and there's a hint of longing in his eyes. It's designer, still in mint condition — layers of sheer red silk. He looks at it the way most guys would look at a Corvette. Then he looks away.

"Come on," he says, "we've got to find those papers."

13

WE DON'T FIND THE PAPERS.

In fact, after searching the entire trailer three times, Aunt Pete gives up and goes back to bed in despair.

"You'll get to school tomorrow. I promise," he says.

That's fine by me. I'm not exactly jumping for joy about starting a new school. The only problem is, this means I have an entire day to fill without texting, e-mailing, or using my cell phone since all my friends are in school and Aunt Pete doesn't own a computer, which is insane. I'm not sure what people who don't own computers do with their lives, but I opt for a marathon of old *America's Next Top Model* reruns because Dad's not around to tell me to "turn that crap off."

When Aunt Pete shuffles out of his bedroom that afternoon, J. Alexander is showing everyone how to perfect their runway walk. He's this large African American man everyone calls the Queen of the Runway, and I have a vague memory of meeting him once in Paris. I wonder if Aunt Pete will say anything about the flamboyantly dressed man strutting down the catwalk in a mini-skirt, but he just squints at me as I lie on the couch eating popcorn.

"Weren't you in this exact same spot five hours ago?"

I nod.

"What are you watching?"

"Nothing," I say, flicking off the TV.

Pete scratches his chin.

"Well, you can't just lie around the trailer all day. I guess we should . . . do something. Uh . . . something together, maybe. What do you normally do after school?"

"I work with Mom at the boutique."

Pete frowns.

"Anything else?"

"Well, I like to go running."

Somehow I can't imagine Pete will want to go running, but he nods.

"Right. Okay. I can do that. I used to run back in the day. Dino and I did a five K once in college, when he was training for the police academy. Just let me get ready."

He ducks into his room, and I try to digest the fact that my uncle is actually going to go running with me. I find my sleek blue Adidas running shorts and brand-new Pro-Wear sneakers in my bedroom, change real quick, then wait outside for him. As I'm waiting, Darleen comes out with her art supplies.

She's wearing overalls and clogs, and it is *not* a fashion statement. It's a mistake. Loulou de la Falaise was once asked which item of clothing she considered an absolute fashion "don't," and she said, "Those things with the straps." Overalls.

"Hi," I say.

"Hello," she says back.

That went well enough, so I decide to say more.

"I'm going for a run with my uncle."

Darleen smiles. "Great."

Now there's an awkward silence, and I hate those, so I say, "You want to come?"

I cringe because that sounded dumb. Obviously she's not dressed for running. I can already see the way her eyes are narrowing and I can tell she's thinking how stupid I am, so I add, "Running is a great cardiovascular workout," because *cardiovascular* is a large, impressive word. Then I add, "It will improve your heart health and help you lose weight."

The instant the words escape my lips, I wish I could stuff them back in.

Darleen's eyebrows shoot up, and she takes in a sharp breath.

"I didn't mean that the way it sounded . . ." I sputter, but she's already turned on her heel to go back inside. When she opens the door to her trailer, I hear her say, "I am NOT fat," and whether she's saying it to me or to herself, I can't be sure.

Crap.

I'm debating about knocking on her door and explaining, but right then Aunt Pete comes out, dressed in the most horrible spandex shorts I have ever seen in my entire life. They're black with a white, blue, and yellow confetti design, and he's got on a bright red muscle shirt.

"Oh god," I murmur, but Aunt Pete is oblivious. He's doing overenthusiastic stretches next to the picnic table.

"This is great," he says. "I haven't gone running in years. This is just the incentive I've needed to get back into it."

I look back and forth between my uncle and Darleen's trailer, but I don't have time to do anything because Pete claps loudly and jumps up and down several times. His beer belly jiggles under his shirt.

"Let's go," he says.

We take off slow, and Aunt Pete sighs loudly. "Ahhh, this is perfect."

We're not even out of the driveway yet.

"The great outdoors . . ." he murmurs as we pass the first trailer.

My legs are barely moving we're going so slow. In fact, I consider just walking, but I don't want to insult him.

"Wait until I tell Orlando about this," Pete adds.

I pick up the pace ever so slightly.

"Have you guys been together a long time?"

Aunt Pete nods. "Off and on since high school."

That's a *very* long time when you're as old as he is.

"So how come you don't live together?"

Pete pauses. "It's complicated," he says, and I frown because people have been telling me this my entire life.

"How complicated can it be?" I ask, trying to keep the edge out of my voice. Pete glances over.

"Well," he says, wiping a layer of sweat off his brow, "sometimes people love each other, but when they try to live together they drive each other insane."

I snort. As if I don't know *that*.

"Is that why Gram and Gramps kicked you out? Because of Orlando?"

Aunt Pete's feet barely make it off the ground. "No," he says, huffing loudly between words. "I got kicked out . . . because your grandfather . . . caught me trying on . . . one of your grandmother's dresses . . . You can imagine how well . . . that went over."

I've got to admit, even I can't top that one. "Where did you go?" I ask. "Afterward, I mean?"

"I went to . . . Orlando's house," he says between gasping puffs of air. "His parents were much more . . . open. They took me in . . . until I finished school."

I'm cutting my strides in half so he can keep up with me. "So that's when you two started dating?"

"Yeah. Of course, his parents didn't know that." *Puff.* "I mean, hell . . . this is the seventies we're talking about." *Puff, puff.* "Open as in caring, tolerant, and generous is one thing. *Open* is another."

He stops for a moment and puts his hands on his knees.

"I've just got to tie my shoes," he says, even though they're clearly tied already. He makes a big deal of kneeling down and untying each shoe real slow, then retying it and double checking the knot.

"We can go back to the trailer if you want," I offer, but Aunt Pete holds up one hand.

"No way," he says. "Are you kidding? This is great. So much fun."

He forces a smile that's so pained, I don't ask any more questions for a long time.

"So your band is pretty popular," I say at last. "How come you live, uh, here?"

That came out wrong, but Pete looks like he's in too much pain to really care. He tries to laugh, but it comes out as a sputter.

"Pineville's where . . . my friends are," he says. "And the band . . . had its heyday . . . a long time ago . . . before glam died . . . a painful death . . ." Aunt Pete stops on the word *death* and gulps in a huge breath. He stands still for a minute with his hands on his knees, then forces himself forward again. "It's a hobby now . . . but that's okay . . . brings in some extra cash . . ." He glances over at me. "Aren't you . . . getting tired?"

"Tired?" I say. "Oh, right. Sure."

"Okay, then," Aunt Pete puffs. We make it the rest of the way around the loop, and then he collapses onto the driveway. His shirt is soaked and he's breathing so hard I worry he's having a heart attack, but eventually he gets up and brushes himself off.

"Great workout," he says as he staggers to the front door. "We'll have to do this again sometime."

14

DAD AND I sit across from each other in the school psychologist's office. We're here to talk about the fact that I've been suspended yet again for accumulating too many detentions.

"Liam, the things you've gotten detention for — talking during lectures, not bringing in your homework, chewing gum, texting, making out with girls in the halls, being late, skipping first period, forgetting your books, sleeping in class — do you see your behavior as a cry for attention?"

I shift awkwardly. "No," I say, crossing my arms over my chest.

"And you, Mr. Geller? How do you view Liam's behavior?"

Dad snorts. "It's certainly not motivated by lack of attention. Liam gets more than his fair share."

He means from Mom, but I don't say that. The psychologist makes a note in her notebook. She asks us a lot more questions about my transition to high school and Dad's job and Mom's past, but then she returns to the attention thing.

"What was the last activity the two of you did together?"

There's a long silence while Dad and I try to come up with one. I can see him getting annoyed, and finally he rolls his eyes.

"Breakfast, lunch, dinner, making sure his homework is done, cleaning up after him, buying him everything he asks for . . . Trust me, this kid is not neglected."

The psychologist nods slowly.

"Liam, what would you like your father to do together with you?"

I uncross my arms and sit up straighter. No one's ever asked me this before, so I feel as if a genie in a bottle just asked for my wish. I think about it a long time.

"Basketball," I say at last.

Immediately Dad shakes his head. "You know I'm not good at sports," he says. Then he turns to the psychologist. "If my son really wanted my attention, he'd choose something he knows I enjoy."

Dad stands up, glancing at his watch. "Time's up."

That night Pete finally locates the FedEx envelope under the couch cushions along with the TV remote.

"Thank god," he breathes. "I was beginning to think it was gone for good." He's wearing a white satin women's nightgown and fluffy slippers and holding a beer. "We'll meet with your principal tomorrow."

I'm feeling out of sorts, so I shrug like it's no big deal. "You can just drop me off. I'm sure I can handle the meeting on my own."

Pete looks appalled. "No way," he says. "While you live here, I'm your guardian. That means I go too."

I don't know why, but I roll my eyes just like Dad would. "You don't look much like a guardian," I say.

Aunt Pete stops drinking his beer and nods slowly.

"Anything else?" he asks.

"What?"

"You should get it all out now. Because after this I don't want to hear it. This is my home and I will do what I want here. Got it?"

"Yeah."

"So?"

"So what?"

"Is there anything else you want to say?"

There is. I want to say thanks for taking me in, and thanks for going running, and maybe tell him that I don't really care what he wears because I've seen men in just about everything you can imagine on the runway, but instead I say this:

"Just that you're not my father."

"I'm not trying to be."

"Good," I say, and I mean it.

The next morning we meet with Principal Mallek. I dress in a new pair of Diesel jeans and a short-sleeve button-down shirt that looks studious, yet cool, because I want to project the look of someone who is about to take life seriously, but apparently Aunt Pete wants to project the look of someone who hasn't changed his clothes in three days, because he arrives home from the radio station wearing the same rumpled outfit he wears every day.

I think about the way he dresses at home — everything satin

and shiny — but the rest of the time he looks like he couldn't care less.

"Let's go," he says when the clock hits eight. This seems way too early to leave, but I follow him out to his zebra-striped Nissan. When we get to the school office, he paces outside the principal's door.

"What's the matter?" I ask.

He shoots me a look. "I don't want to screw this up."

When the door to the principal's office finally opens, Pete and I file inside and take the two large leather chairs across from his desk.

"So, you're Liam Geller," the principal says, sizing me up. "My secretary tells me you're transferring from Westchester. I'm not sure if you're aware that school actually started yesterday here in Pineville."

I nod. "We couldn't find the papers . . ." I start, but Pete gives me a look, so I shut up.

"Well, I trust you have the papers today," Principal Mallek says. I nod and look to Aunt Pete to hand them over. Only he's looking at me.

"I don't have the papers," I say. "I thought you were bringing them."

Aunt Pete's eyes get big, and he starts to sputter.

"Do I look like I'm carrying papers?" he asks. "They were on the kitchen counter. I thought you took them!"

Principal Mallek takes a deep breath.

"We can't move forward without the paperwork, so perhaps you'd like to go get it?"

Pete stands up. "Of course," he says, glaring at me. "You wait here. I'll be right back."

I open my mouth to protest but think better of the idea. Instead, I sink back into my chair, preparing to make myself comfortable, but Principal Mallek clears his throat.

"You can have a seat out in the secretaries' office while you wait."

"Oh," I say. "Right." I get up and move to one of the stiff plastic chairs in the outer room. I keep myself busy drawing doodles of Principal Mallek's long neck and tiny head, which look even worse because of the vertically striped shirt he's wearing. If I could, I'd tell him to wear only solids and preferably things with collars, and I imagine a whole new Principal Mallek wearing a dark gray, double-breasted overcoat with a solid black turtleneck, but just as I'm thinking this, Principal Mallek walks past me and sees the drawing of his long neck and pinhead.

Crap.

By the time Aunt Pete arrives with the papers, Principal Mallek is grouchy, and when he finally hands me my locker number and schedule, he says, "You're off to a bad start, Mr. Geller. Hopefully you can improve upon this."

"He will," Pete says before I can answer.

A loud bell rings, and Principal Mallek says, "That would be the homeroom bell," so Aunt Pete and I shuffle out of his office.

"Catch you on the flip side," Pete says, and he heads back out to the Nissan. I wish I could follow him, but instead I make my way through the halls, trying to find my locker. Which isn't hard since this school is ridiculously small.

Then I spot Darleen.

Her locker is right near mine, and when I come walking up, she looks totally disappointed to see me — like maybe she was hoping I wouldn't be going to school this year.

"Nice to see you," I say as Darleen walks away. She doesn't turn around.

I see her again because we both have physics first period. The fact that I even *have* physics is appalling. I suck at science and math, and physics involves both of those things, so I'm doomed.

Still, I make a point of waving to Darleen again in the hall before class, but she doesn't wave back. She goes directly inside and starts talking to the teacher. *The teacher.* Then, as if that's not bad enough, when the teacher turns around, it turns out it's . . . Principal Mallek. I look at my schedule twice.

Since when does the school principal teach physics?

Principal Mallek nods when he sees me.

"Mr. Geller," he says. "Since you couldn't make it in yesterday, you've missed some important information, so I'd advise you to sit down and pay strict attention."

I nod.

The only empty desk is in the front by the window, so I take it. Since class hasn't started, I decide to take a lesson from Darleen and I ask Principal Mallek a question.

"Do you always teach this class?"

"Excuse me?"

Suddenly the room gets really quiet. Just a minute ago, when I asked the question, people were talking, taking out their books . . . but now they're all sitting quietly. I rearrange my stack of pens as everyone stares in my direction.

"I just meant, because you're the principal and all, I didn't know if you were also a teacher. Like if you had a teaching degree too, which would qualify you to teach physics, or . . ."

This is coming out all wrong.

Principal Mallek turns beet red. It starts on his neck and climbs to the top of his tiny balding head.

Crap. Crapcrapcrapcrap.

"I didn't mean . . . uh . . ."

Principal Mallek swallows hard. "If I were you, Mr. Geller, I'd worry about your grade. Not my credentials."

Now some kids are outright laughing. Principal Mallek takes out a single piece of paper, walks over, and slaps it on my desk.

"The rest of the class took this pretest yesterday." He's all business now, but his eyes seethe. "Write your name on the top. It *is* timed and it *does* count toward your grade. Since I'm assuming you had to pass chemistry in order to leave eleventh grade, this should be no problem. The rest of you turn to page eight."

I stare at the paper. Timed tests make me nauseous. Plus, I only passed chemistry with a C–, which would have been a D except for the final test I paid some kid to help me study for. I'm looking at the paper, but my mind goes blank and all the words blur together. Principal Mallek's voice is grating in my ears, distracting me, and I wonder what Darleen will think when she finds out how stupid I am.

That's when I start to panic. I think how each thing will affect the next — how I'll get these questions wrong, which means I'll fail the quiz, which means I'll fail the class, and if I fail the class, I might fail school, and then I'll never get a job and end up homeless.

The only letters that aren't blurring into the paper are H_2O, so I write the word "water," then I stare at the clock and wonder how many minutes I have left.

"Time's up," Principal Mallek says, hovering over me.

What? Time can't be up. If I'd known it was going to be such a quick pretest, I wouldn't have wasted all that time counting minutes. Principal Mallek picks up my paper and carries it to the front of the classroom.

"Let's see what our new student has impressed us with today," he says. "Hmmm. Looks like he has answered exactly one question. The question reads, what elements combine to form H_2O, and Mr. Geller has responded . . . 'water.'"

The class snickers, and I sink low in my chair.

"Very clever, Mr. Geller," Principal Mallek says. He walks over so that he's standing directly above me. "Let me tell you something. There are no free rides in this school. You're not going to coast by. I expect you to work hard, and if I see that you're doing that, I'll work with you, but if you expect to sit here and give me attitude all year, you'd better think again." He drops the paper onto my desk and turns away.

"All right, class, the rest of you turn to page ten."

Day One, Class One, and already I have screwed up.

15

EVERYTHING AFTER PHYSICS IS A BLUR. I sit through French IV, civics, and health, but my mind has shut off. People say hi to me in the halls and introduce themselves. A girl named Jen makes a point of welcoming me to school, and two kids, Joe and Nikki, invite me to sit with them at lunch — but all I can think about is how I messed up.

It only gets worse. During math I blank out at the exact moment the teacher asks me to solve a problem on the board, and in economics I think I can turn my day around by impressing everyone with my vast knowledge of the World Bank, but I get it all wrong. I thought I could say what it was, since Dad does a lot of work with third-world debt, but the truth is he's never really explained it to me. How is it that Dad can give national lectures about this stuff and I can't even define it?

I'm starting to feel really tired, and then I get lost on the way to my last class and end up in the choir room. I could probably make it if I run, but by this point I think, *Screw it.* So, I take my time and finally step into the open doorway of classroom number twelve about four minutes late. I pretend to be reading my schedule, like I've been studying it hard this whole time or something and *that*'s why I'm late, so I don't look up right away.

"I got a little bit lost, but I've got my schedule right here, and I promise it will never happen —"

I look up and my jaw drops. Orlando is standing in front of my English class. I glance at the number on the classroom door, because now I really do think I read my schedule wrong, but sure enough, this is the right room. My schedule says English IV — Mr. DeSoto. Apparently, that would be Orlando.

He walks over and takes the schedule out of my hands.

"Liam," he says.

I'm frozen in place. How is it possible that no one thought to tell me Orlando taught senior English? I mean, they said he was the high school English teacher, but why would I assume he taught *senior* English? Unless, of course, he's the *only* English teacher . . .

"You can take a seat in the front," Orlando says. "We're doing some freewriting, so in the future you'll need to bring a notebook, but today someone can lend you some paper and a pencil. Jen, would you mind?"

Orlando is tapping on an empty desk, but my feet are lead. I'm thinking, *I can't take English from my uncle's boyfriend.* How should I act? Should I pretend we've never met? Say hello?

I walk slowly across the front of the classroom and take the seat Orlando's pointing at. He turns back to the class.

"Okay," he says. "As I was saying, yesterday we talked about writing personal essays for college applications. Today I want you to write a practice essay. I've come up with a pretty broad topic for this first one, something you've all done a million times, so I want you to write at least two pages. You can work at your own pace, but I want your pages handed in at the end of class." Orlando walks to the chalkboard and writes: "The best part of my entire summer was . . ."

Crap.

There's no way I can write about that. My summer sucked. There was no best part. I got grounded immediately, and Mom was going to take me to Milan for a fashion show but Dad said no. Actually, I heard them fighting and what he said was, "It's not worth going all that way just to take Liam."

I've got to think of something, so I write, "The best part of my entire summer was the party at Mike's house." Then I erase it because actually I got drunk, ended up sleeping with Andrea, who later told everyone it had been a mistake. Then somehow my dad heard something from Andrea's mother, who said it was all my fault and . . .

I chew on the top of my pencil and decide I hate essays. They're so much work, and for what? Not everyone is going to college. I stare out the window. Eventually, I write, "The best part of my entire summer was when I went to Hawaii to see my friend Julio." Only, when I got home I overheard Mom talking to Dad and she said, "You only sent him to Hawaii because you don't want to look at him anymore." I erase that, too.

Then I put my head down on my desk.

"Time's up. Papers forward. Tomorrow we're going to read the first act of *Hamlet*, so bring your books." Orlando's stacking our papers into one big pile. The bell rings — *finally* — and I am *sooo* out of here, but Orlando steps in front of me.

"Liam, may I see you a moment?"

I nod and he points at my desk.

"Have a seat." He's holding my paper, and he looks like he can't quite decide what to say. "You've written the word 'the,'" he says once I sit down. "I gave you an entire class period and a broad topic and you were only able to write the word 'the.' Do you want to talk?"

The answer to that question is definitely no.

"Is it because I'm dating Pete and now I'm your teacher? Is that a problem? I want you to know I intend to keep school stuff at school. You can trust me on that."

I nod as if it's no big deal.

"I'm not going to treat you any differently than I treat my other students," Orlando continues. "Every other student managed to hand in two pages of writing on the assigned topic. *Every* other student."

He waits a beat.

"I need you to hand in two pages on the assigned topic." Orlando hands me back my paper. "I've got some lesson plans to go over, so we can sit here until you're done."

I stare at the blank paper. All day I've been counting the seconds until I could leave, and now he wants me to sit here trying to answer an unanswerable question?

"I can't think of anything," I say, but Orlando doesn't look sympathetic.

"You don't have one good memory of your entire summer?"

I shake my head, but I don't really want to get into it, so I sigh and pick up my pencil. Guess I'd better make one up.

16

IT'S SUMMER and we're living in California for a year. I'm eight years old, and Dad and I are out back, behind our house, enjoying the most perfect June evening ever. He got home from work on time, and Mom's out running errands, so rather than make dinner, Dad suggested we pack a picnic instead. It'll be light out for a couple more hours, so we traipse out to my tree fort with a backpack full of peanut butter sandwiches and juice boxes.

Dad brings *Treasure Island* and reads it out loud. I'm trying extra hard to be good and sit still, but when Dad isn't looking I inch closer and closer until I'm pressed up against him, looking at the pages over his shoulder. I put my hand on his arm, and he feels warm and solid. Sometimes, as Dad reads, I watch his face instead of the book.

"'Fifteen men on the Dead Man's Chest — Yo-ho-ho, and a bottle of rum! Drink and the devil had done for the rest — Yo-ho-

ho, and a bottle of rum!"' Dad's voice rings out. *A warm breeze blows through the tree branches and a bird flies out of the leaves. We both jump, and I hold my breath in case he gets angry, but then Dad laughs. The laugh fills the tree fort, and finally I laugh, too.*

"'Yo-ho-ho, and a bottle of rum!'" we say together.

I am completely happy.

When I get home from school, I call Dad. I know I shouldn't, but I do.

I take my cell phone out to the picnic table and call him at work, and his secretary puts me through.

"Hi, Dad?" I say. "It's me, Liam."

"Yes?" Something about the restrained quality of his voice makes me think there's probably someone near his office. That and the fact that he's not hanging up.

"I thought maybe we could talk," I say. "It's been a while since I left, and I want to apologize for everything that happened with Delia. And for calling Pete instead of Gram and Gramps. I know I've made a mess of stuff. Again."

At first Dad doesn't say anything, but then he clears his throat.

"Things aren't going well for you at your uncle's?"

He sounds almost hopeful.

"Uh . . . everything's fine," I say, not sure if this is what he wants to hear or not.

"I'm sure it is," he says. "What do you need? I don't have all day."

I stutter, trying to remember why I called. Talking to Dad always throws me, because he's so much smarter than I am. He says stuff that means two things at once, and while I'm thinking about that I get distracted, so then what I say comes out sounding dumb.

"I thought maybe I could come home," I blurt out, even though I didn't mean to say it yet. "It's only one more year, and I've learned my lesson. I really have. I'm —"

Dad interrupts before I can finish.

"Liam," he says, "let's not waste our time here. The answer is no. You're not doing well. You haven't learned any lessons. Let's not go through this whole charade."

"Dad . . ." I start.

"I'm hanging up now," he says. End of discussion.

"Do you even notice I'm gone?" I ask, just to throw him off. "Do you miss me at all?"

But the whole time I know he's already hung up.

I lie on the picnic table with my head hanging over one edge and my earphones on, and stare up at the clouds, feeling the warm breeze blow over me.

"'Yo-ho-ho, and a bottle of rum,'" I whisper, letting all the air collapse out of my lungs. I'm trying to calm myself down with deep cleansing breaths — and I'm doing a pretty good job — until someone stands over me and yells.

"Could you please move over?"

It's a disconcerting feeling when you're hanging upside down and someone sneaks up on you like that. I nearly fall off the picnic table. I try to turn the volume on my iPod down, turn it up instead, and have to yank the earphones out of my ears.

"You practically killed me!" I say, sitting up fast enough to get a head rush. Darleen is standing above me and she's not the least bit apologetic.

"Of course I didn't," she says loudly. "You're three feet off the ground. And you're taking up the whole picnic table. I need you to move."

"Sorry," I tell her, sliding over. She sits down as far from me as she can get.

"I saw you in school today," I add, for lack of anything better to say.

"Thanks for the bulletin."

"I didn't intend to imply that you're fat. The other day, I mean."

Her eyes narrow, but she says nothing. After a long time I say, "Do you want to know anything about me? Since we're neighbors and all."

She opens her sketch pad and shakes her head. "You're Pete's nephew." The way she says it implies she's heard bad things. "You got kicked out of your house and now you need a place to stay until your rich father allows you to come home again."

"How do you know that?" I ask.

"Because," Darleen says, "Eddie is my dad's cousin. Eddie told Dad, and Dad told me. Said you were some sort of juvenile delinquent who had no place to go if Pete didn't take you in. They

[81]

seem to think I should be really nice to you as an act of charity, but I don't think that will be necessary."

"What?" I say. "Why? And just so you know, I'm not a juvenile delinquent." I think about telling her the whole sordid story of how I ended up here but think better of the idea. "It's not true about having no place to go, either. I *asked* to live with Auncle Pete."

Darleen shrugs. "Whatever."

She keeps on sketching, adding charcoal lines to the pencil outline of Pete's old boots, which are sitting by the steps. I can't help staring because she's transforming these old, cruddy boots into something amazing.

"That looks good," I tell her.

"Thanks," she says, but it's flat.

I wait for a long time without saying anything else, but then I can't stand it.

"It's pretty cool that we have some classes together, don't you think? I mean, today didn't go so well, but . . ."

"I'm trying to concentrate," she says sharply. "If you want to sit here, don't let me stop you. Just don't take up the whole table."

The way she says it reminds me of the way Dad says, "I'm busy, Liam," so I think, *Fine. Forget it then.*

"Maybe I'll go inside," I threaten. I take a step forward, thinking she'll feel guilty and call me back, and when she doesn't I turn and glare at her. "You know," I say, "I don't need your charity, but sometimes people are friendly to other people who are new in town just . . . well, because they might need some friends."

I expect a look of remorse, but instead she chuckles. Laughs right out loud at my indignant speech. She stops and finally looks at me.

"Somehow," she says, "I don't imagine you'll be lonely for long. You look like one of those guys who should be doing underwear ads."

She says this like it's a bad thing.

"And didn't I see you talking with Joe and Nikki, Pineville's power couple, today in the hall? Wasn't that Jen, the head cheerleader, helping you find your classrooms? And if I'm not mistaken, a group of girls hung out at your locker and said they were the Pineville Welcoming Committee? Well, here's another news bulletin. There is no Pineville Welcoming Committee. So if you want me to be all nice to you because you're in need of friends, I really don't think that's going to be necessary."

"How can . . . I don't . . . I'm not at all like what you think, and if you gave me a chance . . ."

She just keeps going.

"Don't try to pretend you're not Mr. Popularity after having been at school eight hours," she says. "I don't mean to be rude here, but you and I can enact this nice social parody of being all buddy-buddy because we're neighbors, or we can save ourselves the time and effort. You'll do what you do, which, if I'm guessing correctly, is to be wildly and naturally popular, and I'll do what I do, which is to concentrate on my art. All right?"

She's giving me that patronizing look I've seen a thousand

times before. The I-need-to-speak-slowly-and-simply-because-Liam's-in-the-room look. But all I can think is, *I'm not Mr. Popularity.*

More than anything in the world, I want to prove her wrong.

"As a matter of fact," I say, "it's not all right, because you have just made a lot of assumptions and . . . suppositions . . . and enacted a discriminating ritual based on the wrong, er, information. I am not popular at all, actually. I'm really very unpopular. Wildly unpopular. I was hoping to hang out with you at school, but now I will eat lunch alone beside the garbage pail or something like that. And furthermore," I say, "I'm going in." I get up and grab my iPod.

Darleen sighs. I wait for her to argue, but she starts sketching again.

"I'm going inside now," I repeat.

"Mmm-hmm."

"You could at least say good-bye."

She puts down her pencil and glares.

"Fine," she says at last.

"Fine?"

"Yes."

"Good."

"Great."

"Okay."

"Bye."

This time I really do go inside. In fact, I stomp into the living room and fling myself onto the couch, which is only half cleared of stuff. Pete walks in, stops short, backs up, stops again, and scratches his beard.

"Something wrong?" he asks.

"No," I say firmly. "Nothing is wrong."

But the truth is, *everything* is wrong.

17

"COME IN, PLEASE. Shut the door behind you."

I slide into my seventh-grade guidance counselor's office.

"Am I in trouble again?"

"No. You're not in trouble. I'm talking with all the students this year about your future plans and how you can achieve your goals. Tell me, what would you like to be when you grow up?"

My mind slides across an image of the runway in Paris and I remember the feel of the colors and lights, but just as quickly I let it fade.

"That life is not for you," Dad always says, and Mom said it too. "Oh, Li, modeling is a crazy business. What about doing something with your hands? You love to build stuff."

I try to think of something else I might become. Maybe an astronaut?

"What are your skills, Liam?" the guidance counselor asks, leaning in. "What kind of aptitudes do you possess?"

I can't think of any skills I have, so after kicking the leg of my chair, I say, "I'm really popular?"

The guidance counselor chuckles.

"Being popular isn't a skill," he says. "I'm looking for something substantial. Do you like math or science?"

"No," I say, frowning. "What do you mean by 'substantial'?"

"'Substantial' means that something has a purpose. A significance. Being popular doesn't mean anything other than that people might like you."

Might? But they do like me . . . don't they? Could they be pretending?

"You need to pick a different aptitude," the guidance counselor says. "Something that can help you unlock your future."

As soon as he says it, I finally understand what Dad means when he says I've compromised my future. Now the image is perfectly clear . . . my future as a locked door.

After talking to Darleen, I decide I'm going to stop being Mr. Popularity. I look around Pete's trailer full of glam-rock records, zebra stripes, chip crumbs, empty cans, and drab brown paneling, and I realize that this is exactly what Dad always warned me about.

This is my future: compromised.

It's possible that it's too late to turn things around, but maybe moving in with Aunt Pete is the wake-up call Dad always said I needed. My last chance to make things work.

So Monday morning, instead of my usual ritual, I stand in

front of my mirror combing my hair down as flat as it will go. I don't have a cowlick, but I try to create one, which is harder than it sounds, and involves a lot of hair gel and a rusty old curling iron Aunt Pete happened to have stuck under his bathroom sink. Just as I've finally mastered the perfect flattened, mishmashed spot on the back of my head, I see Pete squinting at me from the kitchen.

"What are you doing?" he asks.

"Fixing my hair. What does it look like?"

He squints harder, so I slip in a casual question.

"Would it be okay if from now on I take the school bus? There's a bus that goes by here, right?"

Aunt Pete frowns.

"You want to take the bus instead of having me drive you? In my day, not too many seniors rode the bus."

I shrug.

Pete has the cereal box poised over his bowl, but he stops and screws up his face.

"Is everything . . . okay?" he asks at last. "I know we don't know each other all that well yet, and I don't mean to imply that somehow I think you're acting strangely if in fact you're not acting strangely, but . . ." He loses his train of thought. "I guess what I mean to say is, um . . ."

He clears his throat.

"Well, were you talking to your father the other day? I wasn't listening in or anything, it's just that you got home and it didn't seem like you'd had a great day at school, so I was concerned, and

I thought maybe before you were lying on the picnic table you were talking to your dad. And then over the weekend you seemed kind of different. So, uh . . ."

My body gets tense, and for a moment I genuinely panic. I run through the whole conversation I had with Dad in my head. If Pete knows Dad won't let me come home, he might kick me out, and if that happens, I'd be moving to Nevada for sure. No other options.

"That wasn't Dad," I say quickly. "Did it sound like it was Dad? Because it wasn't. It was my friend Brad. He's a good friend but we fight sometimes, and that's who it was."

I'm a horrible liar.

"Your friend Brad?"

"Yeah."

"And you're not acting even a little bit odd? I mean, you always spend your weekends reading the dictionary?"

"I'm improving my vocabulary."

"Okay," Aunt Pete says with a resigned sigh. He finally pours the cereal. Then he looks like he's going to eat it, but he doesn't. "I just hope you aren't trying to be someone you're not. That's something I've always tried not to do. A lot of people say, hey, why do you live in a dumpy old trailer in a small hick town, but you know what? That's me. I like my job; I like my friends; I like my band . . . and you've got to be true to what *you* like. No one else."

I nod, but the whole time Aunt Pete's talking I'm thinking about the red dress, wondering why he doesn't wear it anymore if he's so liberated. If there's one thing I actually know about, it's clothes, and Aunt Pete's boring old T-shirts and jeans are *not* him.

"You can't let others dictate what you think about yourself," Pete's saying. "In fact, there was this one time —"

"So, is it okay if I get dressed now?"

There's a long pause. "Sure," he says at last. "Don't let me stop you."

"Cool. I'll be right out."

I shut my bedroom door and stand in front of the curtain rod I've turned into a makeshift clothes rack. I need to pick out something uncool to wear, but not a single piece of clothing is by itself unattractive, and since I only wear clothes in my personal color spectrum, even odd combinations of clothes end up vaguely related.

Crap.

Day one and already there are obstacles.

I go out to the kitchen.

"Pete? Can I borrow one of your T-shirts?"

He gives me an exasperated look, but I interpret that as a yes.

"Thanks," I say, jogging down the hall to dig through the clothes on his bedroom floor. Unlike my room, Aunt Pete's room actually has a closet, but it's full of musical equipment, so all that hanger space is wasted.

Mostly Pete has T-shirts, which are great for my purposes, because unless it's a really retro T-shirt, they totally say you're not trying. None of Aunt Pete's T-shirts are retro. In fact, he only has two variations. One of them is black with white lettering and the other is white with black lettering. They all say WXKJ on them because he gets them free at the radio station. The only variation from this rule is that occasionally one of the T-shirts has a red lightning bolt through the WXKJ letters. I choose one of those.

"Pete?" I holler.

"Yes?"

"Could I borrow some shoes?"

None of my shoes are uncool.

"Hunhunhh? Come on now . . ."

"Thanks."

I dig around under a pile of silver and gold leotards until I locate a battered sneaker. I pull it out and search for the match, but Aunt Pete peers in the door.

"What the hell are you doing?"

"I don't have anything to wear."

It's surprising how fast an old guy like Pete can move when he wants to.

"Out!" he hollers, coming around behind me and pushing me toward the door.

"But . . ."

"OUT!"

I don't have time to find any shoes, but at least I have the T-shirt. It'll do. In fact, it will be perfect. I take it into my room and try it on with my worst pair of pants. Gap khakis. Then, since I didn't get the sneakers, I slip on my oldest shoes. Suede loafers.

I examine myself from every angle and decide I still look good. The outfit needs something. I tuck in the shirt and, as much as it pains me, I resist the temptation to balloon out the front and back. *Much better.* Now all I need is a studious accessory. This one almost stumps me, but then I see the pack of pens sitting on my floor. Now I'll be unpopular *and* have pens to write with.

Excellent planning.

I put the pens in the back pocket of my pants and go outside to wait for the bus. I haven't ridden the bus since elementary school, and I've forgotten whether I'm supposed to do something to flag it down. I don't do anything and it passes me by, but it stops at Darleen's trailer, so I head over. The bus driver glares at me as I climb the stairs. He's short and stout with huge ears.

"You're not on my list," he says.

Am I supposed to reply to that?

The driver nods at Pete's trailer.

"That's Rockin' Pete's place, isn't it?"

I nod.

"And that would make you the ne-pha-ew?"

He says the word *nephew* as if it has three syllables and is a synonym for serial killer. I nod more slowly, and the bus driver looks like he's considering kicking me off the bus already. How is that possible? Do I emit some sort of scent? Ode de Screwup?

"I don't put up with any attitude," he says. "Got that? Don't try any funny business or I'll send you packing. You got that?"

Yes, I got that. Honestly, I can't imagine what kind of funny business a person would try on a bus, but I certainly won't be racking my brain to come up with any. All I want is a quiet seat in the back of the . . . nooo, wait. Make that the front of the bus. I'm in luck. There's an open seat next to Darleen.

"Mind if I sit here?"

She nods. "Yes," she says. "I do."

I look around for another seat, and fortunately the girl sitting behind Darleen says, "You can sit here." She moves her books, spilling half of them, and I can't help but notice she's got bright red hair and purple braces. Since she's stuck with the braces, she should dye her hair a dark brown and invest in lots of clothes with small touches of purple somewhere on them, like these purple camouflage pants I saw once online. Nothing solid because that would be too much, but . . .

I realize I still haven't sat down, so I slide in next to her.

"Hi," I say. "What's your name?"

"Rebecca," she answers. "You can call me Becky. Are you Liam?"

I wonder how come she knows my name, but maybe she works in the front office or something.

"That's me," I say. Then I decide that probably sounded too cool, so I change tactics. "I mean, uh, yeah. I'm new here. Just moved to Pineville from Westchester. I don't know anyone yet."

The girl giggles.

"My mom heard from Annette, who heard from Donna, who heard from Eddie that you got kicked out of your house because you slept with a model," she whispers. "Is that true?" It's a loud whisper and I can sense the ears perking up all over the bus.

"What?!" I blurt out. "That's not true. I mean, I slept with this girl, but she wasn't a model."

"Oh," she says. "Then it wasn't that Vanessa girl from the cover of *Elle*?"

I snort. "Vanessa Hart? I wouldn't sleep with her in a million years. She came to my mom's boutique once with her stylist, and she's a real bitch when she's not doing press."

"You actually *know* her?" the girl asks, leaning in.

Crap.

"No. I mean, yes. But I didn't sleep with her. I wouldn't . . . or I mean, she wouldn't sleep with me. That's what I meant."

Now everyone on the whole bus is leaning forward. We hit a speed bump and everyone jumps.

"The truth is," I say, trying to dig myself out of the hole I just created, "I got kicked out for sleeping with a really unpopular girl. She wasn't even pretty but she was the best I could do . . ."

Oh, god, that sounded horrible.

" . . . and I was drunk at the time, which is very uncharacteristic of me, because usually I'm very focused on academics. So, anyway, I don't know what you heard, but the truth is I'm just grateful for my aunt Pete . . . I mean, uncle Pete! Did I say aunt Pete? I meant uncle. Uncle Pete."

I am literally starting to sweat. I can feel it dripping down the back of my T-shirt, and I cannot wait for this bus ride to be over. For the first time it occurs to me that being unpopular might be harder than I think.

18

ONCE WE ARRIVE AT SCHOOL, I am determined not to screw up.

I follow Darleen off the bus and try to make conversation on the way into the school building, but she's preoccupied with hanging up flyers on all the school bulletin boards before the bell rings. This looks like a good opportunity for me to be enthusiastic, so I stand next to the library board waiting for her.

"Hi," I say, when she shows up.

She sighs and hangs up a flyer.

SAVE THE ARTS! SAY "NO" TO HOMECOMING! URGE THE SCHOOL BOARD TO REALLOCATE FUNDS!

"No" to homecoming? Who would be against homecoming? I'm confused, but I plaster a grin on my face anyway.

"Great cause," I say, nodding at the flyer. She glares just as a guy in a football jersey reads it. He looks like he's ready to tackle someone — namely, Darleen — so I step in between them.

"Funny," I say, loudly. "This is a great joke."

The football player looks me over. I'm hoping maybe he'll punch me or something, because then right away I will have gotten beat up by a football player, which would be perfect, but instead of tossing me into the row of lockers, he says, "You're new here, right? You should join the football team. Just sign up with Coach if you're interested. We always need players so there aren't any tryouts or anything."

"Uh, thanks," I say.

"No problem."

He walks away, and when I turn back Darleen is staring at me with her arms crossed over her chest.

"I should have expected that from you," she says.

Then she turns and stomps off to class.

"Did you at least notice my outfit?" I call after her, but I can't tell if she hears me and she certainly didn't appear to notice that I look like a dork.

In fact, no one at school seems to care. It turns out that Pineville High is a very friendly place. Especially the girls.

That girl Jen, from my first day, asks me to sit with her at lunch, and I totally want to because she's hot, but I remember Darleen said Jen is head cheerleader, so I shouldn't get mixed up with her. But she catches me just as I come out of the lunch line with my tray, and I'm not sure where else to sit.

"Over here!" Jen hollers, waving me down.

I walk over real slow. "I shouldn't," I say, shifting my weight from one foot to the other.

Jen looks confused. She's got light blond hair pulled back in a ponytail, and her eyes are a perfect clear blue. Plus, she's matched her shirt to their exact shade.

"Why not?" she asks.

I glance around the cafeteria and spot Darleen reading a book. I think it might be our physics textbook.

"Well, uh, just because."

"Because why?"

That's when Joe Banks slides his tray over to make room for me.

"Come on," he says. "We're cool."

That's what I'm afraid of. Joe Banks is the captain of the football team, and his girlfriend, Nikki, is hanging over his shoulder.

"It's Liam, right?" she says.

"Yeah . . . but you can call me . . . uh . . ." There aren't any awful nicknames for the name Liam. ". . . well, Liam."

Suddenly I'm exhausted, so I sit down just for a minute. I pop open my milk with one hand and take a huge gulp as Jen eyes my tray.

"How come you only have hamburger buns?"

I glance down, forgetting what I took from the lunch line.

"Oh, that. I'm a vegetarian."

Jen gasps. Then she claps. She actually *claps* for me.

"That's so cool," she says, giggling. "Guys are never vegetarians." She leans in close. "I'm thinking of becoming a vegan. Is it hard?"

That's a silly question. It's not hard at all if you think about what's in meat products these days.

"My mom's a vegan," I say. "Dad's vegetarian, but only because of Mom. He sneaks meat whenever he can. I never even tried meat until I was twelve years old, and then it was by accident because I went to someone's house and they made lasagna with meat sauce. I thought the meat was tofu, so I ate it and it made me sick. Meat's pretty gross."

Joe makes a face. "Gross?" he says. "I live for meat." He makes a muscle. "Got to bulk up."

"Hey," I say, "everyone's got what they like. I guess if I liked meat, I'd eat it, but . . ."

It suddenly occurs to me that I'm having way too casual a conversation with these people. I glance over my shoulder and Darleen is watching me over her book.

"You know, I really should go," I say. "I've got some, uh . . . studying to do. I'm aiming for a four-point-oh this year. Got to buckle down."

Jen looks disappointed.

"Okay," she says. "Maybe we'll catch you later."

I pause. I don't want her to feel bad, so I smile. "Yeah," I say. "That would be great."

Of course, I don't really have any studying to do, so I end up in the guys' bathroom, killing time until the bell rings. That kind of sucks. Then when the bell rings, I accidentally bump into Darleen in the hallway on my way out. Twice.

Actually, she bumps into me. She sort of trips over the long skirt she's wearing and her books go flying. I help her pick them up, even though she's acting like it was my fault she tripped, and then just when she's got them all together, she starts to walk and trips again because really her skirt is way too long *and* she's got on clogs, which are hard to control. I make a mental note to trip more often.

"Enough already," Darleen says when I try to help her up, and then she stomps off down the hallway as if somehow it's my fault she tripped.

There's something unnerving about being blamed for stuff you didn't do. The only thing worse is getting blamed for things you *did* do. In English, Orlando hands me back the essay he made me stay late to write, and it has a C– marked at the top along with the words "More supporting details."

Great.

And that's only the beginning. First it's, "Sit up, Liam," then it's, "The chalkboard would be in the front of the room, not out the window," then, "Where's your notebook?" He nags me about every little thing, and even makes me read out loud. Apparently we're reading Shakespeare, which I hate. When it comes to class, my plan was to keep my mouth shut because people always assume quiet people are smart and studious, but Orlando calls on me three times and I get every answer wrong.

To make matters worse, Jen catches me as we're leaving.

"Mr. DeSoto is a really tough teacher," she says, "but once

you get caught up, you'll like him." This is nice of her, only Darleen walks by right when she says it. Jen's leaning toward me, looking sympathetic, and Darleen smirks knowingly, and I know what she's thinking.

Don't try to pretend you're not Mr. Popularity ...

I am doomed.

19

THE NEXT MORNING when my alarm goes off, I force myself not to hit snooze. I crawl out of bed, take my towel down the hall to the bathroom, and get ready to shower. I turn the water on so it's steaming up the room, but I run my hand over the mirror and stare at my reflection before I get in. I want to see some shred of Dad staring back at me, but all I see is Mom.

I let the reflection cloud back up again, and for a moment I want to heave, but I step in the shower instead and let the hot water wash everything away.

While I'm in there, I give myself a pep talk that goes something like this:

Damn it, Liam, you idiot, this should not be so hard. Stop screwing the fuck up.

It's not much of a pep talk, but by the time I get out of the shower I've resolved that today people will actually notice how uncool I am.

Once again things start out okay. When Pete isn't looking, I sneak into his closet and dig around to find an outfit even worse than the one I wore yesterday. I'm in luck because he owns both an actual fringed vest and some very old pants that have bell-bottoms. This seems too good to be true, and when I try them on they're too short and way too wide, which is even better because then I can wear an ugly belt. I flatten my hair, gel my cowlick, stick my pens prominently in the pocket of the vest, and wait for the school bus.

The bus driver goes right past Pete's trailer and stops for Darleen, so I jog over and trip going up the stairs. Then just for good measure, I trip again as the bus doors shut. The driver glares at me, as if my tripping insults him.

"No funny business," he reminds me, and I nod, sliding into the seat next to Becky. It's odd though. Yesterday everyone was sitting in the back of the bus when I got on, but today they're all sitting up front, almost as if they're waiting for me.

A guy in a football jersey gives me a nod and kicks his feet up on the bus seat.

There's also this girl sitting behind me who is dressed all in black, and she's got on the perfect Goth makeup. She sizes me up, then looks back out the window.

"Hey, Liam, I heard you're in Jen Van Sant's English class," some guy in a fedora says. "She's hot, huh?"

"Yeah, I love that class," I say, dodging the hot issue. "I am going to *ace* English this year."

"Are you sure?" Becky asks. "Because I could tutor you if you need help."

Darleen smirks at me over her shoulder.

"That's okay. I won't need help," I lie, but the fedora kid interrupts.

"I heard Mr. DeSoto is in a band with your uncle. You seen 'em?"

Now there are two ways to play my cards here. I could pretend that I'm horrified by Pete's band and hope that makes me uncool by association with something horrific, or I could pretend to love Pete's band and hope that makes me uncool by virtue of having bad taste. I go with bad taste.

"Yeah, I've heard them," I lie. "Great stuff. I love seventies music. Stuff like ABBA and Bowie . . ." I can't think of any other musicians from the seventies. "And Bowie . . . and ABBA."

"Is it really a drag band?"

I think about what Mom told me when she was reminiscing about the band. "Nah," I say. "It's a glam-rock cover band, not a drag band."

Everyone looks blank, so I feel compelled to repeat her lecture.

"A drag band dresses up like women, but a glam-rock band just dresses up. You know, crazy stuff. Leather pants. Sequinned jackets. Feather boas. It's gender-bending. Very retro Manhattan."

Once again everyone is staring, so I run my fingers through my hair the way I do when I want it to look tousled. It's a nervous habit, but then I remember I don't want it to look tousled, so I smooth it all back down again.

"They're still a bunch of fags," mutters a voice, just loud enough to be overheard. My first thought is to wonder what kind of teenager still thinks like this when we live in the twenty-first century. But then it sinks in. The bus driver is staring at me in his rearview mirror, simultaneously pretending he didn't make that comment and challenging me to do something about it.

I feel the blood rush to my face.

No one's going to mess with Aunt Pete.

"I suppose some people might put them down," I say loudly, as if I'm still talking to the kid who asked the original question, "but that would be pretty ignorant. Every rock and roller dresses up. My uncle's got more balls than most men in this town; that's what I think."

The Goth girl sits up and makes a fist. "Yeah," she hollers. She's looking at me like she has newfound respect, and then she slips me a cigarette real sly, like we're friends now. This might have felt good, only the cigarette barely touches my hand before the bus comes to a screeching halt.

Crap.

The bus driver stands up. "No smoking on the bus," he growls. "I want you off."

"What? I wasn't even smoking!"

"Off."

"But I don't know the way to school."

This time the driver actually grins. "I warned you," he says.

"Isn't this against the law or something?"

The driver steps forward and glares. "Are you threatening me?" he asks, real low and quiet. "Because if you're threatening me, you'll find out what I'm capable of. Besides, you weren't on my list in the first place."

I may not be the smartest guy in the world, but I know when it's time to shut my mouth, so I get off and stand on the side of the road. The bus peels away, and my perfect look gets showered in a dirt cloud.

The situation has now hit maximum fucked up.

20

"DON'T TURN HERE! Slow down. Are you even paying attention?"

I'm fourteen, and Mom, Dad, and I are on our way to visit some friends of Mom's who live in the country. Mom is driving, and I'm sitting up front with her because just before we left the house, when Dad was about to slip into the front seat, Mom said, "Oh, Allan, let Liam sit there."

So Dad slunk into the backseat and now he's been in a bad mood ever since. Mom and I are having a great time though. Mom is driving real fast on the deserted country roads, and every time she takes a turn she laughs and laughs.

"This is just like that time we were late delivering that evening dress to Mrs. Arnauld in Tremont, isn't it, Li? Remember how fabulous that dress was?"

I do. It was practically couture. Brown suede with fur trim, designed specifically for the buyer.

"Yeah. Remember how she threw it in her closet like we'd delivered the dry cleaning?"

Mom laughs until she snorts, and I see Dad watching her from the backseat. There's something far away in his expression, and for an instant I feel sorry for my father.

"It was an amazing dress, Dad," I say, turning toward him. "Mrs. Arnauld is this rich old lady who likes to think she knows about fashion, but she really doesn't, so Mom always does this thing where . . ."

The expression on Dad's face disappears.

"Pull over," he says to Mom. "You're lost, Sarah. You're driving way too fast and you have no idea where you're going."

Mom stops laughing and looks surprised.

"But, Allan, we're . . ."

"Pull. Over. Honestly, if the two of you could stop talking for two minutes and pay attention to your surroundings, we might not end up going in circles."

Mom looks for a spot to pull the car over, but the country roads are narrow and there's no place safe. She slows way down, but Dad leans forward impatiently.

"Liam," he says, "tell your mother to pull the car over!"

"Ma . . ."

"I'm trying. I'm trying!"

"There. You could have pulled over right there." Dad points over Mom's shoulder, and Mom's hands grip the steering wheel so tight her knuckles turn white.

"I didn't see it," she says, just as I yell, "There's a spot,

Mom!" *So first she swerves right and then she swerves left, and no one sees the minivan coming toward us until Mom plows into it. There's a loud metallic grinding noise and then a hiss as steam escapes the front of our car. Dad slams his fists against the seat cushion as the driver of the minivan gets out and heads toward us.*

"Now look what you've done! Why couldn't you just watch where you were going? Would that have been so hard?" Dad gets out to smooth things over, slamming the door hard behind him.

I should watch where the bus is headed as it drives away, but instead I stand on the side of the road staring at my shoes. I can feel that my cowlick is drooping, so I run my fingers through my hair again, and this time I don't bother to flatten it out. I take off Pete's vest and sling it over my shoulder and untuck my shirt. I'm pretty sure that by the time I arrive school will have started, and that means, at best, I can show up late and get detention. And if I get detention, that won't look at all studious, so all the bad things everyone thinks of me will be confirmed.

So I might as well give up.

There's a plaza up the road on the right, which seems as good a place to stop as any. There's an animal feed store (dull), a liquor store (tempting, but I resist), and a hair salon (usually great, but this one advertises cuts for only $10 and they use old Vidal Sassoon photos in their windows — obviously pathetic). I'm beginning to give up on this place, but the fourth shop catches my eye.

HIS AND HERS APPAREL.

When I open the front door, I'm greeted by the sound of

chimes. There's an impressive display of lingerie on one wall, and an entire rack devoted to men's boxer shorts — nice brands, too. Tommy Hilfiger. Ralph Lauren. Nautica. I pick up a pair of black silk, no-button fly shorts, and I'm examining the waistband when I hear a voice from the back of the store.

"We're not actually open for another . . ."

I drop the boxer shorts, then hurry to pick them up again.

"Liam?"

"Oh. Uh, hi, Eddie."

I try to look casual, but that's hard to do when you're holding black silk boxer shorts in the middle of the morning on a school day. Eddie looks surprised. He glances at my too-short bell-bottoms and frowns.

"What are you doing here?" he asks. "Aren't you supposed to be in school?"

Hmmm. Right. School.

"Well, yeah, but there was this incident on the bus this morning . . ."

Eddie's holding an entire stack of multicolored women's thongs, and he dumps them on the checkout counter the minute I say "incident."

"Oh no," he says. "Do not tell me you got kicked off the bus."

"Well, I wouldn't except . . ."

"Why? What did you do? Ohmygod! Petey's going to have a fit and then your father's going to go insane!"

This is not helping.

"No one needs to tell my father," I say quickly. "And it wasn't my fault. I swear! I got kicked off for smoking, but I hadn't even smoked yet. I would've gone straight to school, but I got lost."

I reach into my pocket to prove I'm telling the truth. One cigarette. Unlit. Eddie picks it up, letting it dangle between his fingers, then he throws it into a garbage can under the register.

"Those are filthy. You shouldn't even have that." He shakes his hands as if they're somehow contaminated. Then he sits down on a stool behind the register.

"What are we going to do?" He looks like he might have a seizure and it's all my fault.

"Maybe you could give me a ride?"

Eddie considers. "No. That will never do," he says miserably. "Mabel Merriman gets her hair done today, and she always comes in here first and spends a crisp hundred-dollar bill. I can't risk leaving." He fans himself. "I could call Petey." Now I'm the one who's miserable.

"No! Don't do that. I mean, he's sleeping and there's no need to wake him up, right?"

If Aunt Pete finds out about this, I'm gone for sure.

"I could call the school and maybe someone would come pick you up?"

I think about that idea, but I don't like it.

"I don't think they do that," I tell Eddie. "Maybe I should just crash here for a while. You could drive me home at noon and I'll tell everyone I felt sick today."

It's not my best plan, but I don't know what else to do. Eddie sighs loudly. He looks around the shop as if he'll find another option hidden in the women's bathing suit section.

"All right," he says at last, "but if Petey has a fit, this is all your fault."

Now, that's a given.

Eddie and I both sag against the counter. I feel pretty bad that I've dragged him into all this, so I try to make conversation.

"You own this shop?" I ask, glancing around. Eddie nods.

"It's cool. I like the way you've blended the lingerie with the pajamas and bathing suits. I'll bet you increase your market that way."

Eddie perks up, but then he deflates.

"Actually," he whispers, "hardly anyone shops here except some of the women who get their hair cut at Mavis's Beauty Shop." He pauses, and then, even though I haven't said anything yet, he nods. "I know," he says. "That place is a disgrace. I mean, Vidal Sassoon posters from nineteen ninety-five? What are they thinking?"

"And ten-dollar cuts?" I add. "Nothing says bad like cheap."

Eddie nods very seriously. "Oh, honey," he says. "You don't know the half of it. Those women get their twenty-dollar perms, then they waltz over here and expect to get a good bra-and-panties set for under fifteen bucks. I tell them — I say, darlings, that is silk you're holding between your fingers. Pure silk with a delicate lace trim and rhinestone detailing. That is a lace and satin, hand wash only, imported corset and garter belt with matching thong. These things are not cheap! And they ask me when I'm having a half-price sale. Can you imagine?"

"You don't . . . do that?" I ask, trying to phrase the question tactfully. Mom always says that good fabrics are never on sale.

"Hardly ever," Eddie says. Then he looks down. "It's just that I don't sell enough some months. I've tried advertising, but we don't get a lot of traffic in Pineville, and I think a lot of the townspeople order stuff online." He looks as if he's just admitted the entire town buys crack. "They order from JCPenney or those country catalogs that sell granny underwear with crocheted red, white, and blue hearts. You know the places."

Yup. Paragons of kitsch.

"It's not your fault," I say. "Some people can't be reached."

He sighs. "I'm sure it wasn't your fault about the bus, either," he says. "I mean, you weren't actually smoking the cigarette, so the bus driver should have at least waited until you lit it."

"The thing is," I tell Eddie, leaning in, "the driver didn't like me right from the start. He wouldn't stop at Pete's trailer, and then he gave me this whole lecture about no funny business after all I'd done was climb the stairs. Then he made a comment about the band . . ."

The look on Eddie's face says that he can guess what the comment was without having to ask.

"Was the driver's name Bernie?"

I shrug. "I don't know. He was a short, round guy with huge ears."

"Yup. That's Bernie."

"You know him?"

Eddie grimaces. "Yeah." He props his white snakeskin boots

on the counter and tips his stool back. "I hate to say it, sugar, but this is a smaaalll town. Everyone knows everyone, and most people have known each other way too long, if you know what I mean. Our friend Bernie used to beat the crap out of Orlando and me when we were in grade school, but then we grew and he didn't, and we started the band when Petey moved to town in high school. He's hated us for years. I'm surprised he even let you on the bus in the first place."

I drum my fingers on the counter.

"So it wasn't my fault he didn't like me?"

" 'Fraid not."

"And he probably would have kicked me off anyway?"

"Probably."

This is the best news I've had all day. I stand up, feeling my second wind kick in. "I'm going to buy us breakfast," I say, because my stomach is growling loudly. Then I remember I don't have any money with me.

"Er . . . or maybe I'm going to go pour us each a tall glass of water."

Eddie pops open the cash drawer and hands me a ten.

"Go wild," he says. "Mae's Pit Stop is down the street. Walk to the post office then hang a right. On your way back, walk to the post office and hang a left. Don't get lost!"

21

"HOW ABOUT THIS ONE FOR THE SHOP WINDOW?"

Mom holds up a gown imported from Italy. It's long and slim with a buckle in the back and a plunging neckline. The fabric is the color of espresso with extra cream.

I wrinkle my nose.

"What?" Mom asks. "You don't like it?"

"Not for the window."

"Why not? I love this one. I would totally wear this. Look at the way the seams cut in at the waist, and feel this . . ."

She hands me a small corner of the fabric, and she's right, it's so soft it's almost liquid.

"I know, but the back waist buckle is the best feature, and no one will see it in the window."

"Mmm . . ." Mom is thinking it over when the welcome bell chimes and Ms. Brock comes in. She's one of our favorite customers.

Young and incredibly hip. She's a personal shopper for some of the richest people in Westchester.

"Ms. B," I say, "would you buy this dress?"

Mom holds it up so that only the front of the dress shows. Ms. Brock fingers the fabric and traces the neckline with one perfectly manicured fingertip. She glances at me and I shake my head very subtly, then make a whirling motion with one finger. Ms. Brock stifles a laugh.

"Let me see the back," she says. Then when Mom turns the dress around she gushes. "Gorgeous! The buckle makes a real statement. How unexpected!"

Mom glares at me, shaking her head, but then she laughs.

"Brat," she says, hanging the dress back where she got it.

I try to look innocent.

"Can I help it if I'm always right?"

I can't stop thinking about Mom. I want to tell her how much I miss the boutique and the regular customers and the way everything always seemed right when I was there, but she never calls. It's like I've dropped off the planet. I sigh and glance around Eddie's shop.

"Mom would like this place."

He looks up, then blushes.

"Really? But Sarah's boutique is so posh! I went to her opening, you know. I'm sure you don't remember . . ."

"Actually, I was grounded at the time."

Eddie pauses. "Oh, sorry," he says. "It was quite the premiere though. Everything was so minimalist, each piece hand selected. I wish I could do that here, but . . ."

"Of course you can't. You're a small-town shop, so your customers need to feel like they can get everything in one stop."

Eddie pauses. "Well, yes," he says. "That's exactly right."

"Plus, I imagine you have to depend on impulse buying, whereas no one buys anything from Mom's boutique on impulse. Not unless they're millionaires."

Eddie smiles. "That's very true."

"Mom would get that," I tell him. "She's a pretty savvy businesswoman."

"Sounds like you're not so bad yourself. Here . . . come take a look at these catalogs with me. I'm trying to decide what to order for the winter, and I'd love a second opinion."

For the next hour we stand there flipping through all the latest catalogs, and I have to say, this is WAY better than school. In fact, we completely forget about him taking me home at noon, and by midafternoon we're having such a great time, I finally work up my courage to tell him about the one thing that's been bothering me since I walked in.

"Have you ever considered getting new mannequins?"

Eddie ordered us sandwiches and he's right in the middle of eating his tuna on a pita when I say it. He glances at the two wooden figures in his shopwindow.

"What's the matter with my mannequins?"

This is delicate. I once told Mom her jewelry display cases

were ugly and she burst into tears. Still, she took my advice and we went from selling almost no jewelry to selling a couple quality pieces every month.

"Well," I say slowly, "for one thing they're obviously very old and the paint is chipping. Plus, they're completely white, and most lingerie and swimwear looks best with tan or brown skin tones." I take the same bra set that's on the figure in the window and hold it up against my arm to demonstrate.

"Also, the lines aren't what they could be. See how the boxer shorts bunch at the sides on the male mannequin? They don't hang the way they're supposed to, and since the mannequin has no face, you're not saying anything about the product. They don't say, 'sexy,' or, 'cool.' It's not that there's anything really bad about them, they're just not doing what they could be."

Eddie stares at me, and for a minute I think I've said too much. Then he smiles.

"Did Sarah teach you all this stuff?"

I nod. "Yeah. I used to go with Mom on go-sees, and she did a lot of research before auditions so she'd know what kind of look the designer wanted to portray, and then when she got there she'd make sure the clothes had just the right silhouette. She always said, 'It's not about the model; it's about the clothes.' I think that's true, don't you? I mean, it's not about how you look, it's about how you make the clothes look, right? Even if you're a . . . uh . . . mannequin."

If Dad could hear me, he'd be saying, "They're clothes, Liam. Nobody saves a life by looking good," but Eddie stands up and studies his window display. He fingers the boxer shorts where they bunch up, then smoothes a crease in the silk panties. Then he walks outside, stands in front of the window, and studies the whole thing from there. Finally, he comes back inside and turns to me.

"I'll tell you the truth," he says. "I looked at those fancy mannequins once, but they are *very* expensive. I'd rather hire a real person to attract some attention to the store — liven things up a bit — but I don't see where I'd find someone in this town who wouldn't mind standing in a shopwindow."

"Yeah," I start to agree. "It would be pretty tough to find the right . . ."

Eddie's grinning. "It would be minimum wage and you'd have to do some stuff around the shop in addition to the modeling, but I could pay you for a full day every Saturday. You could earn some good money."

Did Eddie just offer me a job?

My jaw drops.

"I'd love to work for you," I stammer. "I'll work really hard, I promise. I won't screw anything up. You won't regret this."

Eddie laughs. "I'm not worried," he says. "I've got a good feeling about this."

I swear, it's the first good feeling anyone has had about me in a long, long time.

22

NO ONE SHOULD EVER HAVE A GOOD FEELING ABOUT ME.

Wary. Foreboding. Frightened, maybe. But not good.

Things start out okay. But they usually do.

Eddie and I are brainstorming ideas for the window display, and we decide to do a trial run. I try on a pair of boxer shorts, because that's probably the most risqué thing I could get away with in a small town like this. If we can make a display that works around those, we can probably pull this off.

It's harder than it looks. There's not a lot to work with in the shop, but we get an old wicker chair from the storage room and put it in the window. I pull a man's bathrobe off one of the racks.

"This flannel is a nice red and gold plaid, which offsets the solid red boxers. If I leave it open people can still see the boxers, but they'll also get a good look at the robe. We could move the bathrobes to the front so people can see them right away when they walk in."

Eddie grins. "Liam, you're a genius," he gushes. "You're like a fashion Einstein." He sets down the shorts he's putting back on a hanger and his eyes narrow. "I must ask," he says. "Are you gay?"

Unfortunately, I'm used to this. "No," I say. "Definitely not."

Eddie puts his hand on my arm. "I know it's a stereotype," he says, "but I had to know. You're just so . . . so fabulous at this! And sometimes stereotypes can be accurate, I mean, just look at me." He twirls theatrically, then winks.

"Yeah," I say, "but I'm straight. I just like fashion. And girls."

Eddie sighs. "All right, then," he says. "Good for you for being yourself." I flush, thinking about my horrible outfit and I almost say something but Eddie keeps going before I get a chance. "I'm sure you will make some young lady enormously happy. A Greek god and a fashion protégé? Straight men don't get better than you, Liam." He notices the fact that my face is bright red and laughs. "I'll go get the little table from the back so we can set it up beside your chair."

He leaves, and I stand there thinking about what he just said. I wish it were true. No one has ever called me a genius in my entire life, and I'm damn sure there are a lot of straight men better than me. I feel like a hypocrite.

Still, it feels good.

That is . . . it feels good until Aunt Pete crashes into the parking meter in front of the store.

My first thought is, *Oh. Crap.* I leap out of the window and tear through the shop toward the dressing room as Eddie hollers about all the clothes I've knocked over.

"What are you doing running through . . . the . . . er . . . Petey . . ."

The words fade and all I hear is the sound of approaching footsteps. Heavy footsteps.

"I can explain everything," I yell, but there's no time for that.

"Get the hell out here."

I zip my pants and fling open the door.

"I know this looks bad, but there's a good . . ."

"Shut the hell up."

Uh-oh.

Aunt Pete sticks his wrist in my face. "What time is it, Liam?"

"Two o'clock?"

"What time do I get up?"

"Three?"

"What time does school get out?"

"Two forty-five?"

"So, at two o'clock — *two o'clock* — I should be sleeping and you should be in school. Yes?"

"Yes?"

"Then why aren't either of us where we're supposed to be?"

It's a good question. A really good question.

Eddie is standing just behind Aunt Pete, gesturing timidly. *Something about making a run for it?* "I could put this all in perspective," he says, making an effort on my behalf, but Pete whirls around.

"Shut up, Eddie."

"Right," says Eddie, "shutting up."

Pete turns back to me.

"Let me tell you why *I* am not where I'm supposed to be," he says. "*I* am not where I'm supposed to be because the school called at nine thirty this morning to tell me my nephew got kicked off the school bus for smoking and had not arrived. Nine freakin' thirty. Nine thirty, Liam. Do you know what that means I've been doing for the last *four and a half* hours? *Do you?*

"Let me tell you what I've been doing. I have been driving every back road in Pineville, trying to decide how I would tell my brother, who already thinks I'm an irresponsible loser, that I'd managed to lose his only son. That's what I've been doing. And just when I was about to go home to make that horrible phone call to your parents, I drive past this . . . this . . ." — for a moment Pete can only sputter — ". . . shop, and I see my nephew in the window in his goddamn underwear." He pauses, then knocks over an entire line of pajama sets. "Aaaaarrrghhh!"

I cringe. This is bad. Really bad. Eddie wrings his hands and we both open our mouths, but Pete doesn't want to hear it. He holds up one hand.

"Shut up," he says. "Do not even speak to me until I've calmed down. Liam, get in the car."

I hand Eddie the boxer shorts, and he executes a covert goodbye wave partially hidden by the fabric. I'd like to wave back, but I don't think it would be the best idea under the circumstances, so I just follow Aunt Pete to the Nissan and climb in the front seat.

"Pete, I . . ."

"Shut. Up."

"Right."

We drive the rest of the way in silence, and I can feel myself sinking into despair. It's clear I've compromised my future. Again.

We reach the trailer, and Aunt Pete holds the car door open for me. He runs his hands through his hair, and when he gets inside he leans on the kitchen counter. I'm waiting for the tirade. The pointing and yelling. I'm waiting for him to tell me that he's just now figured out how worthless I am, and how could he have agreed to let me live here. He looks up.

"I thought something happened to you," he says. The words are angry — furious — but kind of choked up. He closes his eyes.

"This is why I should never have kids. People warn you about this stuff, but you don't think it's true until it happens." He's not even talking to me anymore. He's rambling to himself. "Right away I almost lose you."

He runs his hands over his face and takes a couple really deep breaths.

"Don't ever do this to me again," he says at last. "Don't you *ever* do this to me again."

23

I'M TEN YEARS OLD and I've gone to work with Dad for the day. I've been looking forward to this for weeks, but he's been on the phone the whole time. We're supposed to have lunch together at a restaurant near Dad's office, but it's way past noon and every time I ask if we can go, Dad says, "Not yet." So I wander out to the vending machine down the hall because I've got some quarters in my pocket and I'm hungry, but when I get there the machine is broken.

I go to another floor, looking for a different machine, but there isn't one, so then I go to another floor and another. By the time I find a machine that works and get back on the elevator, I've forgotten which floor Dad's office is on.

I wander around looking for anything familiar, but all the floors look alike and there are forty of them in Dad's building. My heart beats fast, and I keep looking at my digital watch. Soon it's been almost two hours. I imagine how mad Dad will be and how he'll have everyone out looking for me.

I'm trying so hard to get back that I'm practically running around each floor I get off on. That's when someone's secretary finally notices me and asks if I'm lost. I tell her who my dad is, and she takes me back to Dad's office. I walk in all sweaty and sniffly and Dad looks up.

"Did you find your snack?"

That's when I realize he never noticed I was gone.

"You didn't even look for me!" I yell. "I got lost and you didn't even look for me. I hate you!"

Dad looks up at the secretary, and his face gets bright red. He gets up real slow, walks her out, shuts his office door, and heads over to me.

"Don't you ever do that to me again," he says.

That night I stay out of Aunt Pete's way, which is hard to do because he's cleaning. Well, not cleaning, exactly. More like he's moving stacks of stuff from one part of the trailer to another, stomping loudly and occasionally dropping things and muttering to himself about how he was not cut out to be anyone's guardian.

I'm waiting for the news that I'm being shipped off to Nevada. My stomach churns and I can't catch my breath. Then around six o'clock, Pete slams open my door.

"I want to talk to you," he says.

My heart starts to pound, and I wonder if it's possible to have a heart attack at seventeen.

He clears his throat.

"The guys are coming over to rehearse tonight. We haven't had a rehearsal since you've been here, but normally we rehearse every other Tuesday. I'm pretty strict about that, so you're going to have to deal with it."

He glares at me. "Now, I don't know how you feel about our kind of rock and roll, but I don't want to hear any jokes about our music. No oldies comments. No snickering. When we dress up for gigs, I don't want to hear any of those clichés about our outfits or men wearing makeup. That's part of glam, and I love this stuff. You got that?"

I stare at him openmouthed. That's it?

"No complaining," Pete says when I don't respond. "If I have to put up with your shit, you've got to put up with mine."

I lie on my bed listening to the guys arrive and I can't calm down, so finally I call Mom and Dad and leave a message on their answering machine. It's a big lie, mostly, but I've got to remind them I exist.

"Hi, it's me. Just thought I'd tell you I'm doing good here. I mean . . . I'm doing *well*. And . . . um . . . I got a job today. Or at least I almost did. I got *offered* a job. I'm studying hard at school. You'd be proud of me, Dad. I'm not Mr. Popularity anymore. I'm making new friends . . . hardly any actually . . . and I'm staying out of trouble and soon —"

The answering machine beeps loudly.

Stupid. That sounded totally stupid.

I flop back on my bed. Out in the living room a guitar screeches and the drums crash. I know I should go out there and show Pete how comfortable I am with the whole band thing, only

I can't help thinking that Orlando is in the band. Not Orlando. Mr. DeSoto. My English teacher.

This shouldn't be a huge problem. I mean, why should I care if my English teacher is in a glam-rock band if I don't care that my uncle is?

But I do care. What if Orlando is wearing skintight leather pants? Or sequins? I think about that picture in Aunt Pete's living room of the guy in the leopard-print spandex. No one wants to see his English teacher in leopard-print spandex.

There's a surge of music, and then suddenly it's loud. *Really loud.* In fact, since my bedroom door is so thin, having it shut makes absolutely no difference. I contemplate climbing out the window but decide I ought to get this over with, so I fling open my door and squint into the living room and . . .

Huh. They're all wearing jeans and T-shirts. Aunt Pete didn't even change. Well, now I'm kind of disappointed. I park myself on the couch to watch them practice. Dino's on drums, Eddie and Orlando play guitar, and Pete's the lead singer.

"Let's play that one by the Dolls," Eddie says when the first song is through, but Pete shakes his head.

"Nah, we always do that one. Liam's not going to want to hear that."

"Liam's not paying us for our gig this weekend," Orlando says, but Pete is insistent.

"Let's play some classic Bowie. Your mom's still a fan, right?" he asks me.

I nod.

"All right, let's do 'Space Oddity' . . ."

"Up-tempo," Eddie suggests, which causes everyone to erupt.

"You can't do that one up-tempo!"

"Why not? We'd be putting our own spin on a classic cover!"

"Because you just can't . . ."

It goes on like this for a long time. Pretty soon I realize that the guys like to argue. Eddie's obviously had way too much espresso, a fact that Aunt Pete uses to stir up trouble. Orlando smoothes things over, and Dino ignores them all and makes crazy rocked-out faces at me from behind the drum set.

Still, when they finally get going they sound good. I never thought I'd be someplace listening to glam-rock seventies hits. Jamming with my English teacher. It occurs to me that this is exactly what an unpopular person might be doing on a school night.

Maybe things are going to work out after all.

The evening is going well until the phone rings. I requested a song by Fergie as a joke, and Pete sings the whole thing in falsetto. The guys are really vamping it up, so when the phone rings I slide across the kitchen in my socks so they won't be interrupted.

"Hello?"

"Is this Liam?"

"Yeah."

"It's Jen. From school. How's it going?"

Huh.

"Good," I say. "Just hanging out with Mr. DeSoto."

There's a long pause.

"Oh, right. He's in your uncle's band, isn't he?"

Damn. Does everyone in this town know everything about each other? Still, it's pretty uncool of me to be hanging out with the band.

"Yeah," I say, "he is. They're awesome. Glam is the best."

Another long pause.

"Uh, yeah."

"So what's up?" I ask, feeling pretty good about my unpopular self. Jen coughs.

"Listen, I hope you don't mind me calling. I got your uncle's number out of the phone book. I heard about the whole bus thing today and . . ."

Oh no.

". . . well, I was wondering if you might want to ride to school with me and Nikki and Joe. I could swing by and pick you up in the morning."

Crap. Now a gorgeous cheerleader with a killer rack wants to drive me to school. What else can possibly go wrong?

"Oh, wow," I say, buying some time. "That's a really nice offer. I mean, you don't have to do that. I'm sure it's out of your way."

"It's not," she says. "I'd be happy to pick you up."

I twist the phone cord.

"Well, see the thing is . . . my aunt Pete, I mean, my uncle Pete, doesn't really trust me to ride with other people."

This is a pretty good excuse, but Pete has come over and he's standing right there. He makes a face, so I add, "He's absolutely justified, so I'd better not risk it." Then I cringe, because I can tell Pete is suspicious.

He ducks under the phone cord.

"You can get a ride with someone," he says, opening the refrigerator. "Given your track record with the school bus, that would actually be preferable." He says it loud, right next to the phone, so Jen hears him. He chucks three beers across the kitchen, and I try to stretch the cord so I can talk in my bedroom, but it won't reach.

"That was him, right?" Jen asks. "He said it was okay?"

I think about lying again, but Pete is watching me.

"Yeah," I say miserably.

Jen laughs. "Great! So, I'll pick you up about eight thirty then."

"Right. Eight thirty."

Now I am sunk.

24

GETTING A RIDE WITH JEN wouldn't be so bad if I didn't live next door to Darleen. I'm tucking a WXKJ T-shirt into a pair of designer pants with one of Pete's rhinestone-studded belts when I hear Jen pull into the driveway the next morning. I run out to the car, but I'm distracted, so first I forget my pens and have to run back inside to get them. Then when I'm halfway out to the car, I realize I don't have my notebooks. Jen keeps beeping, so I'm running, and that's why I momentarily forget about the fact that Darleen's not supposed to see me catching a ride.

Then I realize she's standing in front of her trailer.

I get into the car and slide really low in my seat. It's not like they could be here to pick up anyone else though, so I sit up again just as Jen pulls out, figuring I'd better take a different approach.

"Hold on," I say, and Nikki sighs.

"Now what did you forget?"

I roll down the window. "Do you want a ride?" I yell. It's

kind of rainy out and now that Darleen's seen me, I might as well offer. Joe's eyes bug out.

"What the hell are you doing?" he blurts, but I ignore him.

Darleen scowls. She's carrying two huge bags of god only knows what, but she doesn't look grateful for the offer.

"No. I'm actually allowed to ride the bus," she says.

"Well, okay," I say, rolling up the window. Jen is already pulling away, and Joe yells "freak" out the window. No wonder Darleen hates popular people.

"You do not want to be friends with her," Joe says once he settles back down. "That girl is a total basket case. I swear, she needs professional help."

Nikki laughs. "God knows she needs fashion help. Did you see what she was wearing? She must have bought that shirt from the Salvation Army."

I squirm because that isn't really fair. The Salvation Army isn't a bad place to shop. You can get some cool stuff there that you'd never find anywhere else. So what if Darleen shops there?

I suddenly realize something about being popular. I didn't get it before, but now it clicks. When you're popular, people give you the benefit of the doubt. Here I am sitting in Jen's car, and no one cares that I'm wearing one of the all-time stupidest outfits.

"Darleen's not so bad," I say. "In fact, she's my friend."

Joe frowns like he can't decide whether or not I'm kidding.

"Darleen is a friend of yours?"

"Yeah," I say. "We share the picnic table."

"Liam's right," Jen says. "You shouldn't treat her like that. Just because she's not very social . . ."

"Not very social?" Nikki gasps. "The girl is going to be voted Class Bitch in the yearbook. I think she *wants* people to hate her."

"Seriously," Joe says. "Last year she wanted to cancel the junior prom so the school could do an art show instead. She made this huge argument to the school board about how there's already a senior prom, so why should class funds go toward having a second prom when our arts and sciences are grossly lacking. That's what she said. 'Grossly lacking.'" Joe laughs and Nikki nods from the backseat.

"The year before that she wanted everyone to boycott the biggest football game of the season because of some dumb comment the coach made about women. No one else would have taken offense, but *Darleen* has to make a big deal about everything."

Jen glances at me, then back at Joe and Nikki.

"I think she just has a lot of hostility since her mom left," she says. "It's not her fault . . ."

But Nikki doesn't want to hear it.

"Well, that's not a reason to be a total bitch. I mean, it sucks that her mother was a loser, but that doesn't mean you can treat everyone else like crap."

"Exactly," Joe agrees. "Trust me on this one, Liam. Darleen Martinek is not someone you want to be friends with."

25

DAD STANDS IN THE KITCHEN talking to Mom. He's leaning on the counter, reading the newsletter my school sends out.

"Can you believe this?" he says, setting down his coffee mug. "The orchestra is losing part of its funding so that the basketball team can take some trip."

He means our trip to Washington D.C. for nationals.

"That's outrageous. Our culture places far too much value on sports. What exactly are we trying to teach our children? That having a good body is more important than having talent? That the arts should be shortchanged for a . . ." He laughs derisively. "A basketball team?!"

Mom glances over at me. Her look says, Let it go. Dad doesn't even remember that I'm on the basketball team.

The only freshman to make varsity.

*   *   *

Darleen Martinek is exactly the person I need to be friends with. If there's anyone who would impress my dad, it's Darleen. For the rest of the week I make talking to her my number one priority, but since she's ignoring me, I don't get a chance until Friday.

It happens when I'm least expecting it. I'm sitting in physics, counting green cars in the parking lot outside the window as Principal Mallek announces lab partners.

"Duane Allen and Cynthia Caroll. Liam Geller and Darleen Martinek. Robert Blake and Tyrone Watson . . ."

I stop, then raise my hand.

"I missed my name. Could you read it again?" Darleen glares and Principal Mallek sighs, but I have to be sure.

"Liam Geller and Darleen Martinek. Table four."

My heart beats faster. *Too good to be true.* I gather my books and wait at table four while Darleen goes to the front of the room and starts a long, animated conversation with Principal Mallek. I figure I ought to read ahead, so I'll know what we're supposed to do.

"Equipment: Two inclined planes of equal length. One Ping-Pong ball. One wooden car. One stopwatch."

Not bad. How hard can it be if there are only four things? I skip ahead to the directions.

"Set each plane at a forty-five-degree angle. One person holds the stopwatch while the other person positions the objects at the top of the inclined planes. When the person holding the stopwatch gives the signal, release the objects, timing from the moment of release to the moment the objects reach the floor. Repeat with varying angles."

Huh. That doesn't sound hard at all. I look up as Darleen sits down across from me. Her eyes narrow, but I grin.

"I'll get our stuff."

"No horsing around, Mr. Geller," Principal Mallek says as he hands me two boards, a wooden car, a Ping-Pong ball, and a stopwatch. "I've paired you with my strongest student, so you'll have a good chance at passing the lab section of this course."

I nod. I nearly drop the stopwatch but catch it in time, then I bring everything back and set it down on our table. Darleen sighs.

"Fine," she says. "If we have to work together you'd better pay attention. I've read through the directions, and I think you should work the stopwatch." She hands it to me. "I'll set up the planes, drop the objects, and measure the angles." She takes out the two boards and secures them against the edge of the table while I study the stopwatch.

"You know," I say. "I wasn't mocking your flyers the other day. I know you think I was, but actually . . ."

Darleen sighs again. She holds the car and the Ping-Pong ball at the top of each plane.

"Are you ready?" she asks.

"I think you're absolutely right about homecoming. I mean, who needs to have a good time? This is school and we're not here to have fun. People should really buckle down and —"

Darleen's jaw tightens. "Would you start timing, please?"

I look down at the watch. "Oh, right. Yes. Okay, go. So anyway, I just wanted you to know that if you need any help . . ."

Darleen ignores me entirely and lets go of the car and the Ping-Pong ball.

"What was the time?" she asks. I look down, but the stopwatch is still running.

"Oh. Sorry. Forgot to shut it off. Let's just do it again."

Darleen groans. She repositions the car and the Ping-Pong ball.

"Go," she says. I don't say a word, just watch very carefully as the two objects roll off the planes. Then I hit the stop button.

"Time?" Darleen asks.

"Three point five seconds."

"For which one?"

"What do you mean 'which one'?"

Darleen grabs the stopwatch and points at the diagram in our lab book. "You're supposed to time them separately," she says. "Separately!"

I look at the picture. How was I supposed to do that when I only have one stopwatch? I figure the answer is probably obvious so I'd better not ask.

"Oh, right. Sorry." I reset the stopwatch. "Okay, I'm ready now."

Darleen picks up both of the objects and positions them once more at the top of the planes. I glance around the room and realize everyone else is already adjusting the angles. I take a deep breath.

Darleen drops the objects and I hit stop. Then I hit stop again. The numbers disappear, and I choke.

"I don't know why it did that," I say. "I just hit stop. Maybe it's, er, malfunctioning?"

Darleen grabs the stopwatch out of my hands. She hits first one button, then another button.

"Fine," she says slowly. "It's working fine. Maybe you should drop the objects. How about that?"

I think this is a good idea, even though she isn't being particularly nice about it. I'm sure I can roll a car and a Ping-Pong ball down a board.

"Right. Good idea."

I position each object at the top of the planes and wait for Darleen's signal.

"Time," she says. I drop both objects and watch them roll to the floor. When I look up Darleen is glaring at me again.

"What?"

"You dropped them wrong."

"What?!"

"You dropped the Ping-Pong ball sooner than you dropped the car."

I'm sure I didn't.

"Well, can't you just write the number down anyway? What difference does it make?"

Darleen's eyes bug out. "That's the whole point of the experiment. To see which one gathers the most velocity at the lowest angle. If you don't drop them at the same time, it totally negates the results!"

I don't see why this is such a big deal, but I nod anyway. I pick up the car and the Ping-Pong ball and position them again at the top. Only this time I'm nervous. When Darleen says time I mean to release them both, but I'm distracted, worrying about releasing them at *exactly* the same time, so I end up holding on to the car by accident. The Ping-Pong ball rolls under another lab table.

"I'll get that," I say real quick. I crawl under the table but can't reach it.

"Here." The blonde at table six bends down and hands me a Ping-Pong ball. "We're done, so you can have this one." I want to kiss her.

"Uh, thanks."

Darleen's waiting impatiently, answering questions in her lab book. I'm sure we're supposed to answer those questions together once the lab is done, but Darleen isn't waiting. She doesn't say anything as I set up the experiment, just holds the stopwatch and without looking at me says, "Time."

I release the car and the Ping-Pong ball at exactly the same time. I'm *positive*. Darleen just frowns.

On the eighth try I get it right. Darleen writes down two numbers in her lab book and I have to peek over to see what they are, then copy them into my book quickly before I forget them.

"What do they mean?" I ask. It seems like a good question — a studious question — but Darleen gives me *the look* again. "I mean, what do those velocities, um, signify, about the stuff?"

"We won't know until we complete the experiment. We've got to do it again with at least two more angles."

"Again?!"

Darleen nods. Then she looks at the clock.

"Oh my god!" she says, and I look around, expecting something to be on fire.

"What?!"

"We've only got three minutes left. You've wasted the entire lab period! I can't believe this. I've never not finished a lab before."

She looks really upset.

"We can get it done quickly," I say. "Just copy what those guys have written . . ."

That's when I notice Principal Mallek is standing behind me.

"That would be called cheating, Mr. Geller."

Crap.

26

PRINCIPAL MALLEK SENDS ME to the guidance office. He also gives both me and Darleen failing grades on the lab.

"I truly despise you," Darleen says loudly as I gather my books, and I know that she means it. Everyone stares as I leave the room, and I feel mildly ill.

I wait in the guidance office through all of second period, but they're busy so they give me an appointment seventh period instead. Then I have to wait twenty minutes to talk to my guidance counselor, only to have him forget my name.

"Yes. Leroy. Tell me about your academic history? Looks like you've moved around a lot. Why was that again?"

By the time I get to English, I'm late and frustrated. Orlando is reading something in front of the class, and he stops and sighs when I walk in.

"You're late," he says. (As if I don't know that.) I dig around in my pocket for a hall pass before realizing I forgot to get one.

"Fuck," I say, under my breath.

Orlando puts his book down. "Excuse me?"

I look up. "What? Oh. Nothing. I mean, I forgot to get a hall pass."

"Where are you coming from?"

"Guidance."

Orlando hesitates. "This once," he says, "I'll let it go, but if it happens again . . ."

I nod and walk across the front of the room to sit down at my desk. Orlando starts reading again, but I can't concentrate. Darleen hates me worse than ever now, and if I can't impress Darleen, I certainly can't impress my dad, and since I've already screwed up once with Aunt Pete, that means he'll be sure to kick me out next time, and . . .

"Liam. Where's your book?"

Orlando is standing directly over my desk.

Book? Aw, hell.

"I forgot it."

"Seems to me like you forgot it yesterday, the day before, and, hello, every day this week."

The class snickers.

"Tell me something, Liam," Orlando says, tapping one finger on my desk. "What's the name of the book that we're reading?"

I pause. What kind of trick question is this? Of course I know the name of the book we're reading. Something by Shakespeare. Something hard to read, so I'm going to tackle it all at once the night before the exam.

"No recollection?" Orlando asks. "How about the front cover? Any idea what it looks like?"

My mind is blank. I'm sure I know the answer, but I can't clear the fuzziness from my brain, so I glance at the girl next to me, and she tilts the book in my direction so I can see the cover.

"White?" I suggest.

"I have an idea," Orlando says, tapping on my desk. "Why don't you go back to the guidance office and not return to my class until you come prepared with the book we are reading— *Hamlet* — as well as the Strunk and White grammar guide I recommended in your syllabus, and a notebook. How about that?"

It isn't really a question, but at least Orlando doesn't wait for an answer.

27

PETE IS SITTING ON THE COUCH watching TV when I get home.

"Good day?" he asks from the living room as the screen door bangs shut. I shrug. I go to the fridge to take out a diet soda, but there's only beer, so I take out the orange juice instead.

"It's Friday night," Pete says, making a whooping noise. "Any plans?"

I shake my head.

"I've got the night off," he tells me. "The radio station is doing some all-request eighties thing. The guys and I thought we might drive over to the Hillsborough Mall to do some shopping. You want to come?"

This is very obviously a setup, but every fiber of my being still desperately wants to say yes. A chance to get out of this trailer is way too good to pass up. There's only one problem.

"Orlando's coming?" I ask.

"Yeah. Something the matter with that?"

I shake my head. "Of course not, I just meant . . . you know, maybe he might be busy or something."

Aunt Pete looks at me funny. "No. He's definitely coming. Is that a problem?"

Some of the orange juice dribbles onto my shirt. It's a Ralph Lauren, because I couldn't find anything worse in my closet today. I swear and rush to the kitchen sink to splash water on the spot before the stain sets, but finally I stop scrubbing and resign myself to the presence of the huge off-colored splotch. I take the shirt off and throw it in the garbage. You can't wear a designer shirt with a spot on it.

"No, it's fine," I say. "I just don't think Orlando likes me. He kicked me out of class this afternoon."

Aunt Pete's eyes bug out. "Orlando kicked you out of class?!"

I nod. "Yeah. Because I forgot my book. As if that can't happen to anyone." I sort through the shirts in my room until I find a suitable alternative. I'm considering a really slick black V-neck when the front door opens and Eddie and Dino wander in.

"I'm sure everything will be fine," Pete says, shooting me a look. "You just concentrate on finding the most perfect shirt in the universe and I'll make sure my boyfriend doesn't harass your totally innocent self. Okay?"

I nod. Only what Pete doesn't realize is that my problem isn't finding the most perfect shirt, it's finding the worst possible shirt, and honestly, I don't own any of those. In fact, my entire wardrobe is way too nice for unpopularity. A shopping trip is definitely in order.

There's a high-pitched whistle from the kitchen, and when I look over Eddie is shaking his head at me.

"Sugar pie, where did you get those abs?" he says. Eddie is wearing an outfit that is entirely silver. I'm not kidding. The shoes, the pants, the shirt, the shades . . . all silver.

"I have good abs," Dino says casually.

Pete snorts.

"It's true," Dino argues. "You can't see them under the beer belly, but every night I do, like, ten sit-ups."

"You've never done a sit-up!" Eddie says, letting the shades slide down his nose.

"Oh yeah? Come on, Liam. I will take you on, right here, right now. I am a sit-up machine."

Dino makes a huge bicep, which is impressive, even if it has nothing whatsoever to do with sit-ups. By the time Orlando arrives, me and Dino are down on the floor and Eddie and Pete are counting off our crunches.

"*. . . five . . . six . . . six and a half . . . seven . . . seven and a quarter . . .*"

"*. . . thirty-four . . . thirty-five . . . thirty-six . . .*"

Orlando comes in and flops down on the couch.

"I don't even want to know what's going on," he says, leaning back and shutting his eyes. He looks like he's had a hard day, and for a moment I feel guilty. Dino collapses onto the carpet.

"We'll have to continue this later," Dino says. "Orlando's here now, so we'd better get going."

"Right. Don't want to be late for the mall," Pete says, real sarcastic. "Only four hours of shopping time left."

I get up, grab a shirt, and follow the guys outside. I'm trying not to make eye contact with Orlando, but he punches me on the arm and says, "My money was on you."

Then everyone is crowding into the Nissan, and I stand there staring in disbelief. We can't all be traveling in the same car. It's bad enough that the car in question is a zebra-striped vehicle from 1990, but there is not enough room for four big guys and Eddie.

Pete beeps the horn loudly.

"Pile in," he yells as I stand there gaping. Then he turns and hollers, "Make room in the back."

I take a deep breath and slide in next to Dino. I pray that Darleen will come outside at this exact moment, but of course she doesn't. Instead, I ride the entire way to the mall holding my breath while the guys sing really loud with all the windows open.

"Join in," Dino says when we're almost there, and then he says, "Let's sing something Liam will know."

I want to melt into the backseat. Fortunately, by the time they think of a song I might know the words to, we've arrived in the parking lot.

"Save it for the way home," Pete says, pulling the Nissan diagonally into a parking space. I open the door and jump out like my life depends on it.

The mall is one of those old malls where everything is on one floor and half the shops have been abandoned for years. When we walk inside it's dark, and there's a huge dried-up fountain with loose change still scattered on the bottom. I look up and down the long hall, and Eddie puts one hand consolingly on my shoulder.

"I'm sorry," he says. "I'm afraid this is it."

My first thought is that I can't believe malls like this really exist, but as I look at the stores — JCPenney, Sears, Karl's Shirt Emporium, Payless — I realize this is exactly the place I need to shop.

"Actually," I say, "it's perfect."

Pete frowns, but he doesn't say anything as I follow Eddie and Dino from store to store. I don't trust my own ability to pick out horrible clothes, but I figure I can't go wrong with these guys.

Eddie pulls a shirt off the rack in the Shirt Emporium.

"If I were you, Liam," he says, "I'd add a little flash to your wardrobe. You have impeccable taste, of course, so I'm not trying to tell you what to do, but you could really wear this shirt . . ."

He's holding a hot pink button-down with black stripes.

"You think?" I say, pretending to consider. "All right. I'll get it."

"What about something like this?" Dino asks, holding up a T-shirt that has a skull on the front.

"Yeah, that's great!" I add it to my pile.

Pete stands to one side, watching me. Every now and then he says, "I'm not sure I can see you wearing that," and before I take my stuff to the cashier, he says, "Are you sure about all this?"

I nod and go up to pay for my huge stack of horrible shirts.

Fortunately, this stuff is dirt cheap. They're having a sale — five shirts for twenty bucks.

"Who's up for shoe shopping?" I ask when I'm done paying. Eddie raises his hand, but Pete and Orlando exchange a look.

"Maybe we should split up," Orlando says. "Me and Eddie and Dino can go look at vacuum cleaners in Sears. Weren't you just saying you needed a new one, Ed?"

Eddie shakes his head, but Pete and Orlando ignore him.

"Me and Liam will head over to the shoe store," Pete says. "We'll meet you guys later at Friendly's."

Orlando kisses Pete good-bye, and then the guys head out, Eddie glancing back over his shoulder. Aunt Pete and I stand there for a minute, and the mall seems suddenly silent and empty.

"Shoe store is this way," Pete says, motioning in the opposite direction.

We walk for a while without saying anything, then when we reach the store he coughs nervously. He stops in front of a table full of women's high heels and fingers one shoe wistfully. He moves around the table but keeps coming back to that shoe. Then he takes a deep breath.

"You know," he says, "you don't need to impress the guys. Buying that stuff, I mean. Assuming that's who you're trying to impress, of course. It's just . . . well . . . we like you the way that you are. I know that sounds corny, but sometimes people don't say this stuff and . . ." He pauses. "Hell."

It's probably the nicest thing anyone has ever said to me. I'm not sure I believe it, but at least Pete made the effort to lie. I swallow hard and turn away for a second. When I turn back I nod at the shoes.

"Those are nice."

Pete looks up and his brow furrows. The look is strangely familiar, and at first I can't figure out why, but then I realize it's the look I use when I can't tell if someone is making fun of me.

"I really like them. I mean, they're a cheap reproduction of the originals, but I'll bet they're modeled after these shoes that were in the spring show in Paris a couple years back. Everything was about glamour that year. Liberace style. Real splashy."

I stop for a minute, remembering. Mom and I had gone back to Paris to visit some friends of hers, and we went to almost all of the shows together. I remember the color and the noise. The lights on the runway. Aunt Pete would have fit in perfectly there.

Suddenly I want to say just the right thing.

"Want to know what makes this shoe great?" I ask, picking it up.

Pete looks at me like I'm crazy. He said all that cool stuff and now I want to talk about shoes? But he nods.

"Sure," he says. "Tell me."

I turn the shoe around so he can really look at it.

"It's not just the rhinestones, although those are really fun. It's the fact that the rhinestones are on a regular high-heeled pump. Glitzing up something common. That's what that season's shows were all about. Adding something flashy to something ordinary."

I hand the shoe to Aunt Pete.

"I think you should buy these. To go with your red dress."

He takes it and holds it in his rough hands like it's something special. For the first time he's not looking at me like I'm some strange fungus that grew overnight in the middle of his life.

"Thanks," he says. "I think I will."

28

ON THE RIDE HOME the windows are open and the night air is still warm. We're all stuffed from greasy food from Friendly's and Pete blasts the radio. He plays WXKJ so it's the all-eighties marathon and the songs are terrible, but the guys belt them out anyway. Then Dino farts really loud and everyone laughs until our stomachs hurt.

When we get back to Pete's trailer, we pile out of the Nissan, weighted down by bags of clothes and shoe boxes. Pete's already wearing his new red heels, and he holds the screen door open with one rhinestoned foot as everyone stumbles inside. The phone is ringing so there's a mad dash to pick it up in time without spilling the packages all over the floor.

Eddie grabs it, then hands it to me.

"It's for you."

I pick up the receiver, still grinning and trying not to trip.

"Hello?" I say, a bit too loud.

"Liam?"

"Dad?"

Pete looks up, and suddenly all the raucous fun comes to a grinding halt.

"Dad?" I say again. "I'm so glad you finally called. I've been wanting to talk to you."

"Cut it out."

Dad's voice is sharp, and I pause.

"Cut what out? I just said I was glad you —"

"What the hell are you doing?"

"I . . . What do you mean what am I doing? I'm doing good, mostly. Did you get my message?"

"Do you know how humiliated I am?"

"What? Wait." I can't keep up. "Why are you humiliated? I said I was —"

"Your guidance counselor called. Wanted to talk to your father because you're having adjustment problems. He said you didn't make it to school the first day, then you lost your bus privileges, and that today he had a long talk with you after you were kicked out of class." Dad pauses. "Adjustment problems, Liam?" he asks. "Have the last seventeen years been adjustment problems?"

I take a deep breath. *Am I supposed to answer that?*

"You want to know when your guidance counselor called me?" Dad asks. "He called during an important meeting. There I am with my colleagues at the conference table, and the secretary interrupts the meeting to tell me my son's school is on the phone. Now, I couldn't very well not take the call after she says that, could I?"

I shake my head, even though I know he can't see it.

"Your guidance counselor tells me that you were also called into the office for cheating, and now they've been studying your files and think you might need counseling. Can you imagine how that made me feel?"

I try hard to keep my face composed.

"I don't know. Ashamed? Dad, please just —"

"You don't know? I've given you everything. I've put up with your partying and your sleeping around, and your drunk driving . . ."

I hold the phone away from my ear. I know how this part goes so I follow along in my mind until I'm pretty sure Dad's near the end of the speech. Then I put the phone back.

"You're right," I say. "I know you're right. I'm sorry they called you at work, but if you just give me a chance, I'm going to do better. I'm making all new friends here. Smart friends. And I'm going to join something academic. A club or something."

Dad sighs. "I hardly think you'll get accepted into an academic club."

That stings, but I let it slide.

"I promise, Dad."

There's a long pause, then Dad breathes out long and slow.

"Tell me something," he says. "Did your mother tell you to call Peter?"

The question catches me off-guard, and I want to ask what this has to do with anything, but I don't.

"No," I say. "Mom didn't even know about it. I was the one who wanted to call Pete."

Dad laughs a tired laugh. "You always defend her," he says. Then he pauses. "Well, obviously it's a disaster, and I could have told you that much if you'd bothered to ask."

I twist the phone cord between my fingers until my circulation has nearly stopped. I hold my breath, waiting to see what Dad will say next.

"One of these days you're going to make a decision you can't apologize away," he says. "You're selfish, irresponsible, and indulgent, and unless you shape up, you won't amount to anything. Do you understand that?"

I nod into the phone.

"I asked you a question."

"Yes. I get that."

"Good."

For a moment there's silence.

"Liam," Dad says at last, his voice cold and calm, "I don't intend to let my brother, who's never done anything responsible in his entire life, turn you into some faggot living in a goddamn trailer park in the middle of nowhere. You need discipline. That's the bottom line. And *Peter* is certainly not the one to provide that. One more slipup and you go to Nevada."

I cringe and glance over at Aunt Pete. I know he can't have heard what Dad just said, but my cheeks still burn. From the looks of things, Dino is physically restraining him from lunging for the phone.

"That won't happen," I say, turning back.

Dad clears his throat loudly.

"I know I'll regret this," he says at last, "and I'm warning you — when you're failing your classes and your uncle is ready to stop trying to spite me by playing this stupid little game . . . When he figures out it's not that *easy* being a parent . . ."

Dad doesn't finish the threat, but I nod anyway.

"I understand," I say. "Thanks for . . ." There's something I'm supposed to thank Dad for, I'm certain of it, but I can't think of what it could be. "Thanks for the call," I say at last.

Dad snorts. His bullshit meter picked that one up a mile away, but he's had enough of me, so he hangs up. I close my eyes for just a second before setting the phone carefully back in place. When I open my eyes, Pete is standing at my elbow.

"What the hell did he say?" he demands.

I shrug. "My guidance counselor called him. He wasn't happy about it."

Pete's eyes narrow. "Did he fill your head with a bunch of crap?" he asks. "Telling you you're not good enough, or smart enough . . ."

I know Pete means well, but Dad only said the truth.

"It's no big deal," I tell him, and at that moment I'm not even lying. It doesn't feel like any deal at all.

"I'm going to bed," I say. "Thanks for taking me to the mall."

Pete drums his fingers on the counter and the guys glance at one another.

"Liam —" Pete starts, but I'm already gone.

29

MONDAY IS MY CHANCE to redeem myself. Maybe my last chance. Armed with my new wardrobe, I show up to school like Rocky preparing for the big fight. There's only one problem. I told Dad I was joining an academic club, and as of now I can't think of one that will take me. I don't play chess, can't debate anything, don't understand politics, and I certainly won't make it into the honor society.

Fortunately, homeroom provides the solution.

I'm drifting off when the announcements begin, so I almost miss that there's something going wrong, and when I finally clue in to the fact that the entire class is in hysterics, I have to lean over and ask the guy next to me what happened.

The guy snorts. "Romer just dropped his microphone and had to climb under the table to get it. The camera zoomed in on his butt. What a geek."

Even in my fuzzy state my ears perk up.

"Who runs the announcements?"

The guy laughs. "The technonerds," he says, snorting. "I mean, AV club." He wads up a sheet of notebook paper and throws it at the screen as another guy coughs into his hand. "Losers."

For the first time I start to wake up. *Dad* was in the AV club. I remember him saying something about how it prepared him for a career in public speaking.

I glance at the front of the room, and Darleen is watching the announcements with her arms crossed. Every now and then she turns around and glares at the people who are making fun of them. I try to embody complete innocence, watching the screen carefully. I want to like these kids, I really do, but they're pretty bad. For one thing, the kid who dropped his mic never sits still. He fidgets like he has to pee, and he hardly looks up from his paper. When he does look up, his eyes bug out. He's wearing a tie and a jacket, even though it's still hot out, and to make matters worse, the jacket is dark gray — a winter color, not a fall color.

"Morons," a girl yawns.

A skinny kid with freckles and braces starts reading the sports. If it's possible, he's worse than the first kid. He says "rehearsal" when he means "practice" and misreads the word *varsity* as *variety.* I shake my head, wondering how come I never thought of this before . . .

I pause, thinking through everything very carefully, just to be sure. *Is there any way this idea could lead to disorderly behavior on my part?* No, I'm pretty certain it could not. *Is there any way this idea could cause me to be late for, miss, or otherwise disrupt class?* No. In fact, I'm pretty sure I'd have to arrive early and that teachers would think it was responsible. Last question. *Is there any way I can screw up?*

I don't think so. If I execute my idea, I'll seem studious and make a whole new set of unpopular friends.

It's settled then.

I'm joining the AV club.

First I need to find Romer.

For the rest of the morning I scan the halls, but I don't spot him until lunch. He's sitting next to the skinny kid at a long, otherwise empty table. I wind my way through the lunch line, thinking I'll join them, but when I step out of line Joe and Nikki wave me over. Jen is sitting on top of the table with a small crowd of cheerleaders. There's a pep rally today, so they're all in uniform.

I stare at the empty space they're creating for me.

"Oh, man, see, I would except . . ."

"What?" Jen asks.

"Nothing. I mean, I promised my good buddies over there that I'd sit with them. Sorry 'bout that." I shrug as everyone's faces melt into confusion.

"Which good buddies?" Nikki asks, staring around the cafeteria. I nod at the two guys from the announcements.

"You know . . . them." I smile. "Catch you guys later."

Everyone's staring like I just said I was going to have lunch in the teachers' lounge, but I carry my tray calmly across the room and sit down next to the announcement guys.

"Mind if I sit here?" I ask. Neither one responds. Romer looks like he has to pee again, and both of them move their trays away from mine.

I let out a deep breath. "Cool," I say, sticking out my hand. "Liam Geller." Neither one takes it, so I settle into the long task of scraping every shred of meat off my sloppy joe bun. I asked for just the bun, but the cafeteria lady only glared at me.

"I'm new here," I say. "Saw you guys on the news this morning, and I thought, *Liam, you should hook up with those guys,* so when I saw you . . ."

The skinny kid stares wildly.

I don't know what he's staring at, but it occurs to me that maybe he's confused by my lunch. Not only have I scraped all the meat off my sloppy joe, but I also scraped all the whipped cream off my chocolate pudding.

"Vegetarian," I explain. "And the whipped cream is pure fat calories and artificial flavoring." I glance at the first kid's tray. "Cholesterol," I say, pointing to the meat and shaking my head. "Plus, you never know what they're feeding animals these days. Steroids, antibiotics . . ." I stop, suddenly realizing that neither of my new friends has blinked in the past five minutes.

"So, what are your names?"

The first kid stutters. "R . . . r . . . Raymond Romer."

The second kid hiccups and looks around the cafeteria again, desperately.

"Simon. Simon."

Simon Simon? I wonder. Or did he say it twice?

"Great," I say, finishing off my carton of milk. "So, how do I join?"

Raymond looks at Simon, and Simon looks at Raymond.

"We're full," Raymond says.

"What?" I ask. "How can you be full? Who else is in the club?"

Raymond coughs and moves his tray another inch away from mine.

"Me and Simon."

Two people? *Are these guys messing with me?* I study my tray, considering. If they are, I have several options. 1. I can let them get away with it and never be able to execute my brilliant idea. 2. I can beat the crap out of them, but that's not my style. That leaves me only one option, and although I hate to use it . . .

I stand up and stretch to my full height, faking a yawn. When I sit back down I sit as close to Raymond as possible and tap one finger against his tray.

"You don't want me in your club?" I ask, tapping a little faster.

"No. We didn't say that," Raymond says.

"He didn't say that," Simon echoes.

I try to appear as if I'm considering this. "Because if I were you," I say at last, "and there were only two of us in my little club and a third person wanted to join, I would let him."

Raymond and Simon nod quickly and repeatedly.

"We only said that because our adviser said . . ."

". . . you've got to be able to work the equipment . . ."

I take Simon's milk off his tray, open it, and drink the whole thing in one gulp. Then I set down the empty carton and start eating Raymond's pudding.

"I don't think I'd have to work the equipment if I were going to read the news, now would I?"

"No. No. Did I say that?"

"We didn't mean *you* would have to work the equipment."

I sit back and grin.

"Good," I say. "That's what I thought. So, when do I show up?"

Raymond looks down.

"Mornings. Eight thirty. I set up the camera and Simon edits the news. We film it live."

"Great," I say. "Eight thirty it is."

30

RAYMOND AND SIMON don't let me read the news right away. I have to show up at the AV room every day for "lessons," even though all I'll be doing is reading the news off a sheet of paper. Fortunately, I can catch a ride with Eddie, who heads to the shop at the same time to do inventory before he opens.

"You really want to do these announcements?" he asks one morning as we're driving in. "When I was your age, it would have taken a pretty big incentive to get my butt out of bed early."

I shrug. "It's all right."

"Well, who else does these things? Is there some hot girl involved or something?"

"No," I laugh. "Actually, it's just these two guys who are pretty terrible at them. They're making me learn every piece of equipment and Raymond even made up a test for me. You'd think they were messing with me, right? Only, they're not. Raymond is just really high-strung, and Simon is like his sidekick. He wants to *be* Raymond. I mean, you wouldn't think a guy like Raymond would have a sidekick, but they both totally love the equipment."

"What about you?" Eddie asks. "Do you love it?"

I shrug again. "I might," I say, "if they ever let me give the announcements."

Eddie pulls the car up in front of the school. "I'm sure you'll get your shot," he says, but he's studying me like he wants to say something else.

"Liam," he asks at last, just as I'm getting out, "are you sure you know what you're doing?"

This is a good question, because most of the time the answer would be no, but this time I smile and nod.

"Absolutely. I've got it all under control."

The following Monday morning is my debut. I've given it a ton of thought, and I've determined exactly what it is that Raymond and Simon do wrong. It's not that the announcements are so bad in and of themselves. It's more that they take them way too seriously. I mean, they're announcements for god's sake, but Raymond and Simon try too hard, which makes them ridiculous.

So, for the first time since my transformation, I abandon Aunt Pete's T-shirts and the clothes I got at the mall, and dress in my nicest brushed-cotton gabardine flat-front pants, a truly awesome slim-fitting jacket from Mom's shop — it's one of a kind, designed by an up-and-coming Italian designer — paired with a Burberry button-down shirt with opposing pinstripes and a slim black tie that accentuates the lines of the jacket. I wear my favorite Cole

Haan Italian-made shoes — polished, of course — and leave my hair unbrushed. The whole thing is so over-the-top for Pineville High, it's absurd. Anyone with a lick of fashion sense will smell "overkill" a mile away.

"Now that's more like it," Eddie says when I come out that morning. He whistles and raises both eyebrows until they nearly disappear.

"It's my on-air debut," I say.

Eddie grins. "Well, you're certainly . . . uh . . . prepared." He laughs. "I doubt anyone's ever worn Burberry in Pineville before. And that jacket . . ." He whistles again. "Are you sure this occasion warrants such a stunning ensemble?"

He's joking, but I don't care. What he doesn't know is that this "stunning ensemble" is going to be my ticket into the out crowd.

"Break a leg," Eddie yells when he drops me off.

I wave over my shoulder, then go straight inside to the AV room. I arrive before Raymond and Simon, so when they finally get there I'm totally ready.

I sit down next to Raymond at the news desk and wait for Simon to position the camera. Our faculty adviser has come with them today since it's my first time on air. She's young and wears funky knit clothes. Most of the time she doesn't show up because the AV room is Raymond's domain, but she has to be there to oversee my debut.

"I'm pleased you've decided to join the AV club," she says, staring at my jacket. "Raymond tells me you'd like to read the news. You look very nice." She smiles, then fumbles with a stack of papers.

"I am all for the news," I say. "News is very important. Essential, really."

The adviser tucks a stray hair behind her ear and touches her throat. "Why, yes," she says. "I agree."

I grin.

"You'd better read these a couple times before we start," Raymond says, interrupting. He hands me several sheets of paper. "Make sure you know all the words. I can help you if you're stuck on any of them. Just read slow and look directly at the camera. It's important that you enunciate. Don't you think, Ms. Peterson?"

The adviser is staring at me. "What?" she says. "Oh, right. Yes. Enunciating."

I nod, and grin at Simon and Raymond. "Never fear," I tell them.

Raymond is skeptical.

"Simon will be working the camera," he says, "and I'll be reading the sports, so if you lose your place, I can point it out for you." He attempts to hook the mic on top of my lapel. "If you need me to take over, just kick me under the table. Lightly. No need to be nervous." For the fourth time in a row, the mic slips out of Raymond's sweaty hands. I pick it up and tuck it neatly *under* my lapel, then slide the wire inside my jacket.

"Got it."

The adviser smiles wistfully and Raymond nods.

"Remember to read carefully," he says again. "Are you nervous? You look nervous."

I shake my head. I'm not nervous. I'm thinking about what

kind of look I want to project while giving the announcements. Dramatic? Sincere? Smoldering? *Yes, that's it.*

"Okay. The light's going to come on any minute. Aaanny minute . . . aaanny . . . oh, it's on . . ."

Raymond kicks me under the table, and I pause dramatically, then lean ever so slightly toward the camera.

"Good morning, Pineville High," I say in my best smoldering voice.

Raymond cringes. I was supposed to say, "Good morning, Pineville High *School*." I ignore him and begin to ad-lib.

"This is Monday morning, and the time is now eight forty-five A.M. I'm Liam Geller, and these are the announcements." I change my angle slightly. "In the news today, the first ever mock NATO delegation will be chosen from aspiring juniors and seniors. This team will represent Uganda." I pause as if this is highly significant. "They will travel to Washington, D.C., to play this all-important role. Historic. Truly historic."

I let the moment linger before fixing the camera with a steady, penetrating gaze.

"In other news, the hot lunch today will be (a significant pause) beef stew, a roll, a pudding cup, and (pause) milk. The bag lunch will be (pause) ham sandwich, an apple, chips, and (pause) milk. There is no vegetarian option, but if one were to purchase both a hot lunch and a bag lunch, one could scrape together a meal consisting of a roll, an apple, chips, a pudding cup, and (pause) milk."

I settle back in my chair.

"Finally," I say with grave importance, "any and all students who have not had their annual physical, *please*, report to the nurse's office before the close of the school day. This is the final day." I allow myself to look truly concerned. "A school physical is crucial."

I look into the camera, but I'm careful not to stare at it. Instead, I look beyond it, imagining my audience.

"This concludes the announcements," I say, then I pause because it's time for the clincher. I glance at the adviser, but she has her chin propped between her hands, so I figure I can get away with one final embellishment if I move quickly.

"In the interest of diversity, the announcements will now be repeated in French." I take a deep breath, imagining myself being inducted into the Unpopular Hall of Fame. Who would have guessed living in Paris would come in so handy?

"Bonjour, Pineville High."

I repeat the entire thing, then look meaningfully at Raymond.

"And now to Rambo Romer for the sports. Rambo?"

Raymond does not move a muscle. He's staring at me, his bug eyes bursting out of their sockets and his sweaty hands crushing his papers. I wait, smiling into the camera.

"Pardonne-moi," I say at last. *"Et maintenant, Rambo Romer avec les sports."*

Raymond turns slowly toward the camera.

"J . . . J . . . Junior varsity cheerleading tryouts will be held today from three o'clock until three-thirty . . ."

I sit back and wait for Raymond to finish. *Brilliant*, I think.

Absolutely brilliant. I wait until the little red light goes off, clap Raymond on the back, and stand up.

"That was great," I say, taking off my mic. The adviser is still staring at me, and Simon's mouth is hanging open. Raymond looks like he might pass out. "See you guys later, then?" I ask. The bell rings and I decide not to wait around. I step into the hallway and laughter bubbles out of the classrooms as students pour into the hall. I grin, waiting for the ridicule to begin.

The voices get louder as more kids spill into the hallway, and a group of girls giggle as they walk past. Then I hear it.

"Way to go, Liam!"

I stop midstride as a guy I don't know slaps me on the back.

"That was cool, man."

There's a moment where I am completely stunned. *What?* I think. *Impossible.* I read the announcements in goddamn French! I took them *way* too seriously.

Joe Banks throws a football down the hall and I catch it without thinking.

"Liam, you were awesome!" he yells. "I almost shit a brick."

Then I get it. I start toward my locker, walking faster and faster until I'm running down the hall, plowing through the people in my way. I'm almost there when Darleen strides past.

"Idiot," she mutters.

I slam into my locker and slide down the wall. *Impossible*, I think again. How could I have screwed up at screwing up?

Only I could do that. Liam Geller, King of the Screwups.

31

IF IT WASN'T BAD ENOUGH that the entire school, with the exception of Darleen, loved my announcements, that day I decide to sit with Raymond and Simon again at lunch, and Joe Banks's entire table comes over and joins us.

One minute it's just me and my AV buddies sitting forlornly in the cafeteria all by ourselves, the next minute there are trays and milk cartons everywhere. Half the football team settles at one end, and at least half the cheerleading squad takes up residence at the other end. Nikki sits on top of the table, and Joe produces a blue Pineville Devils football jersey and holds it up dramatically.

"We took a vote, Rambo," he says, "and we think you should wear this Devils jersey when you do the sports. You can be an honorary member of the team."

Raymond looks like he's about to piss his pants, and I can't help but wonder who "we" is. *Didn't anyone else think I sucked?*

"And these," Nikki adds, pulling out a pair of shades. She places them seductively on Raymond's face, leaning far over so that her cleavage shows. Raymond Romer beams. I moan.

"Damn, you guys were cool," Joe adds, sloshing down his milk. "When Liam started doing the announcements in French, I was laughing so hard I couldn't breathe."

"I was in Madame Gorka's homeroom, and she was practically drooling!" A curvy redhead in a halter top drapes her body over the table. "She is totally in love with you, Liam."

Great, I think. All I need is a salivating French teacher.

I'm about to deny that any teacher could be in love with me when Darleen walks into the lunchroom. I haven't seen her since this morning when she called me an idiot, and I'm positive that if we just had a moment alone together, I could explain everything.

Darleen snakes through the line, emerges with her tray, and then she stops, staring at the spectacle of Raymond Romer wearing a Devils football jersey and shades, surrounded by every popular senior at Pineville High. I watch her, wishing she'd sit with us, but Joe follows my gaze and moos loudly. He picks up a slimy orange seed and chucks it at Darleen's back. Raymond takes off the shades, and I open my mouth to say something, but Joe is already moving on.

"Simon should have some sort of guest spot every now and then, don't you think?" He's asking me.

"Huh? Oh, yeah, I guess."

"Hey, Dougie, think up a look for the Simonizer."

Everything's happening around me, and I ought to be fending it off somehow, but all I can think is that now Darleen is convinced I've turned the announcements into a mockery. And maybe I have.

Mr. Popularity strikes again.

Under the circumstances, it's pretty amazing that I make it to English at all, but Orlando glares when I come in a half second late. He's handing back essays, and my latest one is marked with a D–.

Whatever.

"We're going to write another essay," Orlando says. "I want you to have fun with this one."

How could writing an essay possibly be fun? I close my eyes and mentally will him to pick a decent topic.

The Top Ten All-Time Best Waves.

Why Tommy Hilfiger Is Becoming Entirely Too Well-Known.

How to Screw Up Everything.

Orlando stands in front of the chalkboard in his blue jeans and vest and writes, "Describe what you are best at."

"Okay, class, you know the drill. Two pages. At least. From everyone." He looks meaningfully at me. "You've got until the end of class. If you finish early, hand your paper to me and read *Hamlet*. If you need extra time, I'll stay after until you're done. Let's make these good, people. College quality. I want to know what you excel at, so impress me." He sits down at his desk, and I stare out the window.

Well, I think, *it could definitely be worse.* I'm pretty sure I can write two pages on what I'm best at. In fact, I'm pretty sure I can write even more than that. I take out one of my pens, and the girl beside me hands me some paper. Orlando sighs.

"Paper, Liam. School supplies. Bring them."

Thirty minutes later I finish page five. I read the pages over, then grin with satisfaction as I walk them to the front of the room. *At least this part of my day won't suck.* I set the pages on Orlando's desk, positioning them on top of the pile, then sit down to stare at the first page of *Hamlet* for the last ten minutes of class. When the bell rings I pop up, ready to go.

"Liam, would you stay after class, please?"

I pause. Maybe Orlando wants to compliment me on my dramatic improvement. He points toward a seat, so I sit. He takes a deep breath.

"Clearly, this is not your best effort," he says.

For a moment I think I've heard him wrong. I peer at the papers on his desk to make sure they're really mine.

"I wrote five pages," I say at last. "You said two and I wrote five. I could have edited it more, but —"

Orlando interrupts before I can finish. He picks up my paper.

"'What I'm Best At, by Liam Geller.'" He pauses, glancing over the top of the paper before continuing to read. "'I would have to say that the one thing I truly excel at is screwing up. I am very, very good at it there are many ways in which I manage to screw up far more than the average person. Whereas most people screw up only once in a while I am very consistent about it and even screw up at screwing up when I mean to be screwing up.'"

Orlando pauses. "This is your essay? Five pages on why you're best at screwing up?"

"I wrote a lot of supporting details," I stammer. "The bit about getting caught in Dad's office — that was pretty good, don't you think?"

Orlando sets down the papers.

"No," he says. "I don't 'think.' Would any college accept this? They wouldn't, so I want you to rewrite it."

My jaw drops. I spent a half hour writing that paper. My hand still hurts. I followed the directions exactly, and I deserve an A.

"It's a good essay," I say, "and if you just reread it . . ."

Orlando pauses.

"I get to be the judge of what's a good essay in this classroom," he says, "and no matter how many times I reread this, it wouldn't be college quality. Every other student managed to write something positive about themselves, and I know you can too."

My face is getting hot. I pick up my paper then put it down again.

"I did everything you told me to, and it's not fair that I have to rewrite it just because you don't like it."

Orlando stands in front of my desk.

"First of all," he says, shifting forward, "it doesn't matter if you think it's fair. Second, you *didn't* do what I said. I made it clear that the purpose of the assignment was to share something positive about yourself and you're a great kid so I know you can do better than this. Tell me something you excel at."

"I excel at screwing up."

"Everyone has things they do well," Orlando says. "You can't tell me there's not a single positive point about yourself that you can put down on paper!"

I glare, willing something to burst into flame.

"You asked what I was *best* at. I answered the question and that's the truthful answer. Now you're changing your mind, which isn't fair."

Orlando takes a deep breath.

"I'm giving you a second chance," he says, "because I want you to succeed. "I'm not giving you an F on the paper. I'm giving you an opportunity to rewrite it, choosing another subject. Something that embodies the spirit of the assignment. I want you to come up with something else."

"Well, there isn't anything else!" I slap my pen down on my desk, and Orlando takes another long, slow breath. Like Zen breathing.

"Liam," he says, "you speak fluent French, for god's sake. Everybody loved your announcements. You've traveled all over the world. Eddie says you know everything about fashion . . ."

I glare. "Those don't count."

"Who says?"

"*I* say. Speaking French is just like speaking English. When you live someplace you just learn it. And the announcements were a major screwup because I meant to screw them up and instead everybody loved them, so that just proves my point."

Orlando closes his eyes.

"Why on earth would you be trying to screw up the announcements?"

I sigh. "That's none of your business. I just was. Besides, even if I wasn't, it still wouldn't be what I'm best at. I'm not rewriting anything, so you might as well just give me the grade I deserve."

Now Orlando crosses his arms. "I'll give you detention, is what I'll give you. You can sit here after school every day until it's finished."

"Detention? There's no way I deserve detention for writing a damn good essay!" I take back my paper. "Fine. What do you want me to write?"

"It's not what *I* want you to write," Orlando says. "It's what you want to write."

I grit my teeth. "I wrote what I wanted to write and you didn't like it, so how am I supposed to know what to write now?"

Orlando sighs.

"I guess you'll have to figure that out."

32

THE FIRST THING I HEAR when I open the trailer door is Aunt Pete's bellow.

"You're late!"

I follow the voice down the hallway to his bedroom, where he's standing in front of the mirror putting on eye shadow. He's wearing black spandex pants, a long silver tuxedo jacket with tails, platform boots, and a white feather boa.

"You're late," he says again when I appear in the doorway. I frown.

"And you're wearing . . . that."

Aunt Pete glowers at me.

"Glitter's got a gig tonight. A private seventies-themed party out in Stonykill. Now, don't change the subject. Where've you been?"

I sit down on his bed. I consider lying, but I'm too tired.

"Detention."

"For what?!"

"Orlando gave me detention because he didn't like the essay I wrote."

"*Orlando* gave you detention?"

I nod. "It wasn't fair. I wrote a good essay — longer than he said — and he told me to rewrite it. For no reason."

Aunt Pete stops what he's doing and scratches his chin.

"No reason, huh? Did you tell him you thought it wasn't fair?"

I make a face. "Yeah. As if that did any good. It doesn't matter what I think. I'm supposed to do what he wants, no matter what. I hate Orlando."

Aunt Pete shoots me a look.

"Watch it," he snaps. "That's my boyfriend you're talking about."

I suppose he has a point. I flop backward onto the bed. "Okay. Fine. Maybe I don't hate him, but it wasn't fair. I'm telling you, I wrote five pages. He said we only had to write two, but I wrote five."

Aunt Pete chuckles. "All right, all right. I believe you. I'm not saying Orlando's perfect. I'm sure it was a great essay and your writing abilities have been slandered unjustly. In fact, being a devoted uncle, tomorrow, wearing this very outfit, I will go down to the school and protest on your behalf until . . ."

I try not to, but I laugh. Then I stare up at the ceiling.

"That's just what Mom would've done," I say after a while. "Not the protesting part," I add. "The part where you made me laugh instead of getting mad."

Aunt Pete puts down the lipstick he just took out.

"Really? That's what Sarah would have done?"

I nod.

"Yeah," I tell him. "You're not as bad at this as you think you are."

Aunt Pete grins, but I sit up. I wasn't going to say anything, but I can't stand it.

"You're pretty bad at putting on makeup, though." I take the lipstick out of his hand. "I thought you'd been doing this a long time."

Pete just shrugs.

"Yeah," he says. "I've been doing a shitty job for a long time. They don't exactly give makeup lessons for men."

I study his face carefully.

"Well," I say, "you're obviously going for something... uh... loud." I pause. "Still, less is more, and the outfit really speaks for itself." I take out a Kleenex and wipe off most of what Aunt Pete put on, then carefully start reapplying it the same way I've watched Mom do it a million times.

"Why do you do this?" I ask after a minute, drawing a sweeping line with the eyeliner. Aunt Pete follows my hand with his eyes.

"You really want to know?"

I nod.

"Decadence," Aunt Pete says at last. "Art, glamour, theater... It's not so different from modeling, really. You get onstage and strike a pose. Plus, I feel good when I dress up, and men don't usually get to experience that. But why shouldn't we?"

I sweep a line of deep crimson across Aunt Pete's eyelid.

"Doesn't it bother you that people don't get it?"

Pete starts to shake his head, then catches himself and holds still.

"Nope," he says. "If you know what you love, it doesn't matter what other people think. Besides, people are challenged when they're uncomfortable. Glam stretches the boundaries. Gender boundaries, fashion boundaries . . . Glam, punk, rap, metal — they all make people stop and stare. It's good for 'em." He looks at me.

"Besides," he says, "I may not be rich or respected like your father, but I've got the three best friends in the world, a pretty decent trailer, a job I love . . . the good life. I don't need anyone's approval."

I set down the eye-shadow brush. I wish I could say that. I stick my finger in a vat of glitter on Aunt Pete's dresser.

"Hold still."

I draw an arc of silver just below each of Aunt Pete's eyebrows. Each arc sweeps up like the eyeliner and the eye shadow, making evil wings on the sides of his face. I turn him toward the mirror.

"What do you think?"

Pete turns first to one side, then the other.

"Damn," he says. "That's pretty good."

I shrug. Every now and then I manage to do something right.

33

I'M GUESSING ORLANDO TALKED TO PETE about my essay, because the day after the gig Pete invites me to have dinner with him and Eddie on Friday night. They have something important to discuss with me. Something they think I'll really *excel* at.

Whatever.

Actually, Pete invites me to *make* dinner, because whenever he cooks it's a disaster. At least it gives me something to do so I won't think about all the ways I'm screwing up lately.

Then I see Darleen coming toward the picnic table. She hasn't been to the picnic table for days, but now she surveys our joint yard, and then she kind of tiptoes out. She's wearing jeans that are way too short and a shirt that looks like one of those things people wore in the eighties with the giant collar. Her hair is pulled back in a sloppy ponytail, and she's got a huge YES TO THE ARTS, NO TO HOMECOMING poster under one arm and a set of paints under the other arm. She sits down and very carefully starts to decorate the edge of the poster.

"Hi."

Darleen jumps a mile. She didn't see me jog out of Aunt Pete's trailer.

"How's it going?"

Her eyes bug out and for a minute I think she might bolt, but then her jaw tightens and she regains her composure. "Fine," she says, even though she's gritting her teeth. I sit down across from her.

"You're in my light," she says, so I move over.

"Did you have dinner yet?"

Darleen shakes her head.

"Do you want to have dinner with me, Eddie, and Pete?"

She shakes her head again.

"No?"

"Yes," says Darleen.

"Yes?"

Darleen sighs again. "I'm busy," she says. "Can't you see that I'm busy?"

I pause. "Eddie is coming over at seven, but I can be flexible. What if we wait until seven fifteen? You might not be busy then, and we'd still have time to eat before Pete has to leave for work." Darleen glares. She puts down her paintbrush, picks it up again, then puts it down one last time.

"Listen," she says at last, as if she's prying the words out of her mouth. "The answer is no. N-O. And *stop* following me around. I don't know what it is you think you're doing, but if you think you're going to become popular by tormenting me, then I have news for you. You already are popular. Understand? You don't need an 'in' with Joe and his idiotic bunch of lemmings, so whatever grand scheme you're concocting is unnecessary. Got it? Unneeded. A waste of time."

She's talking loudly and slowly as if I won't be capable of understanding.

"I'm not popular," I say. "I joined the AV club."

Darleen stops midbreath. "What?" she says, wrinkling her nose.

"I know you think I'm mocking the announcements, but I'm not. I'm really taking them very seriously, because, well, equipment is my life. I can understand if you think I'm dumb, but in reality I'm very smart. Studious, I mean."

I hope this might make things better, but instead it makes things worse.

"What are you talking about?" Darleen asks. "You couldn't even work the stopwatch. Equipment is your life? You're studious and smart? What does that have to do with anything?"

She picks up her poster even though the paint isn't dry.

"Fine," she says. "You want the picnic table? You can have it."

That's when I crack.

"Wait!"

I say it louder and more desperately then I intend, but at least she stops.

"Please, just . . . I'm trying to be nice. Dinner was Pete's idea. He thinks you and I could be friends, and he and Eddie really want

[183]

you to come. They think it will be fun. Aunt Pete's been looking forward to it all week. If you say no, they'll never forgive me."

This is probably overkill, but Darleen considers.

"Eddie's coming?" she asks suspiciously, even though I just said that.

I nod.

"And this was Pete's idea?"

"You'd be doing him a favor. He's worried I'm not making friends."

Darleen scoffs.

"I'll tell you what," she says. "I'll do it on one condition."

"You name it."

She looks me straight in the eyes.

"I'll come to dinner tonight if you will leave me alone after this."

I can't help wondering how I'll leave her alone when she already avoids me all the time. I'm about to point this out, but instead I simply nod. Best not to complicate things. Besides, when she sees how smooth I'm going to be tonight, she won't care about that anymore.

I grin. "Great. Seven fifteen. You won't regret this."

Just like that, I've got a date with Darleen. Well, okay, maybe not a date in the traditional sense of the word, but the most unpopular girl at school will be having dinner with me, and that's got to count for something. If she were to become my official girlfriend, Dad would be way impressed. I think.

I decide I'd better call Eddie to make sure I don't screw anything up. I get the number off the bulletin board and dial the phone. It rings once, twice, three times . . .

"Eddie here."

I exhale loudly.

"Eddie. Thank god you're home."

"Liam? Is something wrong? What happened? What's going on?" Eddie's voice shoots up two octaves.

"I'm inviting Darleen for dinner tonight. I need your opinion about some stuff."

There's a long silence, so I add, "It's important."

"Well, okay." He sounds a bit confused, but I don't have time to explain.

"I'm making tofu stir-fry. Do you think she'll like that?"

Eddie pauses. "Sure," he says. "I don't see why not."

This is good since it's already made.

"What kind of stuff does Darleen like to do aside from art and protesting?"

Eddie makes a hmmm-ing noise.

"Well, she's also into music."

That's right. The cello.

"Does she watch any TV shows? What kind of books does she read?"

"What? Why do you want to know this stuff? And the answers are that I don't know. It's not like she and I spend a lot of time together just hanging out. I think she reads thrillers, but that's just a guess."

"That's good, Eddie." I don't answer his question about why I want to know. "Oh, and one more thing. Do you think I should invite her dad too?"

Eddie pauses. "Well, no. I mean, Phil works most evenings. What's all this about?"

"Nothing," I say. "Just, you know, being friendly. Okay. See you around seven." I hang up before Eddie can ask any more questions. I'm feeling pretty smug because now I know I should work thrillers and music into our conversation, and maybe we can commiserate about being all alone in the evenings.

Perfect.

Now to set a nice atmosphere. I look around for candles, but all I find are two citronella bug-repellent ones in the broom closet. They aren't the greatest, but they'll have to do.

I survey the kitchen and wish Pete had a table. There's only a counter with four bar stools and no matching table settings — just four plastic plates with the Buffalo Bills logo on them. There's nothing to drink except beer, water, and orange juice, and the food has already been on the stove too long. I take a deep breath. This is okay. Mom always says that nothing can spoil good conversation.

I finish making dinner, then continue my pacing until Eddie pulls in the driveway at 7:12. I let him in, then light one of the citronella candles. I have to put it behind the sink so the smoke will waft out the window.

When he steps into the living room, Eddie stops midstride. "What smells so good?"

I wish he'd said that *after* Darleen arrived, but maybe he'll say it again. There's a knock on the door, and when I open it Darleen is scowling at me. I'm guessing she waited to knock until after she saw Eddie arrive, but that's okay.

"Let's get this over with," Darleen says, which would normally be daunting, but I just smile. Smiling can't help but rub off on people.

"Everything's ready," I say. "I made stir-fry. With tofu. It's very good for you."

Aunt Pete shuffles into the living room. He's just gotten out of the shower, so his hair is dripping all over the floor and his radio T-shirt is mostly wet. He looks surprised to see Darleen, but he hides it well. Everyone grabs a seat at the counter while I dish the food, and I'm expecting there to be a lot of conversation, but there isn't. I can tell immediately that Aunt Pete is uncomfortable around Darleen. They say hello like two people who ought to know each other but don't. And Eddie isn't much better. He asks her about school, but other than that no one talks.

As soon as the food is dished out, Eddie takes a huge bite.

"Liam, this is so good!" he says. "You made this? I can't believe you can cook."

I shrug.

"You like it?" I ask, but I'm not looking at Eddie. I'm looking at Aunt Pete and Darleen. Darleen eats a small bite, but Pete keeps poking the tofu with his fork.

"What is it again?" he asks.

"Soy. It's good for you. Excellent source of protein."

Aunt Pete nods. He breaks off a minuscule piece of tofu and swallows it whole.

"You have to chew it," I say. "Just try it."

He sets down his fork. "Hey," he says a bit too cheerfully. "I wanted to tell you why we asked you to dinner."

I cringe because I forgot I told Darleen they were asking her to dinner so I'd make friends. She gives me a withering look, but Pete is oblivious.

"Eddie and I have been talking about it and we've decided you should work at his store like you guys discussed. I was pretty mad after the whole school bus incident . . . but I've decided that modeling for Eddie would be an excellent opportunity for you. Assuming you still want to do it."

I do, but I'm distracted because Pete isn't eating.

I nod. Then I jab some broccoli on his plate. "Try this," I tell him. "This is just broccoli in a teriyaki sauce. It's good."

Darleen eats a bite of hers. "It's not horrific," she says, but Aunt Pete isn't listening.

"Yeah, so Eddie says you've got a real eye for modeling. Said you're just like Sarah."

I blush and stop jabbing Pete's broccoli.

"Who's Sarah?" Darleen asks.

Pete has a piece of carrot halfway to his mouth, but he sets it down gratefully. "Liam's mom," he says. "She was a runway model. Used to do fashion shows all over the world until Allan got jealous. Oops, I mean, got a job as a CEO."

I set down my fork.

"Dad was never jealous of Mom," I say. "Mom stopped modeling because she got too old and my grades were bad. That's why we moved back to the States."

Aunt Pete coughs the word "bullshit" into his napkin.

I glare.

"It's not bullshit. Mom told me herself. Modeling is a hard business and you can't do it anymore once you get old. Besides" — I turn to Darleen — "Dad is the smartest person you'll ever meet. He's in Mensa and everything. That's why he couldn't pass up a job that would use his full potential.

"He runs one of the top businesses in the country," I add, "and on the side he takes all these top corporate executives to the country club and convinces them to give their money to different charities. He's probably the most selfless person ever to —"

Aunt Pete pushes his plate away.

"Bullshit," he says again, this time without the napkin.

Eddie cringes. "This is really good, Liam. What did you say was in it again?"

I barely hear him. My face is getting hot, and I dig my fingers into the counter. Why does Pete have to act like this? Why now, with Darleen sitting right next to me? And why can't he just eat the damn tofu?

"What do you know about it?" I say, harsher than I mean to. "You haven't exactly been around for the last, what, seventeen years?"

Darleen and Eddie exchange glances, and Eddie starts to say something about school, but Aunt Pete leans forward and points at me. He actually *points* at me, and I think, *See? I knew there'd be pointing sooner or later.*

"You want to know why I haven't been around?" Pete asks. "Because you're wrong about the seventeen years part. Up until you guys moved to Paris I did everything with you and Sarah because your father treated her like crap. And now he treats you like crap, and you defend him. Just like your mother."

I nearly choke. I can't believe he just said that in front of Darleen.

"I can defend my own father," I say loudly, "and he doesn't treat me like crap. I behave like crap so he gets frustrated, and I don't blame him because he's given me lots of chances, and even you get frustrated, so don't pretend it isn't true."

"Liam, for god's sake."

Now we're both being loud. Pete stands up and takes his plate into the kitchen.

"I can't eat this," he says, dishing it back into the fry pan. He stands there for a long time, staring at the stove while Eddie and Darleen study their food.

Eddie reaches over and puts his hand on my arm.

"Don't be mad," he says quietly. "He didn't say it to make you mad."

I shake off Eddie's hand and push my plate away. *Ruined. All this planning and everything is ruined.*

Aunt Pete runs his fingers through his hair. "I'm sorry," he says from the kitchen. "I shouldn't have said that. I'm sure your father loves you. He works hard, and it's none of my business what you think of him. And the food looks good," he adds as an after-thought. "I should have eaten it."

It's supposed to feel great when someone apologizes to you. But it doesn't.

"Shit," Pete says. He pauses. "Listen. This was supposed to be a fun dinner. Eddie and I agreed it would be great for you to work at the store, and I figured you'd be pretty happy about that. He can pay you for eight hours every Saturday. Starting tomorrow if you want. I know this didn't go off the way I planned . . ."

The way *he* planned?

". . . but I hope you'll still do it." He pauses. "I've got to finish getting ready for work," he says, nodding at Darleen. "Sorry."

She shrugs, then stands up.

"Thanks for dinner," she says. "I should go, too. I've got to get back to my poster."

I can't believe this. Now they're both leaving.

"Wait," I say. "You can't go yet! We haven't had dessert and . . ."

She smiles in a preemptive sort of way. "Thanks. Good night."

Darleen lets herself out and I sag against the counter. I put my head down. Only Eddie is left at the kitchen table.

"Didn't go quite how you wanted, huh?" he says.

I groan. "She hates me."

"I'm sure she doesn't hate you," Eddie starts, but I raise one eyebrow.

"Well, she'll come around then. It's not your fault things

went haywire. Petey has strong feelings about your dad. It's hard for him to talk about this stuff."

I roll my eyes. "Yeah," I say. "Just because he and Dad don't get along. As if that's so horrible."

Eddie pauses. He looks like he's going to say something, but he stops. "Maybe you should talk to Petey about that."

Yeah, right, I think. As if I'm going to talk to Aunt Pete about anything now.

34

IT'S NEW YORK FASHION WEEK, the biggest event of the year, and tonight is Mom's last runway show. She's decided to go out with a bang. It's my first official Fashion Week, although Mom's told me all about them, so I'm excited. We arrive in Bryant Park early on the final day of the week, just me and Mom. It's raining, and this is difficult because I've got on suede shoes and a tailored suit that shouldn't get wet.

"Everyone has to look good for Fashion Week," Mom says. "Even if you're seven."

We take a cab, and when it pulls up next to the curb we jump out and huddle under her umbrella. The tents are all set up, and behind them the skyscrapers look like a backdrop someone painted for a movie set.

"Look, Li," Mom says, "every one of those tents has runway shows going on all day into the night."

Mom takes my hand and pulls me along until we're out of the rain. We duck inside a huge tent full of white plastic chairs with a long runway going down the middle. There are bright lights everywhere and people are milling around. They are the best-looking people I have ever seen. Not because they're all models — some of them don't look like models at all — but because they're all wearing beautiful clothes with shoes that have heels high off the floor. They carry handbags with fancy beads and sparkles that catch the lights.

Mom isn't watching the people though. She walks to the end of the runway and stops. She's holding my hand so tight it hurts, but I don't complain. Sometimes I know when to be quiet, and this is one of those times.

"I remember my first show," Mom says at last. "I was so nervous my knees shook all night and I worried I'd never be able to make it. I kept thinking about all the fashion editors and designers and celebrities sitting right here in the front row and when I walked down the runway all their eyes would be on me."

"What did you do?" I ask.

Mom laughs, then she lifts her chin. "I'll tell you what I did," she says. "I put on the most delicious red Persian lamb gown with a gorgeous plunging neckline and I told myself I would be that gown." She pauses, then shakes her head. "I was so, so young."

"Did you make it?" I ask. "Without falling down?"

"I did," Mom says. "I've made it many, many times without ever falling down."

"So why will you stop now?"

I look up at Mom and she has tears in her eyes.

"Sometimes other people need to shine for a while."

"Like the other models?"

Mom cocks her head to one side and laughs. She kneels down and looks at me. "Noooo," she says, teasingly. "You don't think any of them are as pretty as your mommy, do you?"

I shake my head so hard it hurts. Mom grins at me, her famous grin that spreads completely across her face from ear to ear, but then so quickly I don't even see it coming, the smile evaporates into a sob and she buries her head on my shoulder. I'm so shocked I don't know what to do. I don't even put my arms around her or anything. I just stand there and she clutches me tight and her shoulders shake.

Finally, I whisper, "What's wrong?"

Mom looks up and wipes away her tears, smudging her mascara. She sniffs and musses my hair.

"The makeup people are going to love me today," she says. She stands and takes my hand again. "Come on, Li. We need to find Maria so I can get ready."

She walks away from the runway, and I trot behind her, pulled along too fast, wanting to ask a million questions like, "What just happened?" and, "Are you better now?" or maybe, "Will you make it down the runway tonight or will you fall?" But I'm not sure which question is the right one, and if I ask the wrong one, Mom might cry again.

We walk backstage, where the designer's second assistant, Maria, is waiting. She's going to watch me tonight. I've met Maria before, but she melts when she sees my suit and the suede shoes. Then she looks at Mom.

"Oh, Sarah," she says. She reaches out and touches Mom's cheek.

"It's all right," Mom says casually. "I'm okay. Really."

"You know you'll always be Tomas's muse. If you ever want to come back . . ."

But Mom turns away before Maria can finish, and when she turns back it's my happy mom looking at us once again.

"No," she says. "I've made the right decision. I've got a wonderful husband and son to take care of. Just look at Liam. Isn't he getting big? He's promised to be very, very good tonight. Didn't you, Li?"

I nod. Then Mom kneels down one more time.

"Soak it all in," she says. "The lights, the music, the clothes . . . you're going to love it. Trust me."

That night I toss and turn, hearing Pete's voice in my head. "Used to do fashion shows all over the world until Allan got jealous. Oops, I mean, got a job as a CEO . . . Treated her like crap. And now he treats you like crap . . . Just like your mother . . ."

I tell myself it's not true. Mom didn't want to model anymore. She told me that herself, and why would she lie? Only now I can't help remembering her last runway show. I haven't thought about that in years.

I lie in bed, staring up at the ceiling, and my mind is going a mile a minute. Maybe Aunt Pete is right. Maybe Dad *wasn't* proud of Mom's career. Did he pressure her to leave modeling because he didn't like her being more successful than he was? If I succeeded at something, would he be proud of me? *He would,* I tell myself. *He just hasn't been able to prove it yet because I haven't done anything right.*

I need to relax — think about something different — so I start planning Eddie's window. We already discussed the display, but all our ideas were small and predictable, and suddenly I want them to be brilliant. I want the store window to be Pineville's equivalent of Mom's last runway show.

I want it to be a success.

When Eddie swings by at eight the next morning, I'm sitting on Aunt Pete's front step with my surfboard. Eddie stops the car and leans out the window. He's wearing silver shades with a black tank top, and he lets the shades slip down his nose.

"Excuse me?" he asks as I position the surfboard so that one end sticks out the back window. I climb into the front seat and drop a beach bag at my feet.

"I know what you're thinking," I say, trying to sound confident, "but I've been considering the window and I think we can do better."

"Better than a fall montage?"

I nod. "Everyone's doing fall stuff. You want to be different, don't you? I think we should do an end of the summer final sale on bathing suits."

Eddie coughs. "It's September," he reminds me gently. "No one buys a bathing suit in September. I thought you liked the fall thing."

I cringe. "I do. It's just not perfect. Besides," I add, "I have inside information about a certain last pool party of the season.

Some guy in homeroom invited me, and apparently it's going to be a big deal. His parents are away for a week, and they're closing the pool after this, so he's inviting everyone over. All the kids from school will be going, so if we can just get some of them down to the shop ..."

Eddie is skeptical. "How exactly are we going to do that?" he asks. "No one your age voluntarily shops at His and Hers Apparel."

I pull out my cell phone. I'm reluctant to do this, but I don't see any other option. "I've looked up everyone's number," I tell Eddie. "I'll call Jen, Joe, and Nikki. Maybe the guy who's having the party. I'll talk it up as if this could be some sort of preparty event. I know this is risky, but I think we can pull it off."

"You do, huh?" I can tell he's still not on board.

"Listen," I say with more conviction than I feel, "fashion is all about fantasy, right? Escaping from reality? Well, what better reality to escape from than school? We've all been there for a while now, so the thrill is definitely gone and everyone's daydreaming about summer. This guy Rob decides to throw one last pool party ... so let's complete the illusion. It's hot enough today that we can wear shorts and tanks. We'll open the store up, maybe make it a sidewalk sale. We could get some lemonade from Mae's and act like it's sweltering out. It'll be a blast."

I'm only half convinced this will really work, but I can tell Eddie's getting interested. He sits up straighter and drives faster.

"It does sound like fun," he says. "And I've certainly got enough bathing suits left over. As long as we push the other stuff too, we could do okay." He nods. "All right," he says. "Why not?

We'll give it a shot. Only don't be disappointed if it's a slow day. This is your first time doing this, so you can't expect a lot of people to show up."

"I know," I tell him, but really I'm thinking people had better show up, because I do not want this to be one more thing I screw up.

I decide to start making phone calls once everything is set up. I know this isn't exactly an unpopular thing to do, but this is business, so it doesn't count.

I help Eddie move all the summer racks from the sale section out to the sidewalk. We've got to put signs on all the fall stuff so older people who won't be attending any pool parties will still have something to shop for. I run over to Mae's for the lemonade, and she remembers me and gives me extra lemons in a big yellow bowl.

Then I've got to arrange the window.

The surfboard is my best prop, so I feature it prominently. I decide to keep the window simple, because too much clutter will detract from the illusion rather than add to it. The great thing about Eddie's window is that it's shiny and clean. It doesn't have that scuffed up look a lot of shopwindows have. This means the display can be just me, my board, and the bowl of bright yellow lemons.

The summer fantasy illusion is completed by several last details. I put on some great music and slather myself in coconut tanning oil so the smell will be in the air. I even make Eddie put some on. He doesn't seem to mind.

"Here," he says, handing me a deep blue Tommy Hilfiger

bathing suit. "I've got way too many of these left over. Start with this one."

The plan is that I will change clothes every hour. I take the bathing suit into the dressing room and try it on. It fits nice and the color is perfect. Then I take out a small makeup kit I got from my mom. It's not something I let just anybody know I own, but it comes in handy.

When you're a guy putting on makeup, you have to do it just right. Only enough to enhance your features, unless you're doing something dramatic, like a fashion spread in a magazine or modeling something avant-garde. Or unless you're Aunt Pete. Otherwise, no one needs to know you're wearing it.

I also pull out my secret weapon. A small tube of hemorrhoid cream. I put a dab under my eyes since I didn't sleep well last night. It shrinks the blood vessels and gets rid of dark circles. Then I make a thin line with the eyeliner pencil. Eyeliner is the best. It totally makes your eyes stand out and half the time people don't know why. They just know they want to look at you.

When I finally finish my phone calls and climb in the window, I'm thinking about Mom. Tired, nervous, fumbling Mom — but the minute she stepped onstage, or got in front of a camera, she was someone else.

I think about all the things she taught me. The way you should imagine a vertical line straight through your center. That line becomes your focus and no matter what you're doing, you should know where your center is, and how to balance it. When you move, everything moves along with that line so that no part of your body arrives before you do. You can't slouch or shuffle. No matter what you're feeling, you have to move with confidence. Shoulders back. Hands free.

It's not all about looking hot, either. Sometimes it's about being shocking, and that's the one advantage I have going for me today. Without even trying I'll be shocking. No one's going to expect me in the window. If I play it right, I'll make people stop in their tracks.

Eddie goes outside to look at my display, and I can't hear his reaction, but I see the expression on his face. First he's busy, thinking of a hundred details he still has to take care of. Then he sees me and his body becomes still. He stares as if we've never met.

I stand in the window, hoping someone will show up. I can't say many people come by at first, but aside from worrying that the day will be a bust, I don't mind. Standing in the window is like lying on the picnic table. I shut a certain part of my brain off and let myself space out. Obviously I've got to change position every now and then, but once I've settled in, it's okay to relax. There's no photographer to vamp for. All I have to do is hold my position.

It's a half hour before the first real customers come by. I hear them out front, but I don't look at them because I'm leaning on my surfboard staring at something far away. I'm not really focused on anything, but I want people to think I'm staring at a wave. Maybe the last wave of the summer.

"What's Eddie up to this time?" a voice says.

Two ladies are walking up from the hairdresser. They approach the window and lean in to get a better look. Then they disappear and I think they've left for good, only they come back with several women in curlers. The small crowd attracts three men from the animal feed store, and soon I notice cars making sharp turns into the strip mall.

"You having some sort of sale, Eddie?"

"What kind of crazy stunt you pulling?"

Before long the door chimes are ringing every two minutes, and I can hear lots of muffled voices through the glass. Mostly I really do think about waves. I try to remember what it felt like to be in Hawaii. Every now and then I listen to Eddie hand selling the most expensive of the suits.

"I understand the swimming season is over, but by the start of next season I'll have to sell these at full price. Why not buy one now and put it away? That one is beautiful. Honestly, it premiered just this season, so it will look fabulous on you next year . . ."

Then Jen and Nikki show up.

"Oh my god! Liam, I can't believe you're in the window." Jen bounces up and down doing cheerleader kicks outside the shop. "You're crazy!" she yells, flipping open her cell phone. "That's it," she says. "I'm calling the squad."

Twenty minutes later the strip mall is crawling with whistling, giggling cheerleaders. A car pulls up and Joe and three other guys pile out. Joe gives me a fist salute and starts a chant.

"Li-am, Li-am, Li-am."

I've been standing completely still for about twenty minutes, so I allow myself a break. I hop out of the window and yell to Eddie. "Want me to sell stuff to these guys?"

"Yes," he says. He whooshes past me, then stops. "Wait. Could you call Darleen? Tell her I need help at the register."

I'm about to step outside, but I stop and whirl around. "What? No!"

Eddie looks up. "She'll say yes," he says. "She's helped me out before." He puts down the suits. "No wait. You're right. You go outside and talk those boys into buying Hilfiger. Push the blue ones. Then I need you back in that window. I'll call Darleen."

I cringe. "She's probably busy," I say, "and I don't think she'll want to get involved with —"

Eddie scowls. "Go!" he says.

I hesitate, but I can tell he's made up his mind, so I grab the CD player and step outside. I hand the CDs to Jen. "Here, pick out something good."

Joe punches me on the shoulder.

"You're a maniac!" he says. I make a mock bodybuilder pose as music blasts out of the stereo. My biceps still look decent, even though I've only been able to do free weights in the corner of Aunt Pete's trailer. I know I shouldn't be vamping, but this is important for business, right? Nikki dances over holding a tiny red string bikini.

"This one for the party?" she says, holding it up seductively. "Or this one?" She pulls an even tinier black one from behind her back. The guys whistle and Joe pretends to faint, but I don't see a bikini; I see my chance. Girls will buy anything just because it's fun and they want something new to wear, but no guy is going to buy a bathing suit in September unless . . .

"Good try," I say casually, "but the guys have the best suits this year." Nikki looks confused.

"It's true. Check it out." I pull out the blue Tommy Hilfiger and hold it up, then turn slightly to the left.

"That is *so* hot," Jen breathes.

That's the reaction I was hoping for.

In the next fifteen minutes I sell five suits — two of them to guys. My goal is to sell everyone suits immediately so they'll leave before Darleen arrives, but it doesn't happen. Remember that thing I said about making this a preparty event? Well, everyone stays forever, talking and laughing and texting more people. I start to get uptight and my next shift in the window isn't as good. I keep glancing at the clock on Eddie's wall.

It's during my break that Darleen shows up. Jen, Joe, and Nikki have left and come back twice because Jen can't make up her mind. People from school are cycling in and out, but a lot of them are actually buying stuff, so Eddie doesn't mind. I've just climbed out of the window to help Jen when Darleen strides past. She looks determined. Determined to ignore as many of us as possible. Starting with me.

My stomach does a flip-flop.

"Who invited her?" Nikki asks, wrinkling her nose.

"I did," I say. Then I realize they're all going to see Darleen at the cash register, so I amended my statement. "I invited her to work here because we're so busy. She's Eddie's cousin." I don't mean it to sound like an excuse, but everyone nods.

"Too bad," Nikki says.

I'm about to explain that this isn't what I meant, when a girl from the cheerleading squad joins our group.

"Who invited her?" she asks, glancing in Darleen's direction.

"She's Eddie's cousin," Joe says in a sympathetic way.

"That's not what I —"

"I just had a brilliant idea," Nikki says, interrupting me. "We have *got* to do this for homecoming. It would be so much fun. We could do an auction and raise money for the senior class. Liam and I could model the clothes and —"

"And me," Jen says. "How come just you two get to model?"

"I'd be a great model," Joe says, flexing. "Don't you think I'd be great?"

I'm thinking only one thing.

Crap. *Crapcrapcrapcrap.*

There is no way I can do this for homecoming.

"I'd have to ask Eddie," I say, buying some time. Unfortunately, Eddie is walking past with an armful of suits.

"Ask Eddie what?"

"We were thinking of doing a fashion show for homecoming," Nikki gushes. "If you'd give us some of your stuff, people could bid on it and we'd make a ton of money for the senior class." I'm making "no way" signals behind Jen's back, but Eddie ignores me.

"Give?" he asks.

"Fifty-fifty?"

Eddie cocks his head. "It wouldn't be a bad deal," he says at last. "People always way overbid at fashion shows, especially if it's a fund-raiser. I could donate a couple items, and we could split the rest. Maybe Sarah would donate something."

I cringe. "I don't think . . . well . . ."

Nikki's bouncing up and down again.

"You *have* to!" she says. "I've always wanted to model. This could be my big break. It'll be so cool."

That's what I'm afraid of.

Eddie grins. "I'd say yes if I were you," he says over his shoulder as he makes his way back to the shop.

"I'm in charge of homecoming events," Jen says. "I'll give you a time slot toward the end of the day, and I'll even sign up the models if you and Eddie get the clothes."

My stomach is twisting tight.

"I don't know, guys. I don't think people would want to see me in a fashion show, really, because, uh, I'm not that popular and . . ."

Jen gives me a crazy look.

"Don't even!" she says. "You are so going to be homecoming king. Everyone's going to vote for you. And of course they'll want to see you in a fashion show. The son of Sarah Geller modeling at Pineville High? Don't think we haven't heard . . ." Jen puts her hand on my arm. "It's so cool that you're modest," she adds.

All the color drains from my face, and for a moment I think I might pass out. My head gets all woozy. I open my mouth to say something, but nothing comes out, and at that same moment the guy across the street puts up a huge sign advertising pizzas for five bucks. There's a cheer, and in the excitement somehow Jen thinks I've said yes.

"Great," she says, turning to Nikki. "Let's pay for this stuff."

The minute they walk away I slump against the bathing suit rack. I glance inside, thinking I'd better get back in the window, but Eddie is in the stockroom, and that means . . . I dash into the store, but Joe is already sitting on the counter pretending to flirt with Darleen.

"Maybe that one would look good on you," he says. "Oh, wait! That's a girdle."

"Do you even wear a bra?" one of the cheerleaders asks. I hurry around the counter.

"Are you buying the suits, or what?" I demand, and this time Jen pushes the others out of the way. She hands me the blue bikini I recommended earlier.

"We're buying," she says, giving me her dad's credit card. "Definitely buying."

Buying is a good thing, right? It ought to be, only the minute they leave Darleen fixes me with a look that could set a small planet on fire.

"Was this whole thing your idea?"

I look down at my feet. "Not the *whole* thing."

"Well, do me a favor," she says, making every word count. "The next time you have a brilliant idea — leave me out of it. I wouldn't have come today except Eddie got Dad on the phone, so I had to come down here and wait on those juvenile imbeciles buying string bikinis and Speedos."

"I didn't sell anyone a Speedo," I say, but Darleen shakes her head.

"We had a deal. Why is it not possible for you to leave me alone? You follow me around school. You totally lied to me about dinner. I really don't see why it's so —"

That's when Eddie emerges from the back. He surveys the empty shop and lets out a deep breath.

"Good timing," he says. "We need a break. The back room is a mess." He turns to me. "You," he says, "are brilliant. That homecoming fashion show was a great idea."

Darleen's eyes bug out, but Eddie is oblivious. He glances across the street to the pizza place. "You want to take a lunch break?" he asks. "Join your friends?"

I look out the window. "They're not really my . . ."

Darleen glares. "Yeah, Liam," she says. "Why don't you join your hordes of *friends?*"

35

AT FIVE O'CLOCK Eddie and I close up shop. Darleen went home without saying good-bye, and I suppose that's just as well. It's not like I can salvage things now. Not if I'm the future homecoming king.

Eddie and I limp out to the car and he claps me on the shoulder. "I ordered pizza," he says. "Two of them. And I invited the guys to hang out at my place. Figured we could celebrate before Dino and your uncle have to go to work."

I nod. "Fine."

Eddie looks at me funny.

"You okay?" he asks. I nod again.

We stop to pick up the pizzas, then drive to Eddie's little split-level. When we arrive the guys are already there, waiting on the front steps. Aunt Pete's Nissan is parked on the curb.

"Nice place," I say as we pull in. I haven't said anything the whole ride here, so I figure I'd better make *some* conversation. Eddie grins.

"Thanks," he says. "I worked hard for this house — back when I was a lingerie buyer for Lord and Taylor and I used to make money on a regular basis, that is. Of course, that's all about to change, thanks to my brilliant new employee." He opens the car door dramatically.

"And parading up the catwalk sporting the new two-for-one pizza design, the fabulous and dramatic Liam Geller."

I blush. "It wasn't that big of a —"

Eddie places one hand over my mouth. "Hush," he says. "Don't be modest. Peter, your nephew is a genius."

Aunt Pete stands in the doorway and grins. Dino claps him on the back, and I can tell they're proud. They're proud that I didn't screw up. Only I did. They just don't know it.

Eddie opens the door, and I follow the guys up the stairs. I'm about to bring the pizzas into the kitchen, but I stop when I reach the top. There's a picture on the living room wall — a reproduction of an Andy Warhol painting. Mom has that exact same print framed in her boutique. I try not to stare, but I can't help it.

I've been trying not to think about Mom all day, but now my chest aches. I keep wondering how she could leave modeling when it's so amazing? I try not to think the last thought that's pushing its way to the surface, but I can't help it. Dad wouldn't take something that important away from her, would he? How could he not be proud of Mom? She was a superstar.

"Don't be shy," Eddie says, slipping into the kitchen and jolting me out of my thoughts. "I'll get the drinks."

Dino grabs the pizza boxes out of my hands. "I'll take those."

"What? Oh, sorry."

I can't stop staring at the painting.

The thing that gets me is that we bought Mom's from a street vendor in New York City. It's a picture of Warhol with a quote on it that says, "I think everybody should like everybody." Mom and I were so excited to bring it home, but Dad took one look at it and said we'd spent way too much for it. It was like he didn't even read the words.

I haven't thought about that painting in a long time, but now all I can think is, *Has Dad ever liked me?*

I don't know how long I stand there. I hear the crash of dishes and the opening and shutting of the refrigerator, and I try to make myself breathe normally. In and out. Deep breaths. I'm concentrating so hard I don't notice that Pete is standing next to me.

"You like Andy Warhol?"

I try to answer but nothing comes out. I nod, then try again.

"Mom has that same print. We bought it in New York City, but Dad . . ." I clear my throat. "I'd better help out," I say, and Pete nods like he was expecting me to bail, but I don't care. I wander into the living room, where I'm greeted by raucous laughter. I've got to lose this mood so I concentrate on Eddie, who's reenacting everything that happened during the day.

"I'm telling you," he's saying, "they bought everything Liam suggested. He'd say, 'You look good in blue,' and the entire Pineville cheerleading squad would buy blue bikinis. I swear, one girl bought three bathing suits. Expensive ones, too."

Dino hands me a piece of pizza. "Very productive," he says in his deep, rumbling baritone. I take the pizza and I should be starving, but I don't feel hungry. I keep thinking about the look on Darleen's face when Eddie said I could take a break with my friends. I could see what she was thinking. *There goes Mr. Popularity.*

There's a lull in the laughter.

"You don't seem very excited," Orlando says, studying me from across the room. "We've demolished one and a half pizzas already and you haven't eaten a thing."

I look up. "What? Oh. Right, I'm excited. Today was great, it's just . . ."

Aunt Pete sits down next to the couch and grabs a slice of pizza. "What?"

I'm not sure how to ask.

"Well, I was sort of wondering something."

"Wondering if you can work for me every day? Why, yes. No problem," Eddie says, pouring everyone a round of wine. I study the carpet.

"No. Not that."

Aunt Pete frowns. "C'mon, spit it out so you can eat," he says. "Eddie told us you skipped lunch, and I don't want to be accused of not feeding you."

"Okay. But don't get mad."

Pete closes his eyes. "Uh-oh," he mumbles, but Dino jabs him in the leg.

"Ask what you want, Liam," Dino says.

"Well, I was just wondering if you guys were ever . . . un-popular."

There's a moment of silence before Aunt Pete opens one eye.

"What?" Pete says. "You want to know if we were un-popular?"

"In high school?" Orlando asks.

Eddie looks offended. "How could you imply that yours truly . . ."

Now all the guys are laughing. Eddie spills wine on the couch, and Dino's covering his mouth with his hand. I scowl.

"Forget it. I just wondered."

Aunt Pete stops smiling and clears his throat. "C'mon guys," he says. "It's a reasonable question." He raises an eyebrow. "You really want to know?"

I nod.

"Eddie was totally unpopular," he says. Eddie smacks him with his empty plate, but then he places his hand over his forehead dramatically.

"Yes, it's true," he says finally. "I was very unpopular in high school." He makes a face. "I know it's hard to believe, but I was the classic skinny little gay kid. A walking cliché. And remember, this was the 1970s. It was not *in* to be *out*. Plus, I wore all the wrong clothes. Even then I had an incredible flair for fashion, only I didn't exactly have your physique, Liam, to carry it off. Plus, I had this annoying habit of bursting into tears at the drop of a hat. I know, I know. Sometimes one is just predictable and there's nothing to be done about it. I tried to be different. Fortunately, your uncle came along, and then, well, no one was as unpopular as him, so . . ."

Aunt Pete's jaw drops. "That is so not true," he says. "I was incredibly popular. I was a musician, damn it. Musicians are always popular. Glitter was really well-known for a while."

Now Orlando's shaking his head. "That wasn't until college, Pete. And we were popular for about six months . . ."

"No way. It was longer than that! Remember senior year? We started the band senior year, and me and Dino started playing together as soon as I moved here . . ."

"Yeah, but having a glam-rock band didn't exactly make us popular in high school. It barely helped in college."

"Aw, shut up. Fine. All right. I was unpopular in high school. I was going through a stage," Pete says, "and no one had any appreciation for modern music at the time."

"Except Dino, and we all know how popular he was," Eddie adds. Dino shakes his head.

"Don't listen to them, Liam. I was maybe a little overweight . . ."

The guys get laughing again, but Orlando's watching me quietly from across the room.

"Were you unpopular?" I ask him. He nods.

"Yup," he says. "Not terribly unpopular, but . . . I don't know. I guess I took everything too seriously in high school. I was one of those kids who wore a suit and tie to the debate club meeting and studied way too hard for the SATs. You know what I mean, don't you?" For a second I think he's referring to the announcements — like he's figured it out — but then he says, "Why do you ask?"

I shrug. "I don't know. It just seems like a good thing to be, but it's not as easy as I thought."

The laughter dies down and Aunt Pete scratches his head. Dino studies the pizza box and everything gets quiet.

"I'll tell you who was unpopular," Pete says at last. "Your father was unpopular."

I nod. "Because he was so smart, right?"

Pete snorts. "No," he says. "Because he was completely and utterly socially inept."

Now that surprises me. "Dad? He's great with people."

"Not always. Your people-schmoozing, donation-wrangling, award-winning father was a freshman the year I was a senior, and I had to rescue him every freakin' day. Trust me, Liam, your father was not always the big man he likes to think he is. Your grandfather was away for months at a time in the service, and your dad was a total mama's boy and everyone knew it. Kids teased him mercilessly. When you're the new kid everywhere you go, you have to be tough or good-looking, and your father wasn't either of those things. I suppose it didn't help that he had a glam-rocking, gay older brother," Pete mumbles.

Then he stops. "We were all sort of unpopular," he says. "Okay, except for Eddie, who was *really* unpopular, but your father was the kind of unpopular people do not get over. That's why he just *had* to have your mother. She was the most beautiful woman any of us had ever laid eyes on. She'd never been unpopular a day in her life — couldn't be if she tried—and he knew if he had her, he'd be in." Pete pauses. "You want to know where he took her on their first date?"

"It was the concert . . ."

"No, that wasn't a date. The first place your father ever took your mother was the homecoming dance at Pineville High School. One year *after* he graduated."

He has got to be kidding.

"What?" I say. "Nobody who's graduated ever goes to those things."

Pete nods. "I know that," he says, "and *you* know that. But your father didn't give a damn. He just wanted to show her off to all the people who used to mock him."

I shift positions, wondering how come Mom never told me. She always acts like Dad was so perfect.

"That's a good thing," I say. "He was proud of her."

Pete considers.

"You think your mom had a good time that night?"

"Well, she married him, didn't she?"

I don't mean it to come out as harsh as it does, but Pete gets up off the couch.

"Yeah," he says at last. "She did."

36

IT'S A RAINY THURSDAY AFTERNOON, and Mom and I are at the boutique. No one's come in for hours, so we're sitting on the counters eating carrot sticks. We ought to just close the shop, but neither of us wants to go home because Mom and Dad were fighting all morning. Mostly about my report card.

I watch the rain make tracks down the windows.

"Mom," I ask after a long silence, "do you love Dad?"

Mom looks up. "What?"

"You and Dad. Do you guys still love each other?"

"What kind of a question is that? Of course we do."

I hop off the counter and walk over to the window.

"But you're so different. You don't even like the same things, and Dad's so . . ."

"Smart?" Mom laughs. "And I'm not?"

I was going to say "angry."

"This rain is making you morose," Mom says. But then she

stops and sets down her carrot stick. "It's like this," she says. "Sometimes two people get together for certain reasons, but over time things change. That doesn't mean you stop loving each other." She pauses. "You know, when your father was pursuing me, I was so flattered. I had a hundred guys knocking on my door, but there was no one like your dad. I just knew he was going to go far, and he has. We're both so proud of him, right?"

"Right." I nod. "It's just . . . sometimes I think I'd rather be like you when I grow up. Maybe I could be a model or —"

This time Mom's face is a hard mask.

"Don't say that," she says. "No one should be like me. Everything I've ever tried to do has been a mess."

I'm thinking, Even raising me? But I say, "Even modeling?"

"Especially modeling. That was a horrible career choice. Your father always says it brought out the worst in my character, and you know what? He's right. I drank too much. I partied too hard. I never concentrated on my marriage . . . I want more for you, Liam," she says. "If you just try a little harder at school, your father can open doors that would make you successful."

She pauses. "Maybe you'll be a world-renowned businessman someday! Wouldn't that be great? You could still travel all over the world, but you'd be doing so much more with your life than I ever did."

I wonder why there has to be more, but I nod.

"Okay," I say. "I'll try."

Mom comes over and puts her arms around me.

"Come on," she says. "Let's close up early and get out of here.

We'll make a nice dinner tonight, and your father will forget all about that report card."

She laughs lightly at the words we both know are a lie.

When Dino drops me off the trailer is quiet. Too quiet. It's eight o'clock and Pete's gone to work. I sit on the kitchen counter in the dark, not bothering to turn the lights on. Instead I dial my cell phone over and over again.

"Mom? Are you there? Can you pick up? I need to talk to you. Are you home?"

Beep.

"I tried the shop, so I know you're not there. How come you're not picking up? This is important."

Beep.

"Mom? Could you pick up this time? Please? Listen, you know I got this modeling job working for Eddie. Well, we did this whole bathing suit sale. I want to tell you about it. Are you there?"

Beep.

I sit in silence and wait for the phone to ring. An hour later it finally does.

"Hello?"

"Li?"

"Mom? Did you get my messages? Where've you been? Why haven't you called me?"

"What?" she says. "I just got in." She sounds rushed.

"Why isn't your cell working?"

"I shut it off."

"How come you never call me?"

"I *did* call you. Just now."

I lean against my bedroom door.

"Did you wait until Dad wasn't home? Is that it?"

Mom laughs. It's one of her fake laughs, high-pitched and too loud. "Why would you think that? I told you I just got your messages."

"But you haven't called me in a long time. I left you a bunch of messages last weekend. And the weekend before that. Did Dad tell you not to call?"

She makes a scoffing noise. "Of course not. I can call you if I want to. I just thought you needed time to settle in. Get to know your uncle and the guys. They're fun, aren't they?"

I frown. "Mmm-hmm. Listen, I want you to tell Dad I'm doing good here. Tell him I joined the AV club, and I got a job modeling at Eddie's shop. Eddie says I've got talent. He says I could do this for a living."

I wait, holding my breath, but the other end of the line is silent.

"Mom? Are you there? Did you hear what I said?"

There's a long pause. "I heard you."

"Well, you're excited, right? I wish you could have seen the display I put together. Eddie said he sold more bathing suits today than the rest of the summer combined. Isn't that cool?"

Mom is quiet, then she says, "That's great, Liam. I could've told Eddie you'd be good at this."

I frown. *Then why didn't you?*

"Will you tell Dad?" I ask. I can hear Mom moving through the house, and her voice gets lower.

"Let's not tell your father yet," she says. "I mean, I'll tell him about you working at the store, but let's not mention the modeling part."

I'm silent for a long time.

"Why?" I ask at last.

She laughs. "Oh, Li," she says flippantly, "it's a fast life, and your dad worries."

I take a deep breath.

"We're not talking about Paris or Milan. We're talking about a shopwindow in Pineville. And I'm good at it. Besides, *you* modeled and Dad was proud, right? Why is it okay for you and not for me?"

There's a long pause. So long I wonder if she's still there.

"Well, it wasn't always okay."

I grate my fingers against the door frame.

"You said it was your decision to quit. You told me you wished you'd made other choices. Is that the truth?"

Mom starts to laugh, then stops abruptly. The sound bursts forth and shatters like glass.

"Aren't you inquisitive today," she starts to say, but I don't let her finish.

"Did you stop modeling because Dad was angry at you? Angry like he always is whenever we try to do *anything* . . ."

Mom interrupts. "I can't talk to you if you're going to be like this," she says, her voice sharp.

I pause. *Like what? I'm not being* like *anything.*

"There are a lot of things you don't know, Liam," she says at last. "If Allan was angry, it was my fault. *Mine.* You were too young to remember everything . . ."

"Mom —"

"We made compromises, your father and I. For your sake. You can't second-guess our decisions."

"Were they though? *Your* decisions?"

Mom is quiet and when she speaks again her voice is steely. "I'm not going to talk to you about this anymore," she says, "because you weren't there and you don't know what it was like."

Only I *was* there. For some of it, at least.

I press the phone tight to my cheek, but it's no use.

"Okay, Ma," I say at last. The silence is heavy between us, but finally I take a deep breath.

"Eddie and I are putting together a fashion show for homecoming," I offer at last. I say it lightly, as if we never stopped talking about my day. Mom doesn't say anything. "Since you guys had your first date during homecoming, I thought maybe you'd want to come."

This time Mom groans. "Oh god!" she mutters. "What a disaster. Did the guys tell you about that?"

"Yeah," I say. "I thought you said Dad swept you off your feet."

She sighs. "Well, he did. Just not that night."

I grip the door frame even more tightly until my fingers begin to pulsate.

"Well, I was hoping you'd come. Maybe you could donate a couple items or something."

There's a long pause. "Of course I'll donate something," she says at last. "I know just what would look good on you. I got these new pants in at the store from a German designer, and there's a jacket that would look perfect with them."

"And you'll come see the show?"

Silence again.

"God, I need a cigarette," she says at last. "All right. I'll think about it."

"And you'll ask Dad?"

"Liam," she says.

I pause. "Mom," I say, "why can't you do this for me?"

Silence echoes back.

37

I SET DOWN MY PHONE, feeling like all the oxygen has been sucked from the trailer. I've got to get out of there, so I step outside into the cool night air. I close my eyes, breathing deep, and that's when I decide that I'm going to the pool party at Rob's house.

All I can think about is getting buzzed.

I call Joe and he agrees to swing by and get me. At first, while I'm waiting, I make up elaborate justifications about why it's actually a *good* idea that I'm going to this party. I promise myself that as soon as I arrive I'll take over some hyperresponsible role. I'll be the guy who takes everyone's car keys and stops people from having sex. I think all this, but deep down I know I'm lying.

Once Joe and I arrive, it takes about an hour before I loosen up. I'm standing there drinking, watching everything through a mellow haze and it's like I'm not really there — I'm this detached observer, a party scientist or something. That's when it occurs to me that there's a lot of pure, untapped potential here. I see it the way I see what a person ought to be wearing. Like when I imagine someone reaching their full fashion potential.

I'm standing there thinking, *This is an awesome night*. The weather is perfect. It's early fall, so the air is crisp but not cold. There's still a summer vibe, but people are just standing around talking. Drinking. No one's swimming. Nothing is organized. And it's segregated. Joe and the football guys are in one group, a huddle of girls are talking about cheerleading, and Raymond and Simon are on the patio looking like deer in headlights. I'm not saying people aren't having a good time, but they're not having the time they *could* be having. I look at the swimming pool and realize there could be contests. The music could be louder. Some of us could be making out in Rob's parents' bedroom.

I stop watching and wander over to where Joe is demonstrating a couple football moves to a crowd of guys.

"Hey, Joe," I say, and maybe I slur just a little. "You ever try to empty a pool by cannonballing?"

Joe stops what he's saying and squints at me. He's completely drunk.

"No, man," he says. "Can't be done."

"Ha!" It comes out all airy. "Why should that stop us? I'll bet it could be done if enough people did it at once. Hell, yeah."

Now I've got everyone's attention. Suggesting brute physical activity to a group of plastered football players is almost too easy. Next thing I know, without my saying anything beyond that one innocent suggestion, the whole football team is lining up for a cannonball run.

I'm not into that sort of thing myself, so I wander over to the grill and try to figure out how to fire the thing up. I pour out a whole lot of lighter fluid, then strike a match. Once the flames die down, all the girls start to clap. Everyone's laughing and someone turns up the music so loud the walls of the house shake. Rob himself brings out some hot dogs and someone sprays beer, and the football guys are hollering out the count, then dive-bombing into the pool. Everything is suddenly raucous, and I smile, thinking there is nothing in the world as satisfying as a drunken victory.

That's when Jen slides up to me.

"This is the best party!" she says, looking pretty in the moonlight. More than pretty. Beautiful. She's wearing the bikini I picked out for her.

I'm balancing on the edge of Rob's deck, next to the grill, pretending to surf, and Jen is impressed.

"Do you really know how to surf?" she asks.

"Yup. I took lessons in Hawaii from a guy who was a professional surfer. I used to think that was what I wanted to be when I grew up, only I've never lived near an ocean. Watch," I say. "I'll show you how."

I lean forward, and as I do I happen to notice that I've now attracted a large audience of cheerleaders.

"First you find your center," I tell them. "Then you place your feet like this and watch for the wave . . ." I pretend to catch a huge one. "It's really hard because you've got to keep your focus the whole time, and the water is rushing all around you. Sometimes it's like you're in a tunnel and you're flying through the air."

I move my body as if I'm really surfing, and the girls shriek.

I tilt forward, lose my balance, and fall into Jen. She screams, and then we're on the ground. She's lying beside me, panting and giggling, so I kiss her. I'm considering taking Jen up to Rob's parents' bedroom when I hear someone hollering.

"Cops," some kid yells. "The neighbor just called the cops!"

He has to yell it about eight times before anyone moves, but then it's mayhem. People literally flood out of the pool, and I catch sight of Joe and the rest of the guys trying to put out the fire in the grill with the remainder of the beer. Bad idea.

Seniors are disappearing like crazy, ducking into the woods behind Rob's house and racing down the street. The house is completely trashed, and there are empty beer bottles everywhere. Rob starts picking them up, but Joe yells, "Leave it. Just leave it." He and Rob run around to the side of the house and Jen and I follow them. They all pile into Joe's car, and Joe starts the ignition. The car lurches forward before anyone notices I'm not inside.

"Hurry. Get in." Jen's waving from the back window, and I start forward, but then I realize Joe is way too drunk to drive. I may be plastered, but I don't have to be sober to know this.

"Wait," I say. "Let's walk. Let's cut across someone's lawn or something. You guys could come with me — crash at Pete's place."

Joe looks at me like I'm insane, but right then the police car is pulling up, so he doesn't have time to argue.

"Outta here," he slurs. He slams on the gas and the car shoots down the road. I can see Jen watching me forlornly from the back window. That's when I turn around and for the first time I see the red and blue lights from the cop car. I start to run, but it's too late for that now. The police car pulls in front of me, blinding me with its headlights and blocking my path. I try to dart in the other direction, but whoever gets out of the car is quicker than I am. Soon firm hands are gripping my arms from behind and pushing me onto the hood of the patrol car.

Crap.

I think I might pass out. My head is spinning and my stomach churns. The cop is saying something, loudly and persistently, but it takes a long time before I realize I'm supposed to be getting up off the car hood. I peel my face from the metal.

"I've got to take you in," the cop says as I pull myself upright.

I'm thinking, *Well, of course you do.*

"You can call my auncle Pe . . ." I start, but then I stop. As soon as I turn around it's clear there's no need to finish the sentence.

This cop knows exactly who to call.

38

A HALF HOUR LATER I'm drinking bitter black coffee in a tiny one-room police station. I'm sitting across from Dino's desk, trying to remember exactly how this happened, but it's a blur. Dino paces from one end of the room to the other in massive strides, causing the desks to shake.

"I should book you for vandalism," he says. "Underage drinking. Extreme stupidity." His expression moves between angry and angrier. His arms flex as he opens and closes his fists. There's nothing I can do but agree. Maybe add a few more charges to the list. *Failing to reform. Becoming unwittingly popular.*

"Are you listening to me?" Dino asks. "You look like you're zoning out."

What? Zooming where?

"I've got to call Pete," Dino growls, "and I should probably call your parents, too."

My head shoots up. Probably? Did I hear a "probably" in there?

Please, god. If there is such a thing as mercy for the undeserving, let this man not decide to call my father. Please, please, please, god. Please. Please.

Please.

I'm not so good at praying.

Dino pauses, studying me.

"Listen," he says with a sigh. "I haven't made a decision yet. I'm going to call Petey first. If he says to book you, then I've got to do it and there's no choice about calling your folks, but . . ."

I can barely force myself to nod.

Please.

Dino picks up the phone, dials, and waits.

"Pete? Yeah, it's Dino. No, I'm working. What? Ha . . . yeah, wait. I've got something to talk to you about." Dino glances at me, but I put my head down on the desk. "I'm not calling to request a song," he says. "It's about Liam. What? Nooo . . ." There's a long pause. "He's here at the police station."

I close my eyes and let the sensation of complete failure wash over me.

"I picked him up at a party about a half hour ago," Dino says. "There were a lot of them there, Petey. A lot of drinking. What? Well, no. Not exactly. There was a complaint from a neighbor.

"Yeah. I know. I'll call Sarah and Allan if that's what you want, but maybe you should come down here first. I know you're working, but he could sleep here, maybe sober up a little, then you could come by when you get off and we could discuss things."

There's a long pause. A very long pause.

"Well, just calm down. The kid feels pretty bad about every-thing . . ."

Then there's a click. I don't even bother to ask. I wait for the sound of Dino dialing my father's number, preparing myself for what I will say. Which is nothing. I've already decided that this time I will say nothing.

There's a moment of complete silence, and I can feel Dino's eyes on me. He reaches over and puts his hand on my forehead.

"You don't look so good," he says. "Why don't you lie down in that cell over there?"

At that moment I can't imagine anything more appealing than lying down in that cell.

"Really?"

Dino nods. "Don't look so happy about it," he tells me. "Once you're in there it locks automatically and I've only got one clean blanket."

It's a gift from the gods.

Now if I can just stay awake and pray all night.

39

WHEN I WAKE UP THE CELL IS DARK. My temples throb, and at first I can't remember exactly where I am. There's a strange voice outside, then music, and eventually I realize it's the radio. I squint through the bars of the cell into the police station. The station is empty aside from Dino, swiveling in his chair, singing along to a song about hot love. I'm thirsty, and I think about asking for a glass of water but decide the sound of my own voice will make me retch. Instead, I lie back down on the thin mattress, thinking that with any luck I'll pass out again. The sound of the radio is a comforting buzz in the background. Until I make out the words.

"All right, folks. That was 'Hot Love' by T. Rex. Before that was 'Life on Mars?' by the young Miss, oops, I mean, Mr., Bowie, and before that, my personal favorite, 'Personality Crisis' by the New York Dolls. I'm Rockin' Pete and we've got your late-night glam favorites right here on WXKJ. Let's go back to the phones now. For those of you who've just tuned in, we've got a listener poll going. The question tonight? Should I spring my nephew from the slammer? Give us a call at 555-WXKJ."

My eyes shoot open. This cannot be happening. Not even to me.

"Let's take the next caller. Larry, you're on the air."

"Yeah, Pete?"

"Yeah."

"I just wanna say I love your show. You're the best, man."

"So kind, so kind. But tell me, what do you think I should do about my nephew? The kid's seventeen. Kicked out of his house. He's already been in trouble with me once, and now he's picked up at a party for underage drinking. I don't know, man, should I send him packing?"

The guy on the other end weighs everything carefully.

"Nah, I don't know. He just sounds like a kid to me, and he ain't been with you that long, right?"

"Correct."

"Yeah, well . . . I think you should give him another chance."

I close my eyes and silently thank Larry.

"You think? Okay, that's cool, man. Let's take another caller. Janet, you still there, darlin'?"

"I'm here, Rockin' Pete."

"Tell us what you think. Give the ol' Petey some advice."

Janet doesn't hesitate. "Let him suffer! Kids like him haven't got any respect, and when they're like that there's no turning them around. You can try and try. Let me tell you, because I've got a son about that age and I've tried everything."

"You tried tellin' him you love him?"

The woman laughs.

"That's . . . well . . . I did that for years, but at this point I don't even like the kid."

I cringe.

"Thanks for sharing, Janet. Let's take another caller. We've got Wayne from Grover County. Wayne? What do you think? Because I just don't know. We've had a lot of callers on tonight's show, and most of them think I should ship him off. You think that, Wayne?"

There's an inaudible crackling sound, during which I silently beg Wayne to say something good about me. Maybe something good about forgiveness in general or . . .

"Fry him, Petey!"

Now I'm truly ill.

"What? You're voting for capital punishment based on . . . Is that what you're saying?"

"Woooo-HOOOO!"

"Wayne, how come I'm thinking you might not be a stranger to the bottle? Am I right in thinking that? Am I right, man?"

There's another loud, indiscernible noise.

"Folks, I think good ol' Wayne's had one too many tonight. All right. Let's wrap this baby up. Let's take one more caller before the six o'clock hour. Whaddaya say? Spring him or send him packing? We've got Vince on the line."

I hold my breath. *Please vote for me.* I feel like one of those reality show contestants who make the cheesy phone symbol into the television camera when their number is on the screen.

"Leave him in jail and call the parents. No question," Vince says. "Pete, I've been a psychologist for twenty years, and that kid needs to learn a lesson. I guarantee he's the way he is today because his parents don't insist on discipline. If he's seventeen, there's not much more you can do, and frankly he's not your problem. Sounds like they've shipped him off because they can't deal with him, and now you're stuck with their headache. You need to set some boundaries."

Aunt Pete interrupts. "Yeah, but you really think there's no hope at seventeen? I don't know. I remember how I was at seventeen. I gave my parents a wild ride. All decked out like the guys from Slade, stealing my mom's mascara. My folks kicked me out, and now they don't even speak to me because they haven't gotten over the embarrassment, so how can I turn around and send that same message?"

Vince is desperately trying to interrupt.

"No, but . . . that's exactly what the problem is. Everyone's so afraid of taking responsibility that the kid ends up a delinquent. You've got to be fair but firm."

"That's true."

"I'm telling you, Pete. That's your answer."

"I hear you, man. I hear you." There's a crackling sound as the signal is momentarily lost, then Aunt Pete's voice fades in again.

". . . so, we've got to close the polls. It's six o'clock and we've got more music coming up with Dean and Donna, all your country favorites, but right now I leave you with Alice Cooper to deliver the verdict. Ooooh. Looks like my nephew is goin' down. It's 'No More Mr. Nice Guy.' I'm Rockin' Pete. Good night, all."

And that's it.

40

THERE ARE FOOTSTEPS outside my cell, but I don't get up. What's the use? I already know the verdict.

"He awake?"

I hear the squeak of the swivel chair.

"Out cold. You been thinking about everything?"

Pete lets out a long breath. "Damn right, I have. He didn't give you any trouble, did he?"

Dino scoffs. "Nah. No trouble. I think he's scared is all. Looked a little bit ill before he fell asleep." He pauses. "So, what's it going to be? I've got to know before the next shift comes in. We're either booking him or I'm sending him home with you, but it's got to be soon."

There's a pause, then a sigh.

"I'm taking him home," Aunt Pete says, but I know it's only temporary.

Dino knocks on the cell bars.

"Pete's here," he tells me. "Time to go."

I pretend like I'm just waking up, but really I should save myself the theatrics. What do they care? Dino and Pete are too busy commiserating about what a burden I am. How much I've screwed up.

I get up and walk out of the cell and Dino shuts the door behind me.

"I don't want to see you in here again," he says. "Let's make this your first and last visit. Agreed?"

I nod. I'm trying to swallow, but it's not working. Really, I feel like I might throw up.

"Come on," says Pete. "We'll talk about this when we get home."

We plod out to the Nissan and I can tell he's as tired as I am. Neither one of us says a word during the ride home. Pete's probably waiting for me to apologize, but my head is pounding and I think, *Why bother?* The entire town voted me off, so what is there to talk about?

When we get inside the trailer Pete says, "You look like hell."

I nod.

"I called your mom," he adds.

"Is she coming to get me?"

He pauses. "No."

"Dad then?"

"Why would you think that?"

I consider telling him that I heard the radio show, but I just shrug.

"That's it?" he says. "You end up in jail. I bail you out. And now you're not even going to talk to me?"

I shrug again and Pete shakes his head.

"Fine," he says. "Well, I'm not asking you nicely anymore. I want to know what the hell happened. I leave for work and you've just had a really successful day at Eddie's shop. You said nothing about going to that party — which, by the way, I might have given you permission to attend had you bothered to ask me — then five hours later I get a phone call that you're in jail. Jail, Liam. So. What. The hell. Happened?"

I'm guessing from his tone that it's time to dish out the apology, even if it won't do any good. And to be honest, if I didn't feel like crap right now, I would feel sorry for Pete. It's not like he isn't justified in kicking me out. Truth is, he lasted longer than I expected.

"It was a horrible mistake," I say. "There's no explaining my actions. I was grossly out of line. I let you down. I let myself down and I let my family down. It's shameful and I am ashamed."

It's not one of my better ones. Aunt Pete taps his fingers furiously on the arm of the couch. He gets up and walks around the room, then finally he sits down across from me again.

"Did you have fun at the party?"

I look up. What the hell kind of question is that? If I say no, he'll know I'm lying, and if I say yes, he'll blast me for having fun. I wish I were smarter so I could figure it out quicker.

"I don't know," I say, and then I sigh, guessing I'd better make a stab at it. "Yes?"

Pete laughs.

"Are you asking me or telling me?"

I wait a long time before answering.

"No?"

Aunt Pete sighs.

"Liam," he says, "we've got to be able to talk. I'm not out to get you; I just need to know you're being honest with me. Can you do that?"

Right. As if he's not totally pretending I have some say in all this.

"What do you want from me?"

Pete shakes his head.

"Why don't you start by telling me why you were the only one caught last night?"

The question catches me off guard. This is the type of technicality no one ever asks me about. Dad always wants to know about the big, moral issues, never the specifics. I pause.

"The person who offered me a ride was drunk," I say at last. "Since I already lost my license for being stupid like that, I'm more careful about it now, so I didn't get in the car. That's when Dino picked me up."

Pete makes a face.

"That's interesting," he says, more to himself than to me. He thinks for a long time and then he looks straight at me. "I was pretty angry when Dino called. I'm still pretty angry. I let you off easy after the school bus incident, and I thought you'd be more careful after that. I thought you'd think things through a little more thoroughly before sneaking out to a party and getting drunk. I have to admit I'm disappointed that you didn't."

"I know," I start to say. "I shouldn't have . . ."

Aunt Pete holds up one hand.

"I don't want to hear what you shouldn't have done," he says. "I want to hear why you put yourself in that position in the first place."

I don't know what he means, but I don't have time to answer.

"You see," Aunt Pete says, "I've noticed you do a lot of apologizing, but very little thinking ahead. In fact, you do very little thinking *at all* half the time, but you're capable of it. Anyone who can learn from his mistakes and decide not to get into a car full of drunk teenagers is obviously capable of intelligent decision making. So, why don't you make those decisions more often?"

For a minute all I do is stare.

"Cat got your tongue?" Pete asks. His jaw is tight and he's leaning forward. "Here's what I think," he tells me. "I think you want to lay everything down like it's an accident. A sad twist of fate brought on by your own stupidity, but I don't think you're stupid and I don't think there are that many accidents.

"Now, I'm going to say this straight out. You and your mother call me up and say you need to spend a couple weeks here. That's a lie and we all know it. I've known it from the beginning. Allan didn't kick you out for a couple weeks. He kicked you out. Period. But we're going to put that aside for the moment. The truth is, I wanted this chance. I wanted it for a lot of reasons I'm not going to go into right now, but suffice it to say I wanted to help you out. I wanted to help your mom out. But there's this big part of me that keeps thinking, *What the hell am I doing with a teenage boy living in my trailer?*"

Aunt Pete's voice is getting louder and he's trying to make eye contact, but I stare hard at an old Doritos chip lying on the carpet.

"Don't tune me out," he yells, slamming his foot down on top of the chip. "I want to make this work for you, and for Sarah, but I think you're pretty angry at your dad."

"What?" I say, looking up. "I'm not."

Pete shakes his head.

"Oh. So, you don't think your going to the party had anything at all to do with your dad?"

"No," I say sharply. "I went to the party because I needed to relax."

Aunt Pete crosses his arms over his chest. "That's it," he says. "You needed to recover from all the sleeping and watching television that you do?"

"If I sleep a lot, it's just because there's nothing to do around here, and maybe that's why I needed to go to a party. It had nothing to do with Dad. Or Mom."

"Riiiight," Pete says, drawing out the word with an exaggerated sigh. "You're not avoiding anything." His voice is pretty loud now, and I notice the lights go on in Darleen's trailer. "You're not trying to be someone you aren't just to please a man you're never going to please, no matter what you do?"

"That's bullshit." The words come out before I can stop them. "That's *bullshit*."

"This isn't anger?"

"No!" I yell. "It's fucking not."

There's a long silence after that and then I snap.

"If I'm angry at anyone right now, it's you. You're the one who's pretending like you want me here when you totally don't. You're the one who told everyone on the air that I screwed up again. Why don't you just tell me to leave and get it over with?"

"What are you talking about?" Pete says. "I'm not —"

"I heard the radio show," I holler. "I know I got voted off."

He stares at me.

"No more Mr. Nice Guy," I mimic. "Why didn't you just kick me out at the police station? Why are you acting like you're still giving me a chance when you're not? You think I'm angry at Dad? I'm not. I'm angry at you!"

Aunt Pete groans. "Aw, Liam," he says. "You never should have heard that. I never should have done it. I just . . . I was furious. I got a phone call in the middle of my show saying you were in jail, and I don't know . . . No one listens to my show. A bunch of drunks and insomniacs. That's it." He puts his head in his hands. "And Dino. God, why didn't I think of that?"

He looks up and shakes his head. "I'm sorry," he says. "I screwed up. But, Liam, you've got to realize that those people who voted you off don't even know you. They don't know anything. Did you honestly think I was going to kick you out because a bunch of people I've never met said I should?"

I don't answer.

"Well, trust me," Pete says. "I'm not going to send you to

Nevada, and I *can't* send you home. After all, that's the whole problem, isn't it?"

He waits, trying to meet my gaze, but I refuse to look at him. Pete sighs.

"I'm not kicking you out," he says. "I promise. But starting tomorrow I expect you to make smart decisions. Don't give me any crap about why you can't do it. I expect you to write that essay for Orlando and to work with him after school every day until you bring your grade up. I expect you to work for Eddie every Saturday for eight hours and you'd better damn well do it no matter what your father says when he finds out, because you're good at it. And I want you to be *yourself*. I expect all my T-shirts back in my room by tomorrow morning. Got that?"

I'm quiet for a long time.

"Answer me," Pete says.

"Yes," I say at last. "I got that."

41

WHEN PETE FINALLY GOES TO BED, I decide I need to get out of the trailer, so I end up outside, lying on the picnic table. I try to focus on the part of the conversation where he said he wouldn't be kicking me out, but instead I keep hearing his DJ voice in my head.

"Looks like my nephew is goin' down. It's no more Mr. Nice Guy."

My life just gets worse and worse.

That's when I hear Darleen.

"What are you still doing here?"

I sit up quick.

"Sitting," I say, even though that's fairly obvious.

Darleen scowls. "Technically, you were lying down," she says, "and I meant why haven't you left? We voted you off."

I don't like her use of the word "we."

"I don't know," I say, sighing. "I really do not know."

Darleen pauses. "Sorry," she says after a moment. "I didn't mean it like that."

I'm thinking there aren't too many ways to mean "we voted you off."

"I heard you arguing with your uncle." She clears her throat. "I didn't hear *every*thing. Just something about you making smart decisions and returning his T-shirts." She makes a face. "You wore your uncle's clothes?"

She's trying to be funny, make the conversation light, but I close my eyes. Right about now I cannot take Darleen mocking me.

"Yeah," I say at last. "It was stupid, okay? I was trying to impress you. Are you happy now? I've been trying to impress you for weeks and I've failed miserably."

Darleen sits down at the picnic table.

"You've been trying to impress *me*? Why in the world would you want to do *that*?"

I don't answer.

After a while she says, "I've been thinking about everything." She pauses. "Actually, I've been thinking about things ever since we had dinner on Friday."

I groan. *Dinner*. Now that was a disaster.

"It wasn't that bad," Darleen says, as if she's reading my mind. "I mean, it was awkward, but the food was good."

This time I laugh, short and bitter.

"You hated it," I say. "You didn't even eat anything and then you left."

She nods. "Well, that's true, but it smelled good. Pete was right. We should have eaten it."

I pause, and it occurs to me that Darleen is trying to be nice. This throws me, and I try to think of something to say other than *Why in the world are you being nice to me?*

I can't.

"Why in the world are you being nice to me?"

Darleen sighs. "I'm apologizing," she says.

I stare, feeling like none of her features makes sense anymore.

"You're apologizing? To me?"

Darleen nods.

"Yeah," she says. "Don't tell anyone at school. I know they're reserving me a spot as Class Bitch in the yearbook. If this gets out, I'll know who told."

I'm pretty sure that was a joke, but I answer just in case.

"I won't tell anyone."

I should leave it at that, but I can't. Darleen is already getting up like she might go inside.

"Wait," I say.

"What?"

"Well, it's just that you're apologizing to me, but I should be apologizing to you."

"How come?"

I think, *Because that's the way it works,* but instead I say, "Because I'm not really smart and studious like I pretended to be."

Darleen shrugs. "No kidding."

"And I have friends. A lot of friends."

She nods sadly. "I know."

"And I don't love equipment. I can't even work any equipment. I joined the AV club so you'd see how seriously I could take things and because I told my dad I'd joined an academic club."

"I see."

I keep waiting for the hammer to fall — for the moment when she'll change her mind, maybe catch me with a zinger, but Darleen just waits.

"Is that all?"

I hesitate.

"No," I say. "There's one last thing."

This time she looks suspicious. "What?"

I don't want to say it, but I have to.

"If I'm still here by then, I might be voted homecoming king."

Darleen takes a deep breath. Her eyes narrow and she fixes me with a sharp stare. "Don't push your luck."

Darleen's right. I shouldn't push my luck. Someone just apologized to me. Two people, actually. That should be enough. But it's not. I take out my cell phone and call Dad.

I get his voice mail and have to leave a message.

"Dad, it's me. Listen. I need to talk to you. I know you don't want to hear from me, but I thought we could talk, and since my birthday's coming up, maybe we could discuss everything face-to-face. I know you only want what's best for me, and . . . well, this is the only birthday present I'm asking for this year. Just a chance to talk about my future. Please?"

Beep.

I stare at my cell phone. Part of me wants to laugh hysterically. I've just bet everything that Dad will come through for me, and the odds are not in my favor.

42

I FINALLY HEAR FROM DAD Wednesday night. I play the message on my voice mail over and over again.

"Liam, it's your father. I got your message and I've been thinking about your future. Please be ready at your uncle's on Tuesday at six P.M. Not a second late. Dress nicely, but don't wear any of that designer crap."

I am determined I will NOT screw this up.

That means I only have until next Tuesday to get ready, so I start right away. I begin by cleaning my room, but my room is as clean as it's going to get, so I move on to the kitchen. I stack all the electronic equipment on the edge of the living room carpet then wash all the counters. I start on the refrigerator but almost gag, so I have to stop and then start again. The food rotting in the back is no longer identifiable — just moldy, sprouting, smelly globs. I keep the garbage can right next to the fridge and take out two bags before the kitchen is done. I mop the floor and straighten the broom closet, then try to shut the kitchen window, which I pried open when I made stir-fry, only it's stuck.

Aunt Pete comes in and sighs loudly. He digs in the fridge.

"Where is my beer? Did you throw away my beer?"

I'm crouched on the floor, washing the cabinets.

"It's in the bottom drawer. The drawer made for cans."

Pete takes out two cans. "It stinks in here," he comments. It doesn't. It smells like Pine-Sol and that can hardly be construed as stinking.

"Well, if it stinks it's because you had an entire cow rotting on your bottom shelf."

"Where are my tools? They were right here a minute ago."

"They're in the closet. The tool and broom closet. Why does it matter? You never use them."

He doesn't answer. Instead, he stomps out of the kitchen. Then he stomps back in again.

"Why the hell are you doing this?"

For once I'm not going to lie.

"Dad's coming."

Aunt Pete chokes.

"What?! Tonight?"

"No. Not tonight. He's coming on Tuesday. For my birthday."

Pete stares like I'm insane.

"Allan's coming next Tuesday, and you're cleaning everything now? A week ahead?"

I nod.

"And how exactly did he happen to decide to come here? Did your mother put a gun to his head?"

He looks like I've blindsided him, and I start to feel guilty.

"I invited him. It's my birthday, so he'll probably take me out to dinner or something. I doubt you'll even see each other." I pause. "I know you don't like Dad, but it's important to me."

Aunt Pete takes a deep breath.

"Allan is my brother," he says. "It's not that I don't *like* him. There are larger issues involved and there always have been. I just find it hard to believe that he would come here to —"

I slam the kitchen cabinet shut.

"You find it hard to believe he'd want to see me on my birthday? Well, he does. Dad and I are going to sit down and work things out."

"That's not what I was going to say," Pete says, but I don't want to hear any more.

"You'll be rid of me soon enough," I mutter, and then I walk out the front door.

The screen door slams shut behind me, and I stomp out to the picnic table.

Darleen's sitting there, sketching.

"You guys should really try a different volume level," she says. "Believe it or not, some people actually converse *without* yelling."

I sit down and rest my head against the picnic table.

Darleen studies me for a minute.

"So, did I hear you say your dad's coming this Tuesday?"

I nod.

"Is that how come you and Pete were arguing?"

I nod again. "Pete doesn't think Dad really wants to visit, but he said he would, and my father is a man of his word. There's no way he'd let me down."

Darleen pauses. "Liam, I . . ."

"He probably doesn't think Dad will change his mind about letting me come home again, either, but there's a lot Dad doesn't know yet. Like how I'm working for Eddie now, and doing better in school. I'm going to get a B on our physics test on Monday so I'll have something academic to show him."

Darleen laughs. "You're kidding, right?"

I've got to admit, this wasn't the reaction I was hoping for.

"You don't think I can get a B?"

She makes a face.

"No," she says. "It's not that you can't do it. It's just that, well, there's a reason all the information is spread out. You learn little bits at a time because all the new stuff depends on the old stuff. It's not like someone can teach you just what's on this test, because if you don't know the original stuff, it won't make sense. You don't seem to remember any of the math we're supposed to use, or the chemistry information from last year."

Okay. Now she's not helping.

"Fine," I say, getting up from the picnic table. "I don't need a B. I mean, I do, but by the time Dad gets here I'll have lots of other stuff to show him. I'll have my, uh, other grades . . . and other stuff."

Darleen pauses. "You're sure he's coming?"

I nod. "I'm leaving him phone messages every day so he knows I'm serious."

She nods slowly.

"Maybe once a week would be . . . ," she starts, but then she shakes her head. "Who am I kidding? The truth is, if I had a phone number for my mom after she left, I would've been calling her every hour until she came back."

Darleen studies her drawing, then she looks up.

"It's not that I don't believe you can get a B," she says. "I don't think you're half as dumb as you think I think you are."

If I was smarter, I'm sure I could figure that out.

43

DAD NEVER RETURNS my phone calls. I call every day at four o'clock, and he never once picks up or calls me back. Even when I ask where to make our dinner reservation, I hear nothing. This is a problem because I can't decide whether to make dinner, in which case I need Pete to make himself scarce, or whether to make reservations, in which case I need a restaurant within a fifty-mile radius that doesn't have Pit Stop in the name. I'm awake all night debating.

Under the circumstances, I hoped to be able to sleep a little later on my birthday — maybe hit snooze a couple times before getting up — but instead I'm woken up early by a high-pitched, piercing screech and the smell of something burning. I test the doorknob and open the door a crack.

Eddie's standing at the stove, scrambling eggs in a fry pan. Dino is mixing orange juice. Orlando's cutting up grapefruit, and Aunt Pete is burning toast. The kitchen is filled with a thick black cloud, and somewhere a smoke alarm is wailing loudly.

"God damn it! It's here somewhere. Where would I have installed the stupid thing?"

"Why isn't it on the wall? Smoke alarms are supposed to be on the wall."

"Or the ceiling."

"Or . . ."

"Well, obviously it isn't, so if you'd stop telling me where it's supposed to be and help me look for the damn thing . . ."

"Did anyone pop up the toast?"

I open my door the rest of the way and try to wave away the smoke as I walk across the kitchen and pop up the toast. Dino finds the smoke alarm under the sink and the piercing wail ceases abruptly.

"What are you guys doing?"

Dino looks up from under the sink, and Aunt Pete peers at me through the haze. Eddie is wheezing by the stove.

"Surprise," they all say at roughly the same time.

"You're making this for me?" I ask as Pete pries a piece of charred toast out of the toaster.

"Damn," he says. "This was supposed to be a really nice breakfast. We've got presents and everything."

"You got me presents?"

Aunt Pete nods.

"We figured since you were busy tonight, we'd surprise you with breakfast." Pete fakes a laugh. "Heh heh. Bet that smoke alarm was a real surprise, huh?"

Eddie is trying to push the smoke out the open kitchen window with the broom.

"Why would anyone put their smoke alarm under the kitchen sink?" he mutters. Then he adds, "Guess we should forgo the candles."

Dino hands me a tall glass of orange juice.

"Presents?" he suggests. My eyes are tearing. Maybe because of the thick smoke.

"Nobody's ever done something like this for my birthday," I say. "This is like . . ." I can't think of the word.

"Mayhem?" Orlando offers.

I nod. It's great.

Aunt Pete carries over a stack of presents and pulls up a stool.

"Open this one first. They're from all of us," he says. "We pitched in."

I open a small square package. It's a CD. *Glam's Greatest Hits*.

"Uh, cool."

"I wanted to get you a feather boa, but the guys said no."

Eddie hands me a large rectangular box.

"This is your real gift," he says. "You might not like it right away, but we're pretty sure you're going to need it someday."

I study the present on my lap. It's wrapped in last week's comics section and tied with a piece of yellow string.

"Well, come on," Aunt Pete says. "You want scissors?"

I shake my head.

"No, it's just . . ."

Orlando hands me the scissors anyway. "Open it."

I cut the string and tear off the paper. The box inside is a fancy black one, with gold embossed lettering on the front. *Emerald Photos — Premier Photo Gallery.*

I lift the top and carefully pull out a large album. It has a black leather cover with clear pages inside. I run my hand gently over the surface.

"It's for your portfolio," Pete says.

I lift the cover gingerly and turn the pages. "I know," I whisper. A thin piece of paper is tucked between the cover and the first page.

"It's a gift certificate for . . ."

". . . a photo session." I touch the embossed gold letters with the tip of my finger.

"This gift certificate entitles Liam Geller to one photo session on the twentieth day of November."

"This is where Mom had her first photos taken," I whisper. I can hardly breathe. Why would they do this for me? I look around and there's Dino, who had to throw me in jail, and Orlando, whom I still owe an essay, and Aunt Pete, who's put up with me way longer than he had to.

Pete nods at the gift certificate. "I remembered when Sarah went there," he says. "I tried to get you an earlier date for the session, but you have to book them way in advance. The only reason they gave me that one is because I told them you were Sarah Geller's son." He pauses, watching me. "Do you like it?"

I try to nod.

"It's perfect," I say at last. "I'm going to talk to Dad about the modeling tonight, so I can show it to him."

The guys look at each other, and Aunt Pete takes a deep breath.

"Good," he says at last. His voice is tense and he doesn't look at me, but he nods. "I'm glad we got it then."

44

I LEAVE THE PORTFOLIO on my bed, still in its box, but I think about it all day. I don't know why, but having it makes me feel like I have a future. One that I haven't compromised yet. I imagine myself pulling it out and showing it to Dad. Telling him I've got a reason to graduate now, and maybe there's a chance I'll do something cool with my life.

Dad will see that, won't he?

I start to get nervous. When I get home, the trailer still smells like smoke, and the living room floor is dirty from where we sat around eating breakfast, so I pull out the vacuum cleaner and push it distractedly. My head aches and my stomach twists, and the carpet won't come clean, so I keep going over the same spot, again and again. After a while Aunt Pete comes down the hall and sighs loudly.

"Will you shut that off already? There won't be any carpet

left if you keep this up." He's carrying a microphone stand and a piece of Dino's drum set. I shut off the vacuum abruptly.

"What are you doing?"

Pete puts the cymbal on the floor.

"Setting up for practice. What does it look like I'm doing?"

The knot in my stomach pulls tighter.

"Remember my father's coming tonight?" It comes out higher and squeakier than I intend, and Pete looks at me.

"So?"

"Auuncle Pete . . ." I say slowly, aiming for casual.

He sighs. "Why don't you just say 'Aunt Pete'? I know that's what you call me. It's not a big deal."

I swallow hard.

"Can I ask you a favor?"

Pete's hardly listening. He's moving stacks of records.

"I will never get these reorganized," he mutters. "They were in order. The early seventies were under the couch. Midseventies next to the coffee table. Late seventies under the TV."

"Are you listening?"

"Yes," he says, knocking over a stack of records. "I'm listening."

I pray silently, knowing there is no way he's going to agree to this.

"Could you maybe *not* practice tonight?"

There's a long pause while Aunt Pete stares at the records he just knocked over, but he doesn't move to pick them up.

"No," he says finally. "I'm sorry, but I could not do that. Not even for you."

I bite my lip. "It would only be one night. And you guys are so good, you don't *need* to practice."

Pete sets the microphone stand very deliberately in the center of the floor and looks straight at me.

"I don't expect you to understand this," he says, "but a long time ago I made a promise that I've never broken. I promised myself I'd never be someone I wasn't just to please my family. Now, I know you want to impress your father and I've tried to be patient with the cleaning and stuff, even when you cleaned my room, which you shouldn't have been in to begin with, but I've got to draw the line somewhere, and the band is it. Allan can come in and listen or he can take you out to dinner, I don't really give a damn, but I don't cancel practice. Not for you, not for the screaming old lady three trailers down, and certainly not for my goddamn brother, who hasn't spoken to me in years. Now don't ask again."

He pushes the microphone stand into the wall and walks back down the hall. I wipe my sweaty palms on my pants.

Okay. That didn't go so well.

I put the vacuum cleaner away and go back to my room to contemplate my wardrobe. Maybe that will distract me from thinking about the guys playing glam-rock seventies hits when Dad arrives.

Twenty minutes later I'm still trying to make a decision. The gray blue Dolce and Gabbana shirt Mom sent for my birthday would look really nice, but Dad told me not to wear anything designer. Of course, he also told me to look nice, so I was planning to go for the more commercial name brands, but now I think I might just wear the shirt.

A car pulls into the driveway and I bolt to the window, but it's only Eddie and Dino. Eddie comes in and stands in my doorway. "You look good," he says, adjusting my collar. "Simple. Professional. Excellent selection."

"You think?" I ask. "Because I could change . . ."

Orlando's car pulls into the driveway, and I go back into the kitchen to stare at the clock. The guys get set up and start to tune, and Aunt Pete comes out of his bedroom wearing one of the worst outfits I've ever seen. High-heeled black boots and zebra-striped spandex pants that should have been retired in . . . well, they never should have existed in the first place. I take a deep breath. Okay. Fine.

Glitter is already into their second number before there's a knock on the door. I've been staring out the window intently for the last half hour, but I got distracted by a huge cockroach that crawled out of the broom closet. I've just killed it when the knock sounds, so I'm standing there with a paper towel full of smooshed cockroach. I panic and throw it in the garbage, but the delay allows Aunt Pete to beat me to the door.

"Yes?"

I slide in beside him. I'm prepared. I look good, and I've got the portfolio ready to go. This is it.

Only it's not Dad. A man in uniform is standing in the open doorway.

"Liam Geller?"

I nod.

"Sergeant Jim Braddock of the United States Army. Pleased to meet you." The man sticks out his hand and I shake it dumbly.

"I can't talk right now," I tell him. "I have company coming any minute. My father is on his way and —"

Sergeant Braddock grins. "Actually, your father is the reason I'm here. I have a lot of respect for your dad, Liam. Allan is a good friend of mine, and I'm sure you know how lucky you are to have him."

I nod, confused.

"Look, what's this about?" Aunt Pete asks, interrupting. Sergeant Braddock glances from Pete to me.

"Liam, your father asked me to come talk to you today, as a personal favor. I understand you've been having some difficulties, and your father thinks you'd be an ideal candidate for the U.S. military. Now, I'd like to discuss your options with you. Maybe answer any questions you might have about the service."

My whole body goes numb. The last words the sergeant says fade to a distant buzz.

Aunt Pete's eyes bug out. "The hell you're going to do that!"

"Liam," the sergeant says patiently, "I'd be happy to take you out to dinner. Maybe we could talk in a less confined" — he coughs — "space."

I want to answer, but I can't focus.

"Would you like to go someplace else?" the sergeant repeats. "Perhaps we could take a walk."

I'm clutching the door frame so hard my fingers ache. I pry them loose and point to the picnic table.

"We can talk out here," I say. The words sound flat even to me. Sergeant Braddock nods, and Aunt Pete swears.

Dino steps up behind us and glances at me. "You don't have to talk to anyone," he says, nodding toward the sergeant.

I try to shake my head, but I can't, so I walk down the steps and sit at the picnic table instead. Sergeant Braddock follows, sits down across from me, and pulls a laptop out of his briefcase. He opens it and brings up a full-color display.

"Liam . . ." Pete says from the door, but I wave him away.

It's okay, I say, but maybe the words don't come out.

"It never hurts to know what your options are, son," the sergeant says. "Your father has gone to some trouble to see that I visited you today."

I blink. Sergeant Braddock just called me son.

Everything swirls together, but every now and then a word slips into my consciousness. *Benefits . . . training . . . GED . . . skills . . .*

Sergeant Braddock takes out a new batch of papers. "You don't have to sign right now. I understand if you want to think it over, but I happen to know that your parents wholeheartedly approve of this decision, so if you want to give me some information in advance . . ."

I look up.

I never heard the trailer door open. I'm not even aware of

Pete's presence until shreds of paper are raining down on the picnic table.

"He's not giving you anything," Pete growls. "It's time for you to leave my property."

The sergeant stands up. He looks Aunt Pete up and down, and for a moment I think he won't leave, but in the end he hands me his card.

"Call me anytime," he says. "Anytime at all."

The sergeant ducks into his SUV, and I watch as he backs out of the driveway.

"Are you okay?" Pete asks. He puts his hand on my shoulder, but I flinch.

"Do you want me to call your father? I'll get on the phone right now, I swear to god, that bastard . . ."

I look up. "Why?"

There's a long pause while Pete scowls at the papers on the picnic table. *"Because,"* he says, "it's your birthday and Allan told you he was coming to visit and then he sent a goddamn army recruiter and that's a miserable thing to . . ."

I shake my head. "No," I say absently. "It was my fault. Dad said to be ready Tuesday night and I assumed . . . well, I shouldn't have assumed anything. I screwed it up. That's all. It's not like he didn't show. He sent his friend."

I turn the business card between my fingers. Once, twice, three times.

Aunt Pete takes a deep breath.

"Hell," he says. "What your father did was wrong, Liam. Period. This is *not* okay."

I put down the business card, but I'm not really listening to him. "Could you maybe go inside now? I'm just going to sit here for a minute."

"*Liam . . .*"

"I'm kind of tired. Probably because of all the vacuuming. You were right about the vacuuming. Next time I don't think I'll vacuum as much."

Pete closes his eyes and runs his hand over his freshly shaven face.

"Liam, we should talk."

"No," I say. I mean to say more, but I don't.

45

I'M SITTING IN THE CROWD at a fashion show next to Tomas Feral. The lights have gone down and the catwalk is lit with deep reds and purples. The music is loud and pounds in my ears. The models emerge from the back one by one, steady, perfect, overlapping . . . I shouldn't be here because I'm too young — only five — but everyone knows Mom always gets what she wants when it comes to Tomas. And I behave. I sit perfectly still while all the color, sound, and motion dances around me. I want to get up there so badly, but all I do is lean forward in my seat.

Tomas is watching me. He ought to be watching the show — his show — but he's watching me, instead. His eyes move over my face every time the light changes, and at last I turn and look back. He leans close so he can whisper in my ear.

"Someday this will all be yours."

* * *

I'm having a beautiful dream, or maybe it's a memory, but it fades the moment I wake up. The portfolio Aunt Pete and the guys bought me is on the floor near my bed, but sitting on top of it is the business card from the recruiter. I turn over and go back to sleep.

Eventually, Pete pounds on the door.

"Get up," he says. "You're late."

I get up and go to school, but it's all a charade. I stare out the window, counting cars in the parking lot. Total tally: ten red, thirteen green, eight blue, eleven gray, sixteen white, six unidentifiably discolored.

Thursday I get up on time and Eddie drives me in, but I barely make it in for the announcements because he keeps asking if I'm all right, so I can't get away from the car. When I finally arrive in the AV room, Raymond and Simon are sitting at the desk and Ms. Peterson is setting up the camera.

"Liam, you're here," she beams. Simon gets up from the news desk.

"Simon could do the announcements today," I say, but Simon shakes his head.

"No way," he says. "You're best at them."

I shrug and sit down behind the desk. Raymond hands me the news, but I don't look at it.

"Aren't you going to read it before we begin?"

I shake my head. Ms. Peterson gives the signal, and I slouch low in my chair. I hardly notice when the red light comes on, and Raymond kicks me under the table. I start talking without looking up.

"This morning somebody has decided we all need to think about homecoming committees. Great. Fine. So join a committee."

"Jen Van Sant is looking for seniors interested in modeling in the senior fashion show fund-raiser at the homecoming festival. See Jen."

"The debate club won its match against Kingston. Yippee."

"The homecoming nominations are in for king and queen. Of course, I'm on the ballot. That just figures. The one thing I wanted was a little unpopularity. Is that so much to ask? Well, apparently it is. Apparently I've failed utterly and completely at being unpopular, so fine. Go ahead. Vote for me. See if I care."

Ms. Peterson is staring, bewildered, but I don't stop.

"Today's lunch is spaghetti with meat sauce, garlic bread, and milk. Bag lunch is tuna on a hard roll, chips, and milk. Once again there is no vegetarian option, but that's okay because I really love eating bread and milk every day for lunch. Wonderful." I set down the papers and finally look at the camera.

"Believe it or not, there are no more announcements, because there is absolutely nothing else going on around here. I would repeat them in French, but it's hardly worth it, don't you agree?" I sit back. "Raymond?"

For a moment Raymond looks surprised. Then he grins as if I've once again come up with something totally new and exciting. He puts on his shades and begins to read the sports. I don't wait. I unclip the mic and slide out from behind the desk.

I'm at my locker ahead of everyone, so I hardly notice when Darleen comes up beside me.

"Your announcements were unique today," she says. "I thought you had a good point about the school lunches. It is rather fascist the way they insist on putting meat in everything, isn't it?"

I have no idea how that's fascist, but right now I couldn't care less.

Jen catches up to me before English.

"Feeling any better?" she asks.

I shrug.

"Well, thanks for making that announcement about the fashion show. I've got a bunch of seniors who want to participate. We're thinking of scheduling it near the end of the afternoon — after the cheerleading exhibition but before the pie-throwing contest. That way the stage will be clear and the cheerleaders can participate in both. Nikki's planning the music, but she wants to know what kinds of clothes you've got."

Crap.

I completely forgot about getting clothes for the fashion show.

"I don't think I'm going to be there," I say, and Jen's jaw drops. Now she's not worried, she's pissed.

"No way! We've got everything planned. I've given you guys a forty-five-minute time slot, and the senior class is counting on the money."

"I'm sure Eddie will still do it. I just don't think . . ."

Jen is horrified.

"No one's coming to see Eddie. They're coming to see you."

The bell rings and I go in, but Jen follows me.

"We're counting on you," she says sharply. "I'll tell Nikki to call Eddie about the clothes, but you'd better be there."

Orlando is hovering next to my desk.

"Jen. Your seat," he says. Jen scowls at me one more time before walking back, but I don't look up. Orlando waits a moment then clears his throat.

"All right. Everyone take out *Hamlet*." He turns to me. "Liam, where's your book?"

"Do you want me to go to the office?" I ask, because obviously I don't have it.

Orlando pauses, then he takes an extra book out of his desk drawer.

"Sit up," he says. "You can use this one today." He tosses it across the room, and I catch it but set it down unopened.

"You said I'd have to go to the office if I forgot my book again."

Orlando is about to write something on the board, but he stops with the chalk halfway up. "I did say that," he says, "but that was before I realized you were going to forget your book *every* day. I'm giving you a reprieve."

The class snickers and I stare at my copy of *Hamlet*.

"I'm never going to remember to bring the book if you give me a new one."

This time Orlando puts down the chalk.

"Do you *want* to go to the office?"

I shrug. "I'm just saying that you said one thing and now you're doing something else."

There's an awkward silence while all eyes shift from me to Orlando.

"Do you want to go to the office?" he repeats. "Feel free, because the door is open." He takes a step back. "I'm not keeping you here," he says, turning to write something on the board. He writes, "Father, Mother, Uncle, Son," then turns to the class.

"Okay. Let's talk about family dynamics. What's going on in Hamlet's family? How does Hamlet's father, a character who appears only as a ghost, change the plot of the story? How does Hamlet's relationship to his mother change from Act One to Act Five? How about the crazy Ophelia? Does she influence things? Is Hamlet a victim or a perpetrator? Anyone?"

I stand up.

"Liam?"

"I'm going to the office."

There's a long pause while the entire class stares. Finally, Orlando nods.

"All right," he says, so I step out of the room and don't look back.

46

THAT NIGHT I WAIT until Pete is at work and the trailer is empty, then I sit by the phone. I pick up the receiver, dial, and hang up. Then I pick up the receiver but don't dial. I wait until the phone starts to buzz loudly before hanging it up again. A half hour later I dial the recruiter. The conversation is short, and he agrees to arrange everything so I can join the army's delayed entry program. I tell him I'm a little bit worried about passing the GED, but he says, "Don't worry, son. You'll do fine."

As soon as I get off the phone I call Dad at his office.

"Hello? Allan Geller, please." It's eight o'clock, but Dad always works late. Hold music drifts across the line. When Dad finally picks up, I recognize the pleasant business voice he uses with co-workers. I try to remember the last time I heard that voice.

"Allan Geller here."

"Dad? It's Liam."

The shift is immediate. "Oh. Liam."

I take a deep breath.

"I talked to your friend. Sergeant Braddock. He came by the trailer."

There's a pause.

"And?"

"And I agreed to join. He's going to arrange everything."

Dad pauses. "That's excellent," he says, and I think, for once he means it.

"I wanted to know if this means I can come home. I'll need a tutor to pass the GED and . . ."

I hear Dad shuffling papers on the other end of the phone line. "Of course," he says, and I can't tell if he means of course I can come home, or of course I'll need a tutor. I tear off a piece of loose plastic from the countertop and jab my finger until a small drop of blood smears its edge.

"When do you want me to come home?"

There's not even a pause. "It makes no difference."

"It doesn't matter?"

"That's what I just said."

"Right. Saturday morning then. Can you come get me Saturday morning?"

Dad's distracted. "Uh-huh. I'll be there."

I want to ask him, *Will you, Dad? Will you be here?* But I don't.

"Can I ask you something?" I say instead.

I picture Dad poised to hang up, then bringing the phone back to his ear.

"What is it?"

I don't know how to ask, so finally I just say it.

"I had something I wanted to tell you," I say. "I thought you were coming on Tuesday, and I was going to tell you then, but . . . Well, anyway, Mom said I should wait, but I thought maybe you'd be . . ." I choke on the word. "I've been doing some modeling. Nothing serious, but I've come up with a couple displays for Eddie's shopwindow."

Silence.

"The thing is, I think I'm good at it."

Silence again.

"Eddie says I have talent, Dad. He says I've got creativity and vision."

I wonder if Dad is still on the line.

"Dad?"

When he finally speaks, his voice is low and gravelly.

"If you think I'd allow my son to parade down a catwalk so people can take his picture then get drunk at all those parties afterward and sleep with everyone in sight . . ."

His voice is getting louder.

"How many times did I tell your mother to keep you away from all that? How many times? Ever since you were tiny she's been dragging you to everything, taking you into the goddamn dressing rooms with all those men putting on makeup, and half-naked women . . . Letting some flaming designer watch you while she waltzes down the runway. Your goddamn mother . . ."

"I don't know why I brought this up," I say. "I already told you I'm enlisting. I just wanted to know what you'd think of the other thing . . ."

More silence.

"Dad, I'm sorry," I say, even though I don't know what I'm apologizing for. I'm doing exactly what he wants.

"I've got another call," Dad says. "I'll see you Saturday morning. I don't intend to go to your uncle's trailer, so meet me at the school. I'll arrange a meeting with your principal so we can take care of things."

He clicks off and the phone buzzes in my ear.

47

FRIDAY MORNING I don't intend to go to school. I roll over and go back to sleep. Twice. Aunt Pete has to wake me up at eight fifteen.

"Why aren't you up yet? You've got fifteen minutes till Jen gets here. You've already missed Eddie, so I called her on your cell as backup." He kicks my mattress. "C'mon. Get up."

I roll over again, but Aunt Pete grabs the corner of my mattress and tips it until I slide onto the floor.

"You're tired? Well, so am I. I want to go to bed; therefore, you need to get up. Got it?"

I consider explaining, but I don't have the energy, so I stand up instead and pick some clothes off the floor. Aunt Pete stops.

"What are you doing?"

"I'm getting dressed."

"Yeah, but you wore those yesterday and they've been on the floor all night. Don't you need to dry-clean them or something?"

I shrug.

"Fine. I'll wear something else."

Pete hovers in my doorway. He looks as if he might leave, but he doesn't.

"Are you okay?"

I nod.

"You're sure about that?"

"Yeah."

Jen beeps, so I throw on some clothes and splash water on my face. I leave the trailer and hop in her car. Joe and Nikki talk about the homecoming football game, and I try to listen but my mind wanders.

"You got a cigarette?" I ask when we pull into the parking lot. Joe takes out a pack and hands it to me. The girls go in, but Joe stays while I light up.

"There's still a six-pack in the back from that party at Rob's," he says. "I had to empty it out of my car because my parents were suspicious. I gave it to Jen, but she'll never drink 'em. You want one?"

I nod. A beer or six sounds pretty good right now. "Want to skip first period?" I ask.

Joe shakes his head. "Can't," he says. "Homeroom though."

Joe crawls into the back and digs out the cans of beer, and we stretch out on the hood of the car. It's cool outside, but I don't mind. Lying on Jen's car is kind of like lying on the picnic table.

"Senior year's the best," Joe says. "Homecoming's going to

rock. We might even win the game this year. We never win, but Redwood's got no defense. And for once our offense kicks ass . . ."

"I'm dropping out."

Joe stops midsentence.

"Whoa."

"Yeah. I'm joining the army."

Joe studies a scratch on the car hood.

"What about the clothes stuff? I thought you were going to do that."

I shake my head. "Nah. I was just playing around. I'd just . . . I don't know. I'd mess it up somehow. The army's not so bad, right?"

Joe looks like he doesn't want to answer. "No. It's not bad, it's just . . ."

The bell between homeroom and first period rings, and Joe slides off the hood. He stands beside the car, kicking a rock. "You want me to hang out?" he asks, but I shake my head.

"Nah. I'll come in later."

Joe glances at the school.

"You want the rest of my beer?"

This time I nod. I watch Joe disappear into the school building, then I take the beers and the pack of cigarettes out to the bleachers. I stretch out along the top bleacher and stare up at the sky.

Three hours later I wake up and watch the cars go by. I drink the rest of Joe's beer, then the rest of my beer. I smoke half the cigarettes then drink the rest of the beers and lie back, listening to the sounds from the school building. I can hear the bells ringing between classes and the voices of the kids echoing through the halls. Eventually, my stomach growls, so I decide to go in for lunch, but by then it's already seventh period so lunch is over. I think about going to class, but I'd be late, so I sit in the boy's bathroom instead. I try to concentrate, but everything's spinning, and the cigarettes are starting to make me nauseated. The bell rings and I get up.

It's time for English. I need to go to English because it's Very Important. I have to tell Orlando that I'm failing, and that I . . . no, wait. Orlando knows I'm failing. I have to tell him I'm dropping out. Now if I can just remember where my classroom is . . .

I try two doors before I get it right. Number twelve. *That's it. Twelve. As in two one, or one two.* I meander across the room and sink low in my seat. The rest of the class is already seated, so I guess I'm a little late. Maybe a lot late? But I don't mind. It's good to sit down.

"Liam," Orlando says, "come talk to me outside."

I don't move.

"Did you hear me?"

"Mmm-hmm."

Orlando is silent.

"Look at me," he says, but I can't focus because my head is spinning. Orlando walks to the front of the classroom and writes something on the board. "Which piece of modern literature has most affected your life?"

"Two pages. Tell me what and why," he says to the class. "Liam, outside."

I don't get up.

"Outside, *now.*"

The class is silent. Not a single pen or pencil moves.

"Don't make me ask you again."

Finally, I stand up. My legs are unsteady, but I walk across the room, and Orlando slams the door shut behind us.

"Are you drunk? You smell like cigarettes and alcohol."

This time I laugh.

"This isn't funny," Orlando says. "You need to pass my class if you're going to graduate, and I'm giving you every chance . . ."

I shake my head. "What chances?" I slur. "What chances have you *ever* given me? You've known from the beginning you were going to fail me, so why do you pretend like you're giving me a chance?"

Orlando's jaw clenches shut. "I *am* giving you a chance," he says. "I'm giving you chance after chance if you'd just take them. I offered to let you rewrite the essay. I've offered to work with you after school. I haven't failed you yet, but if you disrespect me this way . . ."

I scowl. "Why shouldn't I? Nothing I do is good enough for you, yet I'm supposed to respect you? You pretend like you care about my future, but that's bullshit."

"Liam, if I hear one more swearword out of your mouth . . ."

"What? What the hell will you do about it? Call my uncle? Call my dad? Do you think I fucking care anymore? I'm sick of trying so hard for you."

Orlando slams an empty locker shut.

"Why don't I ask you a question?" he says. "How about this

one? Why don't you tell me why you're so afraid of my class? You haven't lifted a finger all year. You haven't brought your book. You stare out the window when I'm lecturing. Leave in the middle of class. You do everything but force me to fail you. Why is that? Huh? What are you so afraid of?"

My eyes are burning. Doors are opening all along the hallway, and a small crowd is gathered at the door of room number twelve. I glare, but Orlando isn't through.

"I'm not your father, Liam," he spits. "I don't know what you think you're —"

"Go to hell."

This time I walk away. I hear Orlando yelling after me, but I don't turn around. I walk right out the emergency exit.

48

I RUN UNTIL MY SIDE ACHES and my head stops spinning. Then I throw up at the side of the road, turn around and walk the rest of the way to Aunt Pete's. It takes me almost an hour to get back. When I arrive Dino's squad car is already in the driveway, along with Orlando's beat-up old Ford. I open the trailer door and I'm greeted by Aunt Pete.

"Where the hell have you been? I warned you not to do this to me again."

He's pacing in the living room, and Dino and Orlando are sitting at the kitchen counter. They all stand up, but I walk past them without saying anything. Pete follows me into my room, but I ignore him. I take out my cell phone and start to dial.

Fine. Dad can pick me up now instead of Saturday.

"Don't ignore me when I'm asking you a question," Aunt Pete growls. "You owe Orlando an apology, and Dino needs to talk to you because you set off a school alarm, so if I were you, I'd be doing some serious groveling about now."

I wait for Dad's phone to ring, but Pete grabs my cell.

"I'm calling my father," I say, grabbing it back.

Aunt Pete snorts.

"The hell you are." He plucks the cell phone out of my hand and in one fluid motion smashes it on the counter so tiny shards of plastic shoot through the trailer like missiles.

"What are you doing?!"

"Don't ignore me," Pete growls. "You think you're going to do whatever you damn well please? Well, two can play that game."

Now he's pissing me off, so I grab the kitchen phone.

"I can make a fucking phone call," I start, but Pete yanks the phone off the wall and throws it out the window.

"Go ahead. Make your goddamn phone call."

I storm into my room and slam the door, which is totally ineffective because Pete just opens it again.

"As long as you're living here, you'd better listen to me."

"Well, I'm not," I say. "It's over." I throw a stack of CDs into an empty box, but Pete grabs it and dumps the CDs onto the floor. Dino puts one hand on Pete's arm, but he shakes it off.

"You guys need to calm down," Orlando says. "Just calm down."

Aunt Pete laughs sarcastically. "Tell me, Liam, where are you going to go?"

I don't answer.

"I swear, you'd better answer me when I ask you a question, and you'd better apologize to Orlando now and I mean freakin' now or else —"

"Why? Why should I apologize to Orlando? Because he gave me detention for an essay I tried hard at? Because he failed me in a class I was never going to pass anyway? Because he acts like my goddamn father?"

"I've never done that," Orlando says from the doorway.

I shake my head. "Well, it doesn't matter now because I'm joining the army. I called the recruiter last night and there's nothing you can do about it, so you can all —"

Suddenly Pete slams my back against the wall so hard the air thrusts out of my lungs. I close my eyes.

"Pete, calm down."

"Petey . . ."

"Shut up." Aunt Pete pushes harder, pinning me against the wall. "What are you trying to do?" he says. "Are you trying to *make* me kick you out? Is that it?"

I turn my head, but Pete moves until he's in my face. "Well, I'll tell you again that I'm not going to kick you out and I'm not going to let you throw your life away, so you can give it up. You got that? Now you'd better tell me right now that you didn't sign a single goddamn paper."

I can feel the tears stinging my eyes. My breathing is shallow and I can barely shake my head. Aunt Pete loosens his grip and I slide down the wall.

"Why do you care if I join?" I say, but it comes out choked. "Why would anyone care? I'm just going to fail at anything else."

Aunt Pete stops; he's breathing hard.

"How can you say that?" he asks.

"Because it's true," I snap. "And I wish you'd quit acting like I have potential or something, giving me that stupid present . . ."

Pete slides down the wall across from me. He reaches over and grabs my hand.

"Liam," he says desperately, "you do have potential. I know you do. I've never stopped thinking that from the moment you walked into my trailer. And I damn well do care if you throw your life away. You're my nephew, for Christ's sake. I love you."

I honestly can't remember the last time anyone said that they love me.

"But Dad doesn't? Is that what you're saying?"

Aunt Pete's face melts, but then he takes a slow, deep breath.

"I never said that your father doesn't love you."

I run my fingers through my hair. It's hot in the trailer and the air is so still I can't breathe.

"I don't know when things changed for your dad," Pete says, "but somewhere along the line they did. Your father wanted to marry your mom for all the wrong reasons, and she wanted to marry him for all the wrong reasons, and he took it out on both of you . . ."

Things are going way past maximum fucked up.

"I don't want to talk about this. You don't know anything. Dad loves her. *Us*. You just hate him because he hates the band."

Pete closes his eyes.

"Is that what Allan told you?" he asks. "That we stopped speaking because of the band?"

I shake my head. "No," I say. "Dad never said that. Mom said that."

This time Pete looks surprised. He runs his hand over the stubble on his chin.

"Your father stopped talking to me because I told your mother to leave him," he says abruptly. "It had nothing to do with the band. Ever. It has to do with how he treats both of you."

I bite my lip.

"That's not true," I say at last. "He doesn't . . ."

Aunt Pete leans across the carpet. "Honestly, Liam, I've never understood why your mother lets him treat her the way he does, and I don't know why you let him treat *you* that way, either. I've never understood."

My hands start to shake.

"Get out," I whisper.

Aunt Pete moves until he's sitting directly in front of me.

"No," he says. "I did that once. I'm not doing it again."

"Leave me alone," I repeat. "Please."

"No," Pete says again. "I won't, because you're a great kid and for the last five weeks I've watched you trying to turn yourself into someone else. Your father, maybe? I don't know, but I know that everything you succeed at you tell me is worthless and everything you screw up you tell me was an accident, but there aren't that many accidents in life.

"I never should have let your parents push me away, but I did, and it was a mistake . . . So, if you think there's a chance in hell I'm letting you go now, you'd better think again. Do you understand that? There is nothing you could do that would make me kick you out. Not a party or getting thrown in jail or some stupid radio show or even getting drunk and walking out on my boyfriend's class."

He's holding my hand tight.

"Your father is wrong, Liam. He thinks he can treat you anyway he wants and you'll never stand up to him. He thinks he's better than you because he has a prestigious job, but that means nothing. Nothing. He doesn't have the right to talk to you the way he does. Ever. And he sure as hell doesn't have the right to tell you to join the army. That's the bottom line."

Aunt Pete takes a couple slow breaths, but I don't say anything. My chest hurts from trying so hard to breathe. The guys are gone now, and it's just me and Pete sitting on the floor. Then he stands up.

"I'm going into the living room so you can have a few minutes alone," he says, "but that's as far as I'll go. Do you get that? I called in sick tonight, so I'm not going anywhere, and when you're ready I want you to come talk to me."

Then he steps out of the room. He leaves the door open, and I want to reach over and shut it, but I can't.

49

I WAIT UNTIL THREE O'CLOCK IN THE MORNING before I leave my room. Aunt Pete is asleep on the couch, and both Dino's and Orlando's cars are gone from the driveway. It's quiet. Really quiet. I walk through the kitchen and living room and open the front door without making a sound, then I walk across the lawn and tap lightly on Darleen's window. When there's no answer I tap harder. I have to knock three more times, but finally the window opens and Darleen sticks her head out. Her hair is messed up and she squints down at me.

"Liam? What are you doing? It's the middle of the night."

"I need to talk to you," I say. "It's important."

Darleen frowns. "It's three o'clock in the morning."

"Please."

She rubs her eyes.

"What's the matter? You look terrible."

"Can I just come in? I could crawl through your window and your dad will never know."

She shakes her head. "No," she says. "I'm trying to sleep. You shouldn't even be out there."

"I have to ask you something. *Please.*"

Darleen sighs.

"Fine," she says at last. "You can come in for *five minutes.* That's it. I don't see why you can't ask me whatever you've got to ask me from out there. And if my dad hears you, he's totally going to freak."

I wedge my foot into the center of a bush, find a good spot, and push myself up. When I'm high enough I throw my leg over the window ledge.

"You're going to kill yourself," Darleen mutters.

I fall on the floor, then stand up, catching my breath.

"What's so important that you had to come all the way up here in the middle of the night?"

I sit down on her bed, not sure where to begin.

"I have to know . . . ," I say. "I've been thinking about a lot of stuff and . . . I need to know if there's something wrong with me or . . . Why don't you like me?"

Darleen scowls. "Right now I don't like you because it's three o'clock in the morning and you've woken me up to ask a stupid question that could have waited until —"

Something in my face must make her reconsider, because she stops.

"This is really important to you, isn't it?"

I can barely nod.

"Is there something about me that is just stupid or bad or . . . I don't know . . ." The words catch in my throat.

Darleen sits down beside me on the bed and pushes the hair out of my face, just like Mom does, and for a moment I think, *Crap, I'm making a fool out of myself, again*. But then she sighs.

"I'll admit," she says, "that I despised you from the moment I first met you. I overheard your phone call with your friend, and you sounded like a typical womanizing jerk."

I cringe.

"And then," she continues, "I didn't like you because you were instantly part of the most popular group at school, but even that wasn't enough for you. You had to keep bugging me, as if I were some sport you needed to master. One more trophy to put on your shelf."

I stand up.

"I'm sorry," I say. "You're right. I've been a total jerk. And now I just woke you up in the middle of the night so you could tell me this, which is even worse . . ."

Darleen grabs my arm and pulls me back down.

"Sit down, Liam," she says. "I'm not done yet."

My stomach twists.

"You want to know what I thought when I saw you sitting in your mom's convertible that day she dropped you off?"

I don't.

"I thought, *This guy is probably just like every other shallow, popular moron I've ever met.*"

I close my eyes and drop my head in my hands.

"And do you want to know what I think about you now?"

I shake my head, but Darleen just laughs.

"Too bad, because I'm going to tell you anyway." She puts one hand on my knee. "I think you try too hard to please everyone, and now you're ready to throw everything away just because there are people like me who judge you by what's on the surface, without getting to know what's underneath."

She pauses, watching me.

"Do you think I couldn't hear you and your uncle fighting tonight?" she asks after a while. "Your dad didn't show up, you decided to quit school, and now you want to join the army. The *army*?"

I flop backward onto her bed and turn away, but she won't stop talking.

"Liam," she says, "we both know this isn't about whether I like you or not."

"What do you mean?" I mumble.

"Sure, when we first met I hated you. But it's not me you've been trying so hard to impress. And you know what? Your father might not like you either, but you have to stop caring so much what he thinks of you and start caring more about what *you* think of you. Otherwise, you'll always be looking for something you're never going to find. I know this sounds harsh, but you've got to let it go."

I'm silent for a long time, and at last Darleen gets up and walks over to her jewelry box.

"I've never shown this to anybody," she says, pulling out a

crumpled paper. "This is the letter my mom left on the kitchen table before she walked out." She tosses it on the bed and I pick it up.

I hold the letter tightly, then unfold the creases and read it twice.

"I'm not showing this to you so you'll feel sorry for me. I want you to read it because it's all about how much she loves me. Can you imagine someone saying that as she walks out the door, knowing she'll never come back?"

"You don't think she does? Love you, I mean?" My voice is sore and hoarse, and I can barely see Darleen shrug in the darkness.

"I don't know," she says. "But it's what I got and I've had to learn to live with that."

I lie back again and close my eyes.

"Listen," she says, "all those things I thought about you? I was wrong. I thought you were just like Joe and Nikki and everyone else, but you're not."

"But I *am* like them," I say. "I'm worse than them. Joe and Nikki aren't that bad, once you get to know them, and at least they do things right. I'm popular and shallow and stupid and . . ."

". . . brave and talented and funny." Darleen frowns. "Liam, your window display at Eddie's shop was . . . Well, no one who's stupid could've put that together." She touches my arm. "Trust me," she says. "You have talent."

She leans back on the bed so she's lying next to me.

"I'm going to tell you one last thing, and, if you ever tell anyone I'm being this nice, it will never happen again."

I open my eyes.

"What?"

"You're okay, Liam," Darleen says. "Don't let your dad, or me, or anybody else make you think otherwise."

She reaches out and holds my hand tight, and for a while we just lie there, side by side, saying nothing. Then at last she stands up and pulls me off her bed, leading me to the open window.

"I know this isn't what you wanted," she says, "but your living room light just went on. I think you should talk to your uncle. He really cares about you." She pauses. "You can't create love, Liam. You just have to take it wherever you find it."

I look out the window at Pete's trailer, and know that she's right.

50

THE NEXT MORNING I lie in bed replaying Darleen's words in my head.

You can't create love, Liam. You just have to take it wherever you find it.

I think about Dad and then I think about Aunt Pete in his glam-rock spandex, and the guys with their cliché clothes and their band still playing seventies hits.

My head pounds, and finally the alarm clock beside my mattress blares. I reach over and turn it off, but I haven't slept at all.

"You up?" Pete asks. He's standing in the doorway in his favorite green kimono and orange tube socks. I nod slowly.

"I'm up."

Pete frowns.

"You don't look like you're up. Haven't changed your mind, have you?"

I shake my head. "No. I haven't changed my mind."

"All right, then. We've got to meet your dad in an hour, so you'd better get a move on. I'm sure you need the world's most perfect shirt for this occasion, and we haven't got all day to pick it out."

I sit up and run my fingers through my hair. I wait for Pete to shut the door, then stand in front of my clothes rack. It takes a long time, but finally I pick out the right clothes. I lay everything carefully on my mattress, then take my time showering. I make sure my hair is just the right degree of disheveled, then pull on each item one by one. Coal black boxers by Turnbull and Asser, simple four-button worsted-wool suit by Pierre Cardin, paired with a classic blue button-down shirt designed specifically to accompany the suit, black patent-leather shoes by Helmut Lang. Cologne — Hugo Boss.

I stand in front of my mirror, and this time I don't see Mom or Dad. Just me.

At twelve fifteen Aunt Pete and I climb into the Nissan and head for the school. The knot in my stomach tightens as we pull into the parking lot. Dino, Orlando, and Eddie are already standing on the school steps, waiting for us. I get out of the car and walk slowly.

"Thanks for coming," I tell them. "I wouldn't have blamed you guys if you didn't." I meet Orlando's gaze. "I'm really —"

He puts one hand on my shoulder before I can say anything else.

"Save it for inside," he says, glancing at the front doors. "Shall we?"

I nod and the five of us make our way to Principal Mallek's office. The light is on and I can see Dad's profile through the window.

This is it, I think.

I open the door and step inside. Mom's sitting in one of the huge leather chairs that have been set up around the principal's desk, and she's fumbling in her purse for something, but she drops it when I step in. The contents spill onto the floor and she kneels nervously to pick stuff up. I kneel beside her, covering her hands with mine.

"Here, Ma. I got it." I lean in and kiss her on the cheek.

"Christ, Li," she whispers, straightening my collar, and I know exactly what she means. I turn to face my father, but Dad's busy glaring at Aunt Pete.

"I don't believe you were invited to this meeting," he says.

I interrupt before Pete can answer. "I invited him. I want the guys here." I speak directly to Principal Mallek rather than Dad, because I know Dad won't push things when there's someone else in the room. Someone who needs to be impressed.

Principal Mallek nods. "It's not a problem," he says. "In fact, I'm glad everyone's here. We'll need to clear up the matter of setting off the school alarm with Officer Walters" — he nods at Dino — "and I believe that no matter what decisions are made here today, Liam, you . . ."

I don't make him finish. "I owe Orlando, I mean, Mr. DeSoto, an apology. I know." I turn to Orlando. "I want you to know I'm really sorry for . . ." I stop. I can feel the familiar sentences bubbling up, but I don't want this apology to be like all the others. I start again.

"What I want to say is that you've been really nice to me ever since I got here, and you didn't deserve my showing up drunk, or making a scene in the hall, or any of that. I know you think I don't care about what you teach, but that's not true. I like your class and I know that we're reading *Hamlet,* and I tried to read it, but I didn't want you to think I was stupid for not getting everything, so I just never brought my book. You're a really good teacher and I'm sorry I acted like I didn't care. I'm sorry about yesterday and I really mean that."

I look up to see if Orlando is listening, but it's Dad who responds.

"You absolutely should be sorry," he says. "The principal filled me in on your behavior, and as usual you've failed to show even the smallest shred of respect toward authority figures and —"

Dad's on his way into the zone, but Orlando interrupts. "Thanks, Allan," he says, "but I believe that apology was directed to me." Dad stops abruptly, and Orlando studies me from across the room. "I accept your apology, Liam. It means a lot to hear you say what you just said, and for the record I think you're a smart kid. *Hamlet* is a hard book, but with some work you'll get it." He pauses. "And I mean *that.*"

A flood of relief washes through me, but Principal Mallek clears his throat. "And the school alarm?" he says, looking at Dino. I've been waiting for this. Dino could go either way on this one. I wouldn't blame him if he comes down hard; after all, he already let me off the hook once.

"Well," Dino says, drumming his fingers on the arm of his chair, "we take the setting off of a school alarm very seriously. This wasn't a funny prank, or even an error in judgment. It was a deliberate act, so I can't be lenient in this matter. I don't think it's necessary to file official charges, and it's the school's decision what repercussions they choose to impose, but I think community service should be a minimum."

Dad nods. "Absolutely," he says. "There are a plethora of excellent service opportunities in the Westchester area. After Principal Mallek's phone call, I anticipated this and did some research . . ."

Dino coughs. "Actually," he says, "I feel strongly that the community Liam needs to serve is this one. Specifically, this school. I think the others will agree." He glances at Principal Mallek and Orlando. "This is where the alarm was set off, and this is where people have been inconvenienced."

Dad frowns.

"I hardly think that's reasonable. It's a long drive from Westchester, and Liam's time will be occupied with extensive tutoring for the GED and a pre-army training program."

I try to breathe evenly, but my pulse is racing. I glance at Mom, then at Pete. Pete nods, so I clear my throat.

"Actually, Dad, I've changed my mind."

Dad stops midsentence.

"Au . . . Uncle Pete and I had a long talk last night, or this morning actually, and if Principal Mallek will allow it, I'd like to finish school here in Pineville. I know there will be consequences for setting off the alarm and drinking on school property, and I'll do whatever I have to" — I look directly at Principal Mallek — "even if it takes me all year to work it out. But I'd like to stay."

This is the part I've been dreading, and Dad doesn't waste any time.

"Your decision is already made," he says. "That's the reason your mother and I drove here this morning." I can see the color rising in his face. I cringe, but it's too late now. Things are reaching maximum fucked up, but for once I want it that way.

"No, Dad," I say. "*You* made my decision, just like you always make all the decisions. I said yes because I wanted to make you proud of me. But you wouldn't be proud even if I did join the army."

Dad's face turns red. First he sputters, but then he stands up.

"You've changed your mind because *he*," — Dad points at Aunt Pete — "thinks he can be some sort of father figure and —"

"Give it a rest, Allan," Pete says. "I'm not trying to be anybody's father, and if your son happens to be looking for one, maybe you should ask yourself why that is."

Dad laughs.

"If my son happens to be looking for one, I don't think he's going to find it in a cross-dressing disc jockey who lives in a trailer park."

Aunt Pete stands up, but Principal Mallek clears his throat loudly.

"I can see this is a point of contention," he says, but nobody's listening anymore.

Eddie's trying madly to say something that begins with "As Liam's employer . . ." and Orlando is subtly blocking Aunt Pete's right arm by standing next to him. Dino looks like he's considering calling in reinforcements, and Mom is fumbling with her purse again. I run my fingers through my hair.

"You've got no say in this whatsoever," Dad's saying, his finger jabbing in the direction of Aunt Pete's chest. "I'm Liam's father and what I say is that he's coming home with me today. Period."

If things weren't so messed up, I could almost laugh. *Now* Dad wants me?

Pete looks like he's about to spit. "Bullshit," he says. "Your wife and your son bend over backward to please you when all you do is treat them like crap, so it's their decision whether or not —"

Principal Mallek moves between them. "Enough!"

An awkward silence settles over the room.

"I'm sure we can work through this if everyone cooperates," Principal Mallek says quietly. He's using his I-am-very-annoyed-with-you tone, and it's great, because for once he's not using it on me. Dad opens his mouth, but Principal Mallek holds up one hand.

"Liam," he says, "do I understand that you would prefer to finish the school year rather than dropping out?"

I nod.

"Mr. Geller," Principal Mallek says, "I can't imagine you wouldn't at least consider Liam's request. It's very unconventional for a parent to insist . . ."

Dad's face changes from furious to controlled.

"Of course," Dad says. "I'm only concerned for my son's well-being, so if Liam wants to finish the school year back home in Westchester, where he can have adequate supervision, that's fine with me."

Principal Mallek nods. "That's fair," he says. "I can arrange the necessary paperwork, and I'm sure we can come up with some way that Liam can still repay this community and everything can be settled accordingly."

I sit up.

"Wait a second," I say, glancing at Mom. "It's not settled." I try to make her look at me, but she won't, so I have to ask. *"Mom,"* I say. *"Please."*

This time she looks up and we lock eyes for a moment. Then I turn to Principal Mallek.

"I know you believe in consequences," I tell him, "but I'll take the consequences. I promise. It's not too late. I mean, I finally made a decision. That should count for something, right? I know what *I* want to do, and if I just get a chance, I might get things right this time."

I'm not done, but Principal Mallek puts his hand on my arm.

"I'm sorry, Liam," he says, "but I believe you need the support of your parents."

That's when Dad stands up.

"Liam, get your jacket."

I don't move.

"Liam . . ."

"Let him be, Allan."

I expect Pete, but it's Mom. Everyone turns and for the briefest of seconds she looks like she used to, on the runway. She stands up and walks over to me, then kisses me on the forehead.

"Your whole life," she whispers, "I've prayed you'd turn out like your father. *Please,* I thought, *don't let him turn out like me.*" Her hand lingers on my face, and it trembles. "But you are like me, aren't you? Except you're stronger than I am, and when I look at you, I don't feel anything but proud."

I close my eyes.

"I'm sorry, Li," she breathes, and then she says it. "I love you more than anything."

There's a long silence, then Dad says, "Sarah, we've discussed this."

"No, Allan," she says. "We haven't."

She turns to Principal Mallek. "I know you need to speak with Liam regarding his conduct yesterday. I'm not asking for lenience on his behalf, but I am asking that you give him another chance in your school. He's eighteen now and he can make his own decisions. If this is what he wants —"

"Sarah, sit down," Dad says.

She doesn't move. "He deserves another chance, because god knows we haven't given him a real one."

"*Sarah!*"

For the first time Mom looks directly at Dad. "We'll take this into the hallway. Right now Liam has things to work out with his uncle, his teacher, his principal, his employer, and the officer who've been good friends to him." She looks at each one of the guys and there are tears in her eyes.

Dad turns to me.

"We'll discuss this again," he says, and I nod. I have no doubt that we will.

EPILOGUE

TWO WEEKS LATER I'm sitting in front of the giant mirror in the choir room putting on eye shadow. The room is crowded with half-dressed cheerleaders and guys wearing boxer shorts and ties. There are supposed to be separate changing areas for guys and girls but the barriers were knocked down and now there's just chaos. I grin. Fifteen minutes until showtime.

Aunt Pete steps up behind me. "That looks good," he says. "How do you make it look like that?"

I finger the brush lightly. "It's layering," I tell him. "The darkest shade closest to the lid, then a shade lighter in the center, and something with a golden tone to sweep up toward the eyebrows. Stands out from the stage and pulls people in."

Jen sits down beside me. "Can I try that?" she asks. She looks really pretty.

I hand her a brush. "You should use a neutral shade on your

eyelids," I say, "but brush the gold across your lips like this. It'll make them shimmer."

Joe Banks tosses a football against the wall.

"There is no way in hell I'm wearing any of that."

Pete laughs. "C'mon, Joe. A little lipstick? Blush, maybe?"

"You guys are crazy."

I would laugh, but I cringe instead.

"Raymond. Simon. You guys aren't reading the chart. You've got to read the chart. You're wearing the PacSun shorts with the Skechers and the shades."

Raymond looks down. "These are shorts," he says. I groan.

"Nikki, will you show Rambo the PacSun shorts? And Stephie and J.T. have the wrong accessories." *Damn, there's a lot to keep track of.* "I've got to get this stuff on," I mutter. "If I don't get this right . . ."

Aunt Pete is studying me closely, and I catch his eye.

"I know, I know," I finish. "It's not the end of the world." Only, maybe it is, because I want to start succeeding for a change. I hold out the eye shadow. "Want some?"

Pete nods.

"Sure. Why not?" He copies my sweeping arcs. I watch his technique, which is improving.

Aunt Pete is wearing the red dress in the fashion show. He's DJing, too, so they've been plugging it big-time. The uncle/nephew modeling team. It's supposed to be a big joke, his appearing in a dress, I mean, but the whole town is coming out to see it,

and what they don't know is that Aunt Pete is taking this very seriously. He's wearing the rhinestone pumps we bought at the mall,
and he's even shaved. His legs.

"Looks good," I tell him, once he gets the eye shadow on. I
pull on my shirt and adjust the cuffs. Joe Banks's football crashes
against the wall and someone drops a tray full of earrings, but I ignore them. There's something I still have to do.

"I'll be right back," I say, getting up.

Eddie walks into the room just as I'm leaving.

"Where are you going? We've only got ten minutes left.
Ohmygod. I think I'm having a panic attack."

He fans himself, but I ignore him. There's someone I need to
see in the hallway.

"Darleen!"

She's walking toward the gym, but she stops when I slide up
beside her.

"How's Pineville's new homecoming king?" she asks.

I blush. The vote was this morning after the parade and I won
by a landslide. I honestly don't know how that happened.

"Good," I say. "I'm good."

"So, they're letting you go to your coronation now that
you've served your time?" She's referring to my week's suspen-
sion and the community service with Dino. Not that community
service is over. I'll be doing that until I'm eighty. It sucks, too. I
have to pick up every piece of garbage in Pineville, but that's not
the part that sucks. The part that sucks is that hardly anyone in
Pineville litters, so I have to *pretend* there's garbage to pick up.

"Yeah," I say. "Me and Jen are even going to a party afterward, but Pete told her I have to be home by eleven. He says he's calling Dino at eleven-oh-one." I shrug and Darleen laughs.

"How's your dad taking everything?"

This time I frown.

"Not so great. He and Mom had a big fight over whether she would come today, so now she's staying home, even though she said she'd be here. It's kind of a mess."

"But you're still here," Darleen says.

Good point. "So, what's with the notebook?" I nod at the sketch pad she's pinning to her chest, and Darleen narrows her eyes.

"Believe it or not," she says, "Jen called this morning and asked if I'd do some sketches of the fashion show." She glares at me. "You wouldn't know anything about that, would you?"

I mean to play it cool, but I grin, and Darleen shakes her head.

"I guessed as much. You're the only person who could convince Jen Van Sant to call and ask *me* a favor. A favor involving homecoming."

"It's a good idea though, right?" I say. "I mean, it'll be good for your portfolio and the sketches will be something different for the school paper. Supporting the arts and all?"

"And just because I launched a massive campaign against homecoming doesn't mean I can't play a pivotal role." She frowns. "I was going to say no, but I decided I'd be a fool to miss my chance."

Normally I'd pretend to know what she means, but I'm trying to do better about that. "What chance?" I ask.

Darleen adjusts her notebook.

"Well, I figure I'll get voted Class Hypocrite in addition to Class Bitch, but even *I* couldn't turn down a chance to sketch the world's next supermodel."

She grins, and I don't know what to say, but in the end I don't say anything. Darleen glances at the choir room door, where Eddie is gesturing madly.

"Speaking of which," she says, "looks like you're on."